BLOODLINES

BLOODLINES

HOUSE OF THE SPIDERKING™

BOOK SIX

MICHAEL ANDERLE

CHAPTER ONE

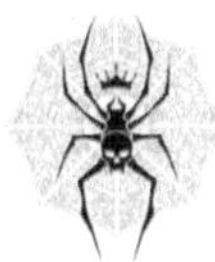

Elana woke before dawn, which wasn't difficult given it was January. She considered trying to get some more sleep, then brushed the idea aside. Her eyes had snapped open with a vengeance. She was ready to face the day. It was time to get shit done.

Unfortunately, that meant attempting to get up and make coffee without waking her new housemate.

Elana slipped out of bed and into her ensuite bathroom. She splashed cold water on her face and ran a brush through her hair to get rid of the worst of the bedhead. It was early enough that she could shower after breakfast and still make it to her meeting with Valeria in plenty of time.

She pulled on a dressing gown and tiptoed out of her bedroom and down the hall. Snoring emanated from the spare room, which was a relief. Vicky had been a sound sleeper through high school.

Elana had once amused herself on a sleepover by making a tower of Cheerios on her friend's forehead. She'd made it to twenty pieces of cereal before Vicky had twitched in her sleep and brought the spire tumbling down. Receiving the Rights had thrown her sleep schedule entirely out of whack.

According to the healers, this wasn't uncommon. The sudden influx of energy and new growth prompted by the sire's nanocytes sent the recipient's body into chaos. One healer had explained, "It's like a second or third puberty, only paired with menopausal symptoms."

Vampires higher up in the Nexus had higher nanocyte counts, and their bodies were more accustomed to functioning in tandem with the specialized proteins they created. On the other hand, brand-new initiates needed *more* sleep to handle the rapid, massive changes. This could take the form of anything from sleeping twelve hours at a time to passing out mid-sentence in a narcoleptic nap. Between those, the mood swings, and the unpredictable hunger pangs, it was easy to tell why many new initiates chose to stay in "nurseries." Many Houses kept a suite of rooms for the purpose.

Elana had no such suite, and to her surprise, the Spider-King didn't maintain a manor house like most vampire Houses. The royal house owned significant real estate in the walled city of Haven but rented out anything residential. Besides, none of it resembled a manor. Valeria owned a personal home and maintained quarters in one of the Citadel buildings in deference to arbiter tradition. Still, she had always functioned as the Arbiter of Shadows, not the official scion of the SpiderKing.

"Where does our House do *business*?" Elana had asked.

Valeria had smirked and gestured in a wide circle. "Think anyone would argue if we commandeered a room?"

Elana supposed that made sense. If the SpiderKing owned the city, he could use it at his will, and no one would argue. On the other hand, it struck her as convenient to have a place of one's own to conduct meetings. It would also allow one to keep guests that didn't require the service of anyone not personally attached to the House.

For the moment, this meant Vicky was staying in Elana's spare room while she weathered the growing pains of a new initiate. However, Elana considered the wisdom of buying or building a manor house with more solemnity every day. The sheer number of private meetings she held on a regular basis necessitated it, especially given that she couldn't otherwise guarantee operational security.

As far as I know, my mom didn't have a manor either. I wonder how she managed it.

Elana eased the freezer door open and retrieved the canister of ground coffee. She'd grown to appreciate fresh-ground beans but wouldn't chance waking Vicky up yet. It wasn't even six AM. The coffeemaker would be loud enough.

She measured a few scoops into the filter, closed the compartment, and hit the button to start the brew cycle. *Maybe I can use nanotech to add more sound muffling. Someone has to have already worked that out.*

Elana grabbed a poppyseed bagel from the breadbox, split it open, and smeared cream cheese on it from the fridge. Then she contemplatively chewed it while watching the overcast sky above her backyard through the sliding glass doors that led to the patio. The in-ground pool was covered for the winter. Elana had entertained the idea of freezing it to make a skating rink after her brief flirtation with vampire hockey. Unfortunately, her pool guys had told her that wasn't wise unless she wanted to replace all the filtration equipment after it thawed.

She'd lamented for months that she didn't yet know how to survive on so little sleep like her extra-powerful vampire friends did. It seemed that ascending in the Nexus had been all she was missing because four nights out of five in the last three weeks had been largely sleepless. Part of Elana wanted to return to needing a solid eight hours a night.

It would have been one thing if she'd been able to distract herself from the insomnia by shooting the shit with Vicky, whether about Haven gossip or their plans for the future. As it stood, Elana felt obligated to keep her mouth shut and do everything she could to help Vicky recuperate from the brutal transformation process. Forty-nine percent of the time, Vicky was ravenous and manic. The other forty-nine percent she was depressed and exhausted. The remaining two percent felt like the real Vicky, the bubbly, confident person who defended Elana against everyone who had called her a freak.

Elana chuckled under her breath. *If only they could see me now—thriving as a vampire and making a point to help everyone I can.*

As it stood, Elana spent most of her nights lately tossing and turning until she got up and wrote out everything spinning around in her brain. Most of the content didn't surprise her, but she was rapidly tiring of the endless hamster wheel not *resulting* in anything. Her REM cycle had subconsciously figured things out when she'd been sleeping regularly. These days, she felt frazzled and on edge.

There's gotta be a way around that. I know the higher levels of the Nexus are less heavily populated, but the more advanced a vampire is, the longer they tend to live. If we burned out from sleep deprivation, that wouldn't happen. I'm missing something again.

The coffeemaker hissed steam as it ended the drip cycle. Elana picked a mug at random from the cabinet above. She filled it with coffee and added milk from the fridge and a spoonful of sugar from the bowl on the counter. Nothing fancy, just a shot of caffeine to give her brain a pick-me-up and hopefully get the gears turning.

She wrapped her hands around the warm mug and considered sitting on the deck, then reconsidered and settled at the breakfast nook. She could look out the glass sliding doors at the snowy backyard without actually having to experience it. Vampires could use nanocyte energy to resist natural heat loss, but that struck her as a waste of resources.

Elana chuckled under her breath, then sipped her coffee. *Guess I'm developing some wisdom after all.*

An eddy of snowflakes whirled by, driven by the slight breeze. The sun was peeking through the clouds some-where, and the gray dawn was slowly brightening. Maybe the wind would shift some of the endless clouds they'd had all week.

Elana drew a deep breath. The aroma of coffee filled her nostrils, paired with the scent memory of snow on the wind. When she exhaled, she let her shoulders drop, and the mental hamster wheel went from breakneck to harried.

Cathy Smith's voice floated through her mind with a gentle rejoinder to be present. The four-thousand-year-old vampire had coached Elana through several crises over the last year, and her weapon of choice was always meditation. Elana had been resistant at first, uninterested in what she'd thought of as "woo-woo" techniques that slapped a Band-Aid over real issues. Cathy had persisted, however, and won Elana over with time, evidence, and research.

For a time, Elana had practiced regularly. Now that she thought about it, she wasn't sure when she'd stopped.

The best time to start is always now. She took another sip of coffee, cradled the mug in her hands, and closed her eyes.

"Morning."

Elana jolted, but something stopped her mug from spilling into her lap. When her eyes snapped open, Vicky was steadying Elana's mug with one hand and holding a fresh mug in the other.

Vicky let go of Elana's mug and pulled the other chair out to sit. "Sorry. Didn't mean to startle you. Did you fall asleep? I hope my snoring isn't keeping you up."

"No, no." Elana set her mug on the counter. "It's all good. I was meditating, and *clearly* my mind got further away than I realized. I'm sorry I woke you. I tried to be quiet."

"You were. The smell of coffee woke me. Everything smells *so much stronger* now. I've had to ditch, like, my entire perfume cabinet."

Elana winced. "Goddammit, I should have known. Sorry again."

Vicky waved away the apology. "Hardly the worst way

to wake up. Besides, my stomach would have growled me awake soon anyway, judging by how much it's contributing to the conversation." On cue, a loud grumble emanated from Vicky's abdomen, and both women chuckled.

Elana pushed back from the nook and stood. "What do you want for breakfast?"

"I could eat a horse, but I don't think you have any."

"I am, alas, entirely out of horses. There's leftover roast beef. I could make omelets or a scramble or something."

"Ooh, a scramble sounds good. Want help?"

"Chop a pepper for me?"

"You got it."

They fell into a comfortable rhythm as they prepared the meal, moving around each other smoothly and with the practiced communication of a long friendship. Soon, the frying pan was full of eggs, hash browns, peppers, and beef. Elana poked it occasionally with a spatula while leaning on the counter beside the stove.

Vicky refilled her mug and returned to the breakfast nook. "Does it get easier?"

"Depends on what you're asking about. The smelling thing?"

"That's what's most on my mind, but I guess I'm asking about all of it."

Elana shrugged. "Yes and no. Everyone's experience is different, or so I've read. I've discovered that it takes a couple of weeks for me to adjust every time I progress. Some people live strictly scent-free lives or have tiny filters implanted in their nostrils.

"On the other hand, I've heard of people who go the opposite direction and revel in the heightened senses.

Stinky tofu at every meal, drowning themselves in perfume, et cetera."

Vicky grimaced. "Urgh. That's definitely not for me yet. I smelled someone's BO the other day and just about dry heaved."

Elana chuckled. "Fair enough. Luckily, all of us can smell those people coming a mile away, so we can GTFO if we want."

"Thank God—or, um, thank the Nexus? How does this work?"

"Ha! Some vampires treat the Nexus like a deity, but it's pretty rare. You kind of sound like a character from a fantasy novel if you talk like that, right? Most of us keep whatever curses we grew up using. In that respect, we're not that different from humans. Honestly, if you ask me, we're not that different from humans at all."

Vicky shook her head. "Could have fooled me. I feel nothing like I used to."

Elana stirred the contents of the pan again, tasted a piece of scrambled egg, and added salt and pepper. "Fair enough. I have to keep reminding myself that I went through what you're going through now when I was a toddler. I don't remember it. Actually, you might benefit from chatting with Matt."

"He was changed as an adult?"

"I don't know exactly how old he was, but he wasn't a kid as far as I know." Elana tested the hash again, nodded, dished it onto the waiting plates, and handed one to Vicky. "Eat up. We have training with Gustav this afternoon."

Vicky groaned but tucked into the plate with gusto.

"I'm glad you're coming with me. I suspect I'm gonna get my ass handed to me on a platter."

Elana snickered, then ate a forkful and smacked her lips. "That turned out perfect. My cooking skills are so much better than they used to be."

"Agreed, but I can't help noticing you didn't do anything to assuage my concern about getting my ass handed to me."

Elana grinned. "You realize I still get my ass handed to me more often than not, right? Like, I've moved from nine-point-five times out of ten to maybe six times out of ten."

"That does *not* inspire confidence."

"You'll get there. I promise. You've never let anything keep you down for long."

"True enough." Vicky stabbed a piece of beef. "So, what's keeping you up at night?"

Elana sighed. "Same old, same old, really. Every time I think I've solved part of this conspiracy, it turns out I've only unearthed a pile more puzzle pieces. For every two pieces I put together, the puzzle gets bigger...and the stakes get higher.

"We shut down House Veridian, but someone's still pursuing their agenda of experimentation and destruction. I stopped Celyn and Edward from kicking off more pandemics, but that same person probably has samples of both viruses—or the means to make more. Arbiter Tarsin's trying to figure out how they created mindless monsters like Steve and Clarissa, but she's not exactly spoiled for options when it comes to research materials. Again, whoever's behind all this did a very good job cleaning up after themselves."

Vicky shuddered. "Those caves were terrifying."

Elana grimaced, remembering the rows of bodies they'd pulled out of the lake under Il Giardino's mountain. "Amen to that.

"When you boil it down, we're facing someone who wants to do a great amount of damage to humans and vampires, but we have no idea *why*. Even when we thought it was 'just' a serial killer, there was never a solid theory as to why they kidnapped the victims they did. No real victimology. No manifesto. No *goal*.

"Now, we know House Veridian was experimenting on creating hybrid human-vampire DNA. Our best hypothesis for the why on *that* is to create those mindless killing machines. But again, we have no *big picture*."

"Usually, when someone starts making supersoldiers, it's because they want to take over the world." Vicky pointed at Elana with her fork. "At least, that's how it works in the movies."

"That's true," Elana admitted. "But at some point, the bad guy still launches into their evil monologue that explains everything. Why build an army? What's the threat? Do they want to kill vampires, or humans, or both? If it's plain and simple megalomania, why are they *waiting*? Typically, those urges aren't easy to control."

Elana shook her head while meditatively chewing and swallowing her last bite of scrambled eggs. "It just doesn't add up. I'm still missing something."

"You could go back to your mom's journals," Vicky suggested.

"I've thought about that. I don't know if there's anything left to find. Mom's archives showed the way to

House Veridian, but they dried up pretty quickly after that. The last major thing I found in there was her letter to me."

Vicky shrugged. "Can't hurt to take another look. Maybe she somehow keyed it to your Nexus level?"

Elana tapped her fork against her lower lip. "I have no idea if that's possible, but I suppose it could be. Maybe I *should* look again."

"Also, don't you have insight powers?" Vicky reminded her. "Can't you just glare at the data and tell it to make sense, and it will?"

Elana burst out laughing. "God, I wish! I mean, I can *sort* of do that. If I focus my insight power on something, I'll usually end up with a gut feeling in some direction. That's why I still think I'm missing a piece—because I *don't* have that gut feeling. There are too many options.

"That, or my brain's sputtering out." Elana grumbled. "I spent months looking forward to not having to sleep as much. Now I don't seem to need it, and I wish I did. Being awake gets *boring* after a while."

"Sounds like you need to relax."

"Yeah, because it's so easy to relax when there's a supervillain on the loose."

"You gotta take care of yourself, Lana! Remember, if you don't have your health, you don't have anything."

Elana snorted. "That line is from *The Princess Bride,* and it's from the most horrible person in the movie."

"Isn't it annoying when terrible people make good points?" Vicky grinned. "I'm serious, though. You're not gonna catch this guy by running yourself into the ground. Maybe all you need is a day at the spa. Relax your body and mind so it can put the puzzle pieces together for you. Wouldn't you tell me to do the same thing?"

Elana rolled her eyes. "Yes, I would, and I know it would work. Damn you and your logic."

"Maybe that's my superpower." Vicky laid her fork on her plate and drained her second mug of coffee. "When do I find that out, by the way?"

"Your power? Usually sometime after you become an adept."

"Boo."

Elana chuckled. "I hear you. I was super impatient too. 'I've already been an initiate for three decades! Why can't I just figure it out?' But your body and your brain will tell you when they're ready. Your job as an initiate is to get used to the first *huge* changes you're going through. Think of it like being a kid again."

"Gross. Wait, does that mean every Progression is like puberty?"

"Sort of? Not really?" Elana squinted at the last drops of her coffee. "Honestly, the biggest jump for me was guardian to sentinel, but part of that was because it was rushed. I can see how you'd draw the parallel. I'd be lying if I said I didn't experience anything like what I remember of puberty, but it's not *quite* that simple."

Vicky grumbled, "I am having serious second thoughts."

"Too bad, so sad. The Rights are not reversible."

Vicky stuck her tongue out. "Thanks for the sympathy."

"Heh. Trust me when I say I get it. I've wished a few times in the last year that I could go back to being 'normal.' I guarantee you're not the only one feeling like this." Elana gathered the dishes and arranged them in the dishwasher.

"I wonder if there are support groups for new initiates. There must be."

"I can ask at the library," Vicky volunteered. "I plan to spend the morning reading, and libraries are always hubs for community stuff."

Elana beamed. "Good call. You're already doing better than I was."

"How so?"

"With all the revelations about my mom and my life up to that point, I flailed like I was drowning. I used up all my initiative on House Veridian stuff, so Valeria, Matt, and Cathy had to slow-walk me to so many revelations. You're seeking answers of your own accord and making connections. That's exactly what you need to do. Make friends."

"How do I know if I'm making friends with the right people?"

Elana shrugged. "Same as you do with humans. Get to know them, listen to your gut, and decide whether they bring the kind of energy you want in your life."

She glanced at the clock on the stove and sighed. "Wanna come help me pick out an outfit for this walk-and-talk meeting? I have a wardrobe full of amazing clothes, and I'm still shit at deciding what to wear."

Vicky bounced off the stool with an ear-to-ear grin. "*This*, I can do. To the closet!"

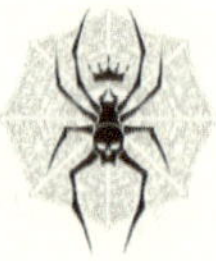

Elana hid a smile behind a well-practiced veneer of professionalism as she approached the knot of consorts milling around the Great Hall's atrium. Elana didn't know why Valeria frequently opted to host her meetings in the spacious galleries of Haven's premier museum, but she wouldn't complain. The backdrop of gorgeous art made the policy discussions far more agreeable. Judging by the scattered grumbling, not everyone felt the same way.

Maybe that's why Valeria does it. Winnow out the consorts with no appreciation for art and history. Valeria is very good at using casual observation to build her opinion of a person.

Elana caught a side-eye thrown in her general direction by one of her least favorite attendees, a slim man who dressed more like a funeral home director than a stylish vampire. This was Raoul Demoissac, the newly appointed Consort of Genealogy. He'd been promoted in recent months from his previous position as a "free-roaming" concubine in the service of the Domain of Legacy.

Figures he works for Zilmann. Elana pasted the professional smile on as thickly as possible in Demoissac's direction. *Slimy bastard.*

Elana's first interaction with Raoul Demoissac had been in her first days in Haven. She'd met Cathy that day too. It seemed like so long ago now. While the atrium hadn't changed, the featured exhibitions had. Different floor-to-ceiling paintings filled the gaps between the columns, and the brochures tucked into the kiosks dotting the circumference of the huge balcony that overlooked the lower floor were different colors.

Elana had visited here on her first day in Haven. Valeria had told Elana to come to the Great Hall after she finished studying in the King's Archives. Upon showing up, Elana had overheard a simpering man implying that Valeria didn't have the balls to take on the SpiderKing's enemies.

I never did find out who or what Otellier was. Or why Valeria didn't want to mess with them even knowing she had the king's backing. I suppose that's what happens when assassination attempts grab your attention and hold it hostage.

For being a lowly concubine at the time, Demoissac hadn't even given Valeria the proper respect of calling her *arbiter.* He'd addressed her as *consort.* While not technically *incorrect*—all arbiters were consorts, but only eight consorts were arbiters—it was certainly impolite. Valeria hadn't skyrocketed through the ranks of Haven's elite royal servants thanks to *nepotism* despite her position as a member of the House of the SpiderKing.

House Scorpion, or House Scorpiones if you wanted to be *extra* proper about it, was a well-respected cadet branch of the House of the SpiderKing. It was small, and primarily produced defenders of the royal family. Valeria certainly qualified.

Elana had attended half a dozen of these walk-and-talks since becoming the Consort of External Affairs and Diplomacy. She'd had the distinct displeasure of attending with Raoul Demoissac on three of those occasions. Each time, she'd come away with an oily film of revulsion lingering in her stomach and the back of her throat. He was conniving and *rude*, and his stringent insistence on formality only emphasized his discourtesy.

You're still being an ass if you're being a polite ass.

The arrival of another consort broke Elana's line of sight on Demoissac. Elana often worked with Raelene Braun, the Consort of Internal Policy and Communications. Raelene was Arbiter Mélissand's right-hand woman, and rumors were rampant that the Arbiter of Vision was grooming her as an eventual replacement.

In Elana's opinion, it spoke well of Raelene's integrity that she had refused to comment on the rumors so far. The Domain of Vision was not only the domain of politics, although Carlysle Zilmann seemed to think the Domain of Legacy held the most sway in Haven's political arena. It was also the domain of arts and culture, a combination that had once confused Elana. How did one square politics and the arts without making the arts overly political? How did you keep it from becoming propaganda?

The SpiderKing's solution seemed to be fairly simple. In keeping with his stated preference for women to hold power and authority in Haven, most of the civil servants working in the Domain of Vision were women. The Arbiter of Vision could not unilaterally make political decisions that would affect the city-state as a whole. Her authority was curtailed in comparison to the other Domains. While most other arbiters required a majority vote of five arbiters to pass legislation in the consulate, the Domain of Vision required six.

Raelene smiled and bowed politely. Her long, straight brown hair fell in a curtain over her shoulder, and she swept it back as she straightened. "Good morning, Elana. How is your initiate settling in?"

"Vicky's doing well." Elana bowed in return. "Still getting used to smelling everything several times stronger than usual. We're eating pretty bland these days."

Raelene chuckled. "You're a kind soul. My head of House once assigned me to the nursery for a decade because I pissed her off, and it was the most annoying job I've ever had. To have your initiate living with you—I can't even imagine."

"I'm sure it would be more annoying if Vicky wasn't already my friend. As it stands, I feel an extra responsibility. I got her into this business in more ways than one, so I need to take care of her."

"An admirable commitment." Arbiter Mélissand's resonant voice broke in, and both consorts turned and bowed deeply. Roxanne Mélissand was dressed in deep red today, in a pencil skirt with a slit that came to her knee and a matching blazer with tails that nearly brushed the floor. A ruby the size of an apricot lay in the hollow of her throat, and her black hair was swept into a deceptively messy beehive.

The look was daring, more in line with an on-stage soloist than a walk-and-talk political meeting. Arbiters were expected to make statements with their fashion as much as their policies. Valeria's nickname of The Ice Queen of Haven had as many facets as a snowflake. Her strict adherence to all-white clothing meant that the extremely rare occasions when she showed up in all *black* struck fear into the hearts of all assembled without a smidgen of effort on Valeria's part.

"Thank you, Arbiter," Elana replied. "It's the right thing to do."

Mélissand clicked her tongue. "Too few vampires think that way these days, in my opinion. Too eager to fob off their responsibilities on their House staff, relying on their name to stand in for personal integrity."

Elana admired Arbiter Mélissand. The stateswoman was a force to be reckoned with and stringently fair in her dealings. Not the type of person most would expect to hold Haven's top political office.

Roxanne Mélissand not only refused to sling mud at her opponents, she walked around every mud puddle in sight. Impolite or uncivil behavior was the fastest way to get yourself kicked out of her caucus of consorts.

Demoissac cut in. His reedy voice made Elana's teeth ache. "Houses represent their traditions!" His tone indicated protest, but his shining, pearly white teeth left no room for misunderstanding. "If we can't lean on our Houses' reputations, why, the foundation of our entire society would become meaningless!"

His ingratiating smile turned on Elana, and she fought the desire to punch him in the teeth. He pleasantly added, "Of course, I can understand why someone of your history would find that less *intuitive* than others might."

Elana forced herself to smile. Her insight power wasn't a secret—vampire grapevines were legendary—so she and Demoissac both knew Elana wasn't fooled in the slightest by his manners.

"Your deference to my *eventful* personal history is kind, Consort Demoissac, but it's unnecessary. I'm perfectly aware and deeply appreciative of my House's reputation. However, I must respect the extra responsibility that befalls me as a member of the royal House of Haven. It would reflect poorly on the House of the SpiderKing if I did not comport myself with the *utmost* integrity and professionalism."

Elana didn't let Demoissac break eye contact at any point while she spoke. She took care to underline the references to just whose House she belonged to, and by extension, how far in the stratosphere she stood on the social ladder compared to him. It wasn't a language she liked speaking because social hierarchies were a pain in the ass, but she'd learned it well.

Demoissac's flawless grin faltered. He appeared to be mustering the courage to rebut her statements, but his gaze flicked over Elana's shoulder, and he withdrew. Elana wasn't surprised. She'd felt Valeria coming thirty seconds earlier and had timed her tiny monologue accordingly.

The Arbiter of Shadows swept in like an icy wind—or maybe that was the outside breeze eddying at her heels. Either way, Valeria Draven knew how to make an entrance. The only people who didn't automatically flinch were Arbiter Mélissand and Elana, and Elana nevertheless bowed politely. She and Valeria didn't stand on ceremony in private anymore since they had too much work to do to waste time, but keeping up appearances was of paramount importance in Havenite society.

Mélissand inclined her head and gestured at the gathered consorts and concubines. "Good morning, Arbiter Draven. Are we ready to begin?"

Valeria confirmed with a terse nod and stepped forward. Mélissand fell in beside her, and the small mob of attendants shuffled into their well-practiced pecking order in their wake.

"I'm hearing further concerns about our defensive measures regarding biological weapons," Mélissand began. "Have you given any thought to last week's conversation?"

"It's the only thing on my mind," Valeria replied sharply. "I can assure you, however, that Haven is as safe as it can be against foreign *and* domestic threats. The Domain of Shadows is working with the Domain of Knowledge to prepare for as many possible scenarios as Tarsin and I can dream up."

"And Tarsin has the most fertile imagination of us all," Mélissand murmured. Amusement rippled through the consorts. In her normal tone, she added, "Will we see increased security on the Wall?"

"We're investing in the newest generation of bioscanners coming out of the Office of Innovation and reducing the length of shifts. Guards will only work four hours at a time moving forward. This will allow them to work harder in the shorter time since they won't have to pace themselves. Therefore, the increased vehicle and personal searches I've ordered won't be done by tired operatives who aren't at their best."

Muttered approval cascaded through the consorts,

many of whom were subtly taking notes on arm-mounted or handheld tablets. Elana wasn't taking notes. Her head was on a swivel, glancing between the arbiters and consorts as she focused her insight power on each of them.

Elana's role in these walk-and-talks was twofold. Nominally, she was there as the Consort of External Affairs and Diplomacy, the outward-facing counterpart to Raelene's office of Internal Affairs and Communication. Raelene handled anything inside Haven that affected its citizens, while Elana managed the messages Haven sent to the rest of the world.

The other half of Elana's job was observation. The arbiters and many long-serving consorts had developed their intuition regarding their colleagues, but nothing compared to Elana's insight power. Valeria had likened it to a laser-focused spotlight, able to strip away pretense with a glance.

Havenite politics was perfectly in line with human politics if you ignored the unnatural life span and supernatural powers. It was incredibly useful for Elana and Valeria to have an "inside view" of the other consorts' motivations.

For instance, Arbiter Mélissand was putting on a good face right now, but she was bored to tears by the incessant complaining that the arbiters weren't doing enough to make the House Veridian problem go away. *She* understood that accomplishing this goal would require the international manhunt that was *already happening* to succeed, and it wasn't in her purview.

Alas, while most of her office shared that attitude, it fell off sharply among the consorts and concubines working for other arbiters—notably the Office of Legacy. Arbiter

Carlysle Zilmann liked Elana about as much as she'd liked Elana's mother, which was to say, not at all.

Zilmann thought Tessa and Elana both had it out for vampires as a whole, which was ridiculous. The prejudice against human-born vampires ran deep in many Old World Houses, and Zilmann thoroughly subscribed to the manifold stereotypes. Unfortunately, this meant Arbiter Zilmann regularly did her utmost to block Elana's projects and initiatives.

Most notable among her efforts was the months-long battle over the deed to a plot of land in Thani, where Elana wanted to build another "coed" vampire-human housing complex. Despite the overwhelming success of the first complexes in Zevenda and Haven's sister city of Ashford, Zilmann remained staunchly opposed to the concept of vampires and humans living side by side.

Elana maintained that the SpiderKing had always intended for Haven's residents to have closer societal ties than it had turned out. It was hardly *his* fault that a bunch of arrogant, whiny assholes too low in the Nexus to know anything real had swindled a second bunch of arrogant, whiny humans into thinking they could overthrow the SpiderKing.

Centuries had passed since the SpiderKing had been forced to annihilate the rebels, but the resulting chasm between vampires and humans remained deep and wide. Haven was *nominally* supposed to be a safe place for humans to coexist with vampires, especially the Citadel at its heart, where humans could walk freely. In practice, very few humans lived within the ring Wall of the vampire city-state.

Given the rampant stereotyping and cruelty that ran between the populations, Elana wasn't surprised, only disappointed. Therefore, she'd jumped in with both feet when she discovered her mother's mission as the Arbiter of Sanctuary to bring vampires and humans closer together.

She had landed in a conspiracy even deeper than the gaping divide between vampires and humans, but hey. Win some, lose some.

"What about the prisoner being held in Citadel Tower?"

The atmosphere in the portrait gallery was suddenly cold as ice. The hesitation in Arbiter Mélissand's voice was clear as day, even to someone without an insight power. She had a duty to voice whatever inquiries were brought to her by the general populace, even when those inquiries made pink spots rise in the Arbiter of Shadows' cheeks.

A few weeks ago, Elana had traveled to Winnipeg, Manitoba, following a tip that someone in Agoracor Pharmaceuticals was using information or furthering research in line with the House Veridian conspiracy. That person was Edward Korynchuk, co-CEO of the philanthropic medical research and development company. His tenure in the company ended years of pent-up resentment and bitterness.

Edward and his business partner, Alistair Sayyah, had also been in a committed relationship for the decades they'd worked together. Alistair was a vampire, a member of the prestigious House Scarapha. Edward had asked many times that Alistair give him the Rights, allowing them to live and work together for centuries beyond Edward's lifespan, but Alistair refused.

In the end, the slight had built in Edward's mind and

heart to such a degree that he'd engineered a lethal virus that would target only vampires. He'd taken Alistair's foster daughter hostage in an Agoracor board meeting and threatened to release the virus unless Alistair consented.

Elana had stepped in lest the virus be accidentally released. Then she'd extradited Edward to Haven. She and her crew of covert operatives had discovered proof that data from House Veridian had aided Edward's research... and that Edward had inoculated himself with synthetic nanocytes as a shield against vampire powers. He had broken the core secret of vampire society. Neither humans nor any vampires below the level of sentinel could learn of the existence of nanocytes.

Elana had expected Arbiter Draven to execute the scientist after interrogating him. Instead, Valeria opted to give Edward the Rights and keep him as a prisoner in Citadel Tower, where he was now working *for* them instead of *against* them. They had done their best to keep the events from becoming public knowledge, but not even the Domain of Shadows was leakproof. It hadn't been long before rumors spread about the scientist in the tower.

On the heels of those rumors came the calls for Edward to be drawn and quartered—mostly figuratively. Havenites were up in arms about the "dangerous man" being held in the Citadel who could have been responsible for the potential death of every vampire on the planet. It was irresponsible to hold him there, they cried. Public opinion was swaying toward Carlysle Zilmann's camp, which drove Elana mad. That said, she wasn't sure *she* agreed with keeping Edward locked up in a tower, either.

"We must protect vampiredom," Demoissac chimed in.

"It's not safe to keep a known enemy so close to the heart of our city."

Elana bit the inside of her lip but focused on the arbiters ahead of her. Other consorts were not so calm and shot dirty looks at Demoissac for speaking out of turn.

Valeria stopped in her tracks, and Roxanne Mélissand halted a step later. She turned back to look at Valeria, but Valeria replied in sharp tones to the impertinent consort without turning to meet his sycophantic gaze.

"Edward Korynchuk is in the custody of the Domain of Shadows. He will remain in that custody, working for us to mitigate the damage he has already caused until we decide whether to end his life. Until that time, Consort Demoissac, you and your mistress may consider the matter closed to discussion."

Silence fell on the restless group of civil servants. Everyone held their breath to see if Zilmann's dog would bark again or if he would tuck his tail between his legs. There was no question in Elana's mind.

"Of course, Arbiter Draven," Demoissac simpered.

Elana wished she could toss him through a wall.

CHAPTER THREE

Elana bit her tongue through the rest of the walk-and-talk. Nothing much came up that she would have to deal with later. Demoissac made a few more side comments hinting at how much Arbiter Zilmann planned to screw Elana over in the upcoming special legislative session of the Council of Arbiters. She wasn't looking forward to *that*.

"How did I end up a politician?" she lamented to Matt while winding toward the Citadel in her sleek Lotus Emeya. She'd never been much for electric cars in her previous life. You couldn't work in demolition and construction without a trusty pickup truck, but vampires opted for the sophisticated look ninety-nine times out of a hundred. She occasionally missed her beloved F150, but the Emeya was much more suited to Haven.

Someday, I'll buy a plot of land outside Ashford, and I'll have as many trucks as I want. Just as soon as we catch the Staker and I can live outside the Wall without fearing for my life.

"You followed in your mother's footsteps, I guess?"

Matt sounded patiently amused, which was a tone he used often in their conversations. "You could leave."

"I definitely can't, and you know it," she retorted. "I'm in this for the long haul."

"Fair enough. There's always next century."

Elana snorted. "Right. How many careers have you gone through now? Have your parents given up on you ever settling down?"

Matt laughed. "They're pinning their hopes on Claudia becoming the next head Chimera. Although I have to say, the last family dinner was considerably less awkward. Head guardian is acceptable, especially in this time of tumultuous unrest."

He spoke the last few words in an exaggerated French accent, which made Elana snicker. Matt was a Richelieu *of* House Richelieu, famed member of the House of Cardinals. The House of Houses had its fingers in every pie from here to Antarctica.

He and his parents had been given the Rights sometime in the last couple of centuries for the express purpose of creating a new branch of House Richelieu to be quartered in Haven. In theory, Matt was in line to inherit the head of House position, which offered him considerable sway in Havenite politics.

However, he couldn't have been less interested in using it, to the unending frustration of his parents and the elders of the House back in Europe. Matt's preferences ran far more to the practical. Over the course of his life, he'd been a social worker, a lawyer, and probably a few other things Elana hadn't wheedled out of him yet.

Elana had met him while he was "slumming it" as a

dispatcher in the guardian offices, taking a shift off from his position as head guardian to reconnect with the people he oversaw.

Now, he spent most of his time in his office in Guardian HQ. The beautiful pagoda-inspired building stood proudly above the fields of Senkyem, the fifth district of Haven and the Domain of Shadows.

Senkyem's dual nature as the agricultural center of Haven and its law enforcement puzzled many until you realized it was a deliberate choice on the SpiderKing's part. Residing in the fields and greenhouses meant the backbone of Haven's work surrounded the guardians. It grounded them.

It struck Elana as a remarkably forward-thinking decision, and Matt couldn't have been better suited as the "foil" for the Arbiter of Shadows. While he was bound to follow her orders, he was a man of sufficient integrity and level-headed rationale that Valeria listened when he voiced a concern.

Elana was deeply grateful Matt had been her first contact with the vampire world and that they'd grown into a sibling-esque relationship. Being an only child, Elana was used to making her own decisions, and that independence had only intensified after her father died. Having someone around to consult whom she could trust to give thoughtful advice took a huge weight off her shoulders.

"What's Zilmann doing now?" he asked lightly, bringing her out of her thoughts.

She halted at the floating stop sign, checked both ways, flicked on her blinker, and turned onto the inner ring road that circled the Citadel. She began looking for a parking spot. "Same old, same old. I really hoped I'd have worn her down by now. This surge in paranoia thanks to the pandemic threat—and the fact that we still haven't caught the Staker—has given her so much leverage.

"According to Demoissac, whose intestines I'd like to wear as a scarf, she plans to drown the council in isolationist legislation. Humans out, vampires in, rah rah rah. Gag me with a spoon. As if that will give us any protection!"

Matt sighed. "Of course. Humans and vampires are cut from the same cloth. When threatened, our first instinct is always to circle the wagons."

"But that only works if the threat is outside the wagons to begin with, and it's not! The Staker *has* to be a vampire. Kicking humans out of Haven won't help."

"And Zilmann knows that perfectly well, which means her next target will be human-born vampires since no one of sufficient pedigree in the Sanguine Nexus could possibly seek to harm vampiredom to this extent." Matt sounded almost bored, but Elana heard the fatigued sarcasm underneath. *The more things change...*

Elana pulled into a parking spot next to the Minor Gate of Secrets, the entrance to the Citadel that sat on the border between Quarto and Senkyem. "That is depressing and infuriating at the same time. How dare you."

"Ha, ha. So, what's your plan?"

She killed the engine and sat back in her seat, staring out the windshield at the Wall that rose past her line of sight. "Hasn't really changed. Find the Staker so we can bring the curtain down on this circus and deprive Zilmann of at least one arrow in her arsenal."

"You know that won't stop her, right? She gave your mother at least as much shit as she's giving you, and there wasn't an active manhunt for a vampire-murdering serial killer going on at the time."

Elana sighed heavily. "I know. I hope I'll be able to sway public opinion with a successful capture. It won't convince the hardcore purists, but I doubt I *could* convince them. When you've been in a vampire-only bloodline for long enough that you've forgotten that your ancestors were human at some point, you're too far down the rabbit hole to be brought up by anything but a bathysphere."

"Deep cut."

"Very funny." She sighed again. "Am I still on the list of Edward's permitted visitors?"

"I haven't been told to remove you, so unless you've seriously pissed Valeria off in the last twelve hours, you should be. *Have* you seriously pissed her off in the last twelve hours? If so, I'd appreciate knowing so I can lock myself in my panic room."

Elana snorted. "You're punchy this morning."

"I'm fielding the same calls Zilmann's staff are. Everybody's punchy."

"I bet. No, I haven't pissed Valeria off, at least not as far as I know, and she's not the passive-aggressive type."

Matt laughed. "You'd definitely know if you'd pissed her off, yeah. You're visiting loverboy, then?"

Elana rubbed her key chain between her thumb and forefinger. It was a scrap of fabric from her dad's favorite tie, cut into a simple rectangle, hemmed, and embroidered with the words *Bishops LLC*. She'd been toying with it so much in the last year that a patch of the maroon silk was doubly shiny.

"Yeah," she finally replied. "He came up at the meeting today. I feel like I'm the only one making sure he's okay."

"You're not. I have guardians checking on him several times a day."

"I mean emotionally. I doubt the guardians are making a point to engage the poor guy in conversation. They're just there to make sure he doesn't off himself."

"They're not there to therapize him, that's true. I'd say I don't understand why you care, but I'd be lying. Your mother would have done the same thing."

"Would my mother have let him be given the Rights and locked in a tower?"

"Good question. I don't know. The possibility never came up."

Elana bit her lip, then sighed a third time. "Yeah. I should go. Talk later?"

"Sure. We still on for supper?"

"Wouldn't miss it for the world. My couscous salad is chilling in the fridge."

"I look forward to it. And Elana?"

"Yeah?"

"Take care of yourself, okay? Don't let the bastards grind you down."

"I'll do my best. Thanks, Matt."

"Any time."

Elana hung up, grabbed her dimensional handbag, and got out of the car. She locked it behind her with a wave, then strode through the Gate of Secrets into the Citadel's courtyard.

Once upon a time, this open space at the center of Haven had struck such awe into her soul that she'd stopped cold before taking a second step past the gate. This was the core of Haven—the beating heart of the SpiderKing's daring experiment to see if humans and vampires could live side by side as equals, and ground zero of the Rebellion. The massive hourglass of the Rebels' Monument flowed inexorably, as pristine as the day the SpiderKing had created it.

Rumor held that the king lived under the courtyard, in a chamber only accessible by the arbiters and only then at the king's pleasure. When you walked across the Citadel, you walked over the king's head, or so went the saying.

Elana paid none of this any mind today. She had grown accustomed to the splendor of the Citadel and Haven. It was home now.

She was used to seeing the floating stop signs, the buildings untouched by time and weather, and the subtle displays of technology beyond human comprehension. Her gaze slid past it all without taking any of it in. She had work to do.

The sheen of novelty had gradually worn off for Elana, but she would have to confess that the vampire world had truly lost a touch of its magic for her when she discovered nanocytes. Knowing there was a banal explanation for everything vampires did, despite having held suspicions to that effect for years, made the wonders around her seem so mundane as to be *ho-hum.*

If pressed further, however, Elana would admit it wasn't the nanocytes that had removed the gleam of wonder. It was what she perceived as selfish secrecy—the solemn, unquestioning adherence to the lie that vampires presented to the outside world. *We are better than you in every conceivable way because we are blessed by the Sanguine Nexus,* or something like that.

No admission that vampires could only do what they did thanks to a genetic mutation that allowed them to access and manipulate a specialized type of cell carried by *every living thing on the planet,* humans included. No admission that vampires held the position they did in the world because their ancestors had gotten *lucky* several thousand years ago.

Most of all, no admission that because vampirism was thanks to a quirk of evolution *that could be transferred,* humans were no different.

We're not special, Elana thought bitterly as her heels clacked across the gorgeous, intricate sigil of the Spider-King inlaid into the consulate's marble floor. *We're just lucky.*

Since bad luck could always follow good luck, it stuck in Elana's craw that vampires around the world believed themselves immune and untouchable. *That's why they're so scared, though. For millennia, their status was assured as long as they kept their secret. Now that safety net is fraying, thanks to the man I'm about to see.*

Elana's frown deepened as she ascended the stairs into the Tower of Shadows. Truth be told, she wasn't sure what her goal was in seeing Edward other than convincing herself that her paranoia was baseless and the man was still alive.

She knew the guardians wouldn't kill him since he was too valuable an asset, but she couldn't imagine the depressive state he had to be in. He'd thrown away his entire life because he'd allowed his fear to eat him from the inside out, and now he had to live with that choice.

He wanted the Rights, and he got them. I wonder how deeply he regrets it.

Elana came to the door of Edward's cell. A pair of guardians in full armor flanked it. Edward was an initiate, meaning he was about as powerful as Elana's pinky toe compared to his guards, but the threat Edward posed was mental, not physical.

After all of this blew over, Elana wondered whether Valeria would execute him or relegate him to a cell deep underground. Out of mind meant he could be out of sight. Right now, Valeria had to look like she was doing something about the situation, so he was up here in the semi-public corridors of the Tower of Shadows.

Elana squared her jaw and tried to steel herself for the imminent confrontation, only to deflate when she realized the only person doing the confronting was her. She was screwing her courage to the wall so she could handle seeing a person in abject misery that she'd had a hand in causing.

Again, she cursed the life events that led her to become a politician. This was *not* how she wanted to spend her days.

Elana cleared her throat and stepped up to the door. "Elana Bishop, here to see Edward Korynchuk," she informed the guards. "I won't be long."

The guard in charge glanced at her and nodded almost imperceptibly. He twitched his hand along the doorframe, and something in the wall slid aside in response to the nanocyte-driven signal.

Another step forward. The door slid into the wall, revealing the small room that constituted the entirety of Edward Korynchuk's world. When Elana walked in, claustrophobia threatened the edges of her mind as her insight power picked up on the mental state of the prison's sole inhabitant.

The room's furniture was limited to a bed and a desk with a chair. The walls included a few small cubbies for storage, and a small separate chamber hid the ensuite, the one concession to privacy. Elana knew the only reason the bathroom had any privacy was because it was so small it would be hard to find a way to kill yourself, which was depressing in itself.

The room and its contents were not uncomfortable, only Spartan. It didn't change that Edward now existed in a twelve-by-twelve box with no access to the outside world. When Elana left the room, the door would merge seamlessly with the wall on the inside. The light cycle was controlled from the outside, and the temperature never varied. It was like he lived in his own pocket dimension.

Edward was sitting at the desk when she came in. He wore gray sweatpants and a gray sweater. They were his clothes since he'd been allowed to bring a selection of his belongings to Haven upon his extradition. He could also request other items since the House of the SpiderKing had seized his estate. His belongings were now in storage in the guardians' subterranean complex. The guardians were going through it with a fine-toothed comb for evidence of his crimes, but he could still get a book if he wanted it.

Thin lines of light glimmered around his wrists and ankles. These were nano-inhibitors, devices designed to limit Edward's use of his newly awoken nanocytes. As Elana understood it, wearing nano-inhibitors felt like wearing thick mittens, socks, and earmuffs, all laden with static. They deadened your senses to worse than human levels, and if you tried too hard to use any nanocyte powers, they would zap you.

The man hunched over his desk, idly dragging documents and illustrations across the built-in interface. Working, presumably, but as miserable as she usually saw him. A far cry from what he'd likely hoped for if he'd ever convinced Alistair to give him the Rights—a free pass into the pseudo-utopia of vampire civilization, where nanotech ran everything.

A scientist's paradise. Knowledge beyond imagining. Like being beamed up by aliens into a science-fiction universe that had always existed just behind the curtain.

Instead, he got prison.

"Hi, Edward."

He glanced up, then back at his work. "Morning, Elana."

"You know it's morning?"

Edward stopped his dull motions on the desktop interface and looked up at her with sparks of disbelief and offense in his eyes. He pointed to the corner of the desk. "I have a *clock.*"

Elana blushed. "Oh. Right. Sorry, that was stupid. Mind if I have a seat?"

He dismissively waved at the rest of the room. "Be my guest."

She awkwardly perched on the edge of his bed, which

was comfortable. Better than any bed she'd had growing up, and Jeremiah Bishop had believed in buying quality mattresses. *Anything that goes between you and the ground is worth spending money on,* he'd taught Elana. The axiom had served her well.

"What are you working on?" She knew better than to ask Edward how he was doing. She'd done that on the first day and had immediately wished she could take the words back when she saw them land like whipcracks. There were no pleasantries here, especially not when half of those present knew the other half could read them like a children's board book.

"Reverse-engineering the genome required to create the nanocyte proteins found in the blood of House Veridian's test subjects." His tone was flatter than a pancake and much less tasty, despite Elana knowing genetic engineering was his enduring passion.

Elana forced a chuckle. "That sounds like it would be seriously interesting, possibly frustrating, and undoubtedly way over my head."

Edward shrugged. "It's a challenge. Keeps me occupied. Better that than staring at the ceiling alone with my thoughts."

"I bet." She folded her hands in her lap and tried not to feel awkward. She'd been visiting Edward every day since he'd been let out of ultra-max security about a week after they'd returned to Haven. Valeria's interrogations had filled a couple of days, but over half of that time had been spent recuperating from receiving the Rights, which hadn't gone well.

Although Valeria was adept at administering the Rights,

having done so several times, they interacted unexpectedly with the synthetic nanocytes already in Edward's blood. As Elana had heard it, he'd spent about a day and a half hovering between life and death.

He still looks like a zombie. Elana did her best to unobtrusively give Edward a once-over, even though she knew it was almost pointless since they were the only two people in the room and he was staring at her blankly. His eyes sat deep in their sockets, he'd lost at least twenty pounds in short order, and his skin was sallow and sagged on his frame. He *looked* the most like someone "undead" that Elana had ever seen.

"Can I get you anything? I know they make sure you have enough food, but I don't know how many options you have. They won't tell me no. Well, not unless you ask me for something to break yourself out."

Edward chuckled, but it was utterly mirthless and dry as a bone. "The inhibitors would just stop me anyway. There'd be no point." He lifted a hand and circled it to indicate the glowing bracelet. "Fascinating bits of technology. Truly ingenious. I imagine they could be recalibrated to inhibit cancerous cell growth."

Elana swallowed. Edward had sounded like this since the first day they'd spoken. He wasn't *literally* dead, but he might as well have been. *Is this really better than death? Is getting the information we need worth indefinitely keeping a man in this kind of existential despair?*

"Potato chips," he added. "If you wouldn't mind. Any flavor. I like to have something to crunch on while I work, and while my meals certainly meet all my nutritional needs, junk food doesn't exactly make the list."

"Potato chips," she echoed. That casual request had somehow thrown the entire exchange into the twilight zone. "Yeah, sure. I can get you potato chips."

"Thanks."

Edward turned back to the desk and bent over the incomprehensible documents. After a moment, Elana stood and left, feeling worse than she had when she arrived.

CHAPTER FOUR

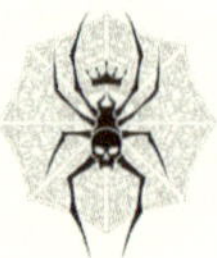

Vicky was a bundle of nerves on the way to the Consorts' Training Grounds. She didn't own a car since up until now she'd spent most of her adult life traveling around the world on Condé Nast's dime. Elana picked her up at home and drove them into the heart of Senkyem.

She'd tried to convince Elana that she would take a glider to the training grounds, but Elana nixed it. "You've barely gotten your legs under you, Vick," she flatly told her. "Remember, I had thirty years to get used to being an initiate, even though I didn't know it. You've had days. Don't think I didn't see you trip yesterday."

"Everybody trips!"

"Sure. Not everybody trips and slides fifty feet down the sidewalk because they're driving a hovercraft. You don't want to spend *more* time in the medical center, do you?"

"No."

"I'll be there in fifteen minutes."

They pulled into the parking lot in front of the elegant

glass-walled lobby, and Elana felt the anxiety emanating from her best friend in waves. She killed the engine, turned to face Vicky, and fixed her with her best eyebrow raise. "What's wrong?"

"Nothing."

Elana's second eyebrow joined her first. "Try again."

Vicky squirmed and covered her face with her hands. "I am *terrified* of making a fool of myself, and I *know* I will. Why couldn't we do this at home or in a regular gym? Why do we have to go to the *Consorts' Training Grounds?*"

"Remember the whole reason you wanted the Rights in the first place?"

Vicky peeked between two fingers. "Because I've wanted to be a vampire since you and I were obsessed with them in high school?"

"Very funny."

"It's true!"

"It's *half* true," Elana countered. "The other half is because you're in my orbit whether we like it or not. You quite rightly figured out that you would benefit from the extra physical and mental abilities that come with being a vampire. If vampires are coming after you because you're connected to me, you need to be able to protect yourself."

Elana pointed at the building outside. "Part of that is training. We're *here* because, again, you're connected to me. Sure, you might get decent training at any gym in Haven, but you'll get the *best* training at the Consorts' Training Grounds. Since you have access through me, you might as well take advantage of it."

Vicky sighed and let her hands fall into her lap. "Damn you and your annoying habit of making sense."

"Sorry."

"Do I at least get to fall on my ass privately? Or did you sign me up for group training?"

Elana chuckled. "It'll just be you, me, and Gustav."

"Gustav? *The* Gustav?"

"The very one. I asked nicely."

An impish grin spread across Vicky's plump brown face. "Well, that's not so bad, then. I can never say no to a Russian bear."

Elana snorted and rolled her eyes as she unlocked the doors. "You don't get to date him."

"You're not the boss of me. I can date whoever I want."

"I'm pretty sure he's gay."

"Have you *asked?*"

"No, but I have the most powerful insight around, barring the SpiderKing. In other words, my gaydar is impeccable."

Vicky pouted. "You're no fun."

Elana laughed. "Hey, who knows! Maybe you'll be the cause of his bisexual awakening. Just don't let your mooning distract you from his right hook. You'll regret it."

She led the way into the lobby. She checked in with the receptionist, signed Vicky in as her guest, and headed down the hall to the palatial locker rooms. There, Elana almost had to drag Vicky away from the Roman-style baths and intricate showers with promises that they would be back before she knew it.

"I doubt that very much," Vicky grumbled. "I have a sneaking suspicion that today will feel like the longest day ever, and I won't want to move an inch when it's done."

"You're probably right. On the plus side, it means the shower room will be even *nicer.*"

"You are enjoying this *way* too much."

Elana chortled as she pushed open the door to the gym where she had her first training session over a year ago. She mostly worked in the back wing now, in the rooms designated for use by Haven's law enforcement elite, like the Shadowguard and Chimeras. Being back in this gym was a nostalgia blast.

"I asked Gustav to come in an hour," she told Vicky. "That'll give us time to warm up first, and it'll give *you* time to start getting used to how your body's changing."

Vicky looked down at herself and made a face. "I don't *look* different, but you're right. I've tripped over my own two feet more times in the last week than I ever have in my entire life. God knows I'm no athlete, but I'm no klutz, either. It's been driving me up the wall."

Elana nodded and sank into a deep lunge, stretching her right calf and curving her torso up and back to stretch her side. "Stretch however you want, but focus on the big muscle groups. Your muscles are more efficient now, so it takes less energy to do more, and your brain hasn't caught up yet. That means you're likely to overshoot your target every time you move."

"That explains the tripping and knocking things over."

"Bingo."

Vicky was no stranger to solo exercise, having seen the inside of innumerable hotel gyms in her career. She easily moved into a familiar routine of stretches and light aerobics, and Elana was pleased to observe that she intuitively began to adapt to her new vampiric abilities. She moved slowly, noted how her body reacted, and adjusted accordingly.

A few minutes in, Vicky opened her eyes, looked around the gym, and frowned. "Do y'all have any exercise equipment? Not, like, treadmills or stair-climbers. Free weights? Barbells? Anything like that?"

Elana finished her jogging lap beside her friend. "Sure, but not really in the way you think—at least, not in this gym. What do you want?"

"Pair of five-pound weights. Everything feels so *easy*, so I'm not convinced my form is right."

"Fair enough. Follow me." Elana trotted to the wall and tapped it. A large waist-high rectangle glowed on the vertical surface and extruded into a cabinet. Another tap made a drawer slide open. Inside were rows of glowing objects, everything from various weights of barbells to practice weapons.

Vicky's eyebrows shot up. "Holy *shit*. Vampire tech is *amazing*. Wait, are those nunchucks?"

"Sure are."

"I thought this was a *gym*."

"It is. It's also a dojo. Want to learn how to use nunchucks?"

Vicky blinked. "I… Huh."

Elana paused, sensing the shift in mood, and tapped the drawer to close it again. She turned to face Vicky head-on and leaned on the glowing cabinet. "Everything okay?"

Vicky didn't answer immediately. Her gaze was stuck on the spot where the nunchucks had been. Eventually, she shook her head and murmured, "It just got real all of a sudden."

Elana reached over and caught Vicky's eye before putting her hand on her friend's shoulder. "Wanna talk about it?"

"Not sure what to say." Vicky's gaze slipped back to the floor, but she didn't push Elana's hand off. "I know you told me about learning to fight. God knows I've been around you enough in the last year to know why it's a good idea—hell, like you said, that was part of the reason I wanted the Rights. But seeing those..." She motioned toward the empty air. "Brought it home, I guess."

"Having second thoughts?"

"Heh. All the time and not at all. It's just scary. I know you get that."

"I do."

Vicky drew a long, slow breath and let it out in a gentle hiss. "It's not even like I haven't already trained in self-defense. It's been a while since I took a refresher course, and I've only had to use it a few times...and I'm not naïve, but..."

"But there's a big difference between basic self-defense techniques and learning to use nunchucks," Elana finished. "Or whatever you choose to learn."

"I kinda want to learn the nunchucks," Vicky sheepishly responded. "Is that weird?"

Elana threw back her head and laughed. "It's not weird. I don't know if Gustav does nunchucks, but I guarantee we can find someone to teach you. I think you'd look badass swinging those around.

"That said, it's vampire tradition, I guess, to learn sword-fighting," Elana added. "Honorable weapon and all that."

Vicky scoffed. "Still boggles my mind why vampires haven't developed uber-evolved guns. If y'all can make glowing cabinets that slide out of the wall, why not make super-powered guns? Wouldn't that solve all your problems?"

Elana raised an eyebrow. "Uh, no? No more than the glut of ridiculous automatic weapons out in the human world solves all of their problems. Besides..." Elana grimaced. "You know this already, but you might not have thought of it along these lines. Most vampires think of themselves as being a cut above humans. Right?"

"Uh-huh."

"Right. So, 'stooping to' the use of guns feels almost *dirty* to a lot of those vampires. Makes it too easy, basically. If you have a problem with someone, vampire law is way more permissible when it comes to having it out with whoever. There are plenty of situations where you can get away with murder. However, your social standing can take a hell of a hit if you don't do it 'right.'"

Vicky blinked, then shook her head again. "Wow. Man, even with all the conversations you and I have had over the last year, I still feel like I don't know anything. The tabloids we used to read were crap!"

Elana snickered. "You're telling me. I remember the first weeks I was here. I spent so much time grumbling about how far astray the tabloids and forums had led me. So much of what I thought I knew was entirely wrong!"

She patted the cabinet again. After the drawer slid open, she poked around until she found a pair of free weights. "Here. If you take nothing else from today, remember this. Very often, you will find it immensely useful to work out all your frustration and confusion in the gym. You won't always be able to use *this* gym, but I can get you a membership to any gym in the city."

Vicky accepted the weights and hefted them, then raised an eyebrow at Elana. "I *do* have money, you know."

Elana shrugged. "Sure, and I've no doubt you'll make scads more than me once you set your mind to it. You have a knack for business—you'll fit into that part of Havenite society way better than I do. For now, I have money burning holes in my pocket, and everything costs five times more than it should here because we *all* have more money than God. Take the money and run, hon."

"Well, it's dumb to say no to a free lunch, so fair enough, and thanks." Vicky settled into proper form for weightlifting and began a series of bicep curls. "God*damn*. How much do these weigh?"

"Five pounds, like you asked."

"They feel like feathers."

Elana grinned and retrieved the next set from the cabinet. "I thought they might. Try these."

"Gladly. I want a *workout*, not to show off." They traded, and Vicky started working with the next set. "That's a little better. I'd ask for the next one up, but if what you say about not knowing my own strength is true, I don't wanna overdo it."

Elana replaced the first set in the drawer. "Very wise. You're already doing *way* better at this than I did when I started."

Vicky scoffed. "I don't believe that for a second."

"It's true." Elana selected a much heavier set of weights and mirrored Vicky's movements. "I was impatient as hell when I started training. Pushed myself in a lot of ways, probably further than was healthy. I thought I had to prove myself since I'd grown up as a vampire without realizing it.

"It didn't help that I was under immediate threat, either." She chuckled. "Assassination attempts tend to kick your motivation into high gear."

Vicky laughed, then focused on finishing her set of repetitions before carefully placing the weights on the floor. "I was like that the first year I worked for the *Traveler*. I rushed into so much shit without being ready for it. I thought if I didn't prove myself faster than anyone ever had, they'd can my sorry ass as soon as they realized I was faking it.

"Luckily, my editor was no fool. She saw right through my idiotic behavior, called me out, and showed me the way forward. Slow, steady, and mindful makes a much better piece. You taste the food better that way, too."

Elana nodded while continuing her repetitions. "Cathy taught me the same thing. Had to grab me by the collar and yank me onto a yoga mat, but she got through."

Vicky crossed her arms and counted Elana's reps. "How much are those? Fifty pounds?"

"Something like that."

"You're not even *straining*."

"Welcome to being a sentinel." Elana winked. "You'll get there someday."

The door to the gym slid open, and a man with a gruff Russian voice called, "Elana! *Moya umnichka!* I have missed your lovely face!"

Elana finished the repetition, set the weights on the floor, and grinned from ear to ear. She opened her arms wide as Gustav approached and wrapped the short, burly Russian trainer in a tight hug. "I hope you've missed more than my face!" she teased.

"*Da,* but if I said what I *really* missed, you'd toss me across the gym!"

They both laughed heartily, then released one another. Gustav clapped Elana on the back and motioned at the weights. "Not bad. I remember when you first tried those. You whined like a baby."

"I did not! Okay, maybe I did."

Vicky chortled. "I can see it. You have a stellar pout."

Elana glared. "Whose side are you on?"

Vicky raised her hands innocently. "The side that ends with my face on the mat the *fewest* number of times!"

Gustav chortled. "Oh, do not be so sure that sucking up is the way to go. Elana can attest to how many times her face ended up on the mat..."

Elana winced. "Let's just say you're gonna *seriously* appreciate your new regeneration abilities."

Vicky smacked a fist into her palm. "Bring it. I wanna learn."

Gustav leaned back on one foot and gave Vicky a once-over, then glanced at Elana. "What would you recommend, Elana?"

Elana's eyebrows rose. "Who, me? I'm just here for moral support. I don't know the first thing about training someone from the ground up. Why do you want my opinion?"

"For precisely that reason. You have not trained

someone before. You have only *been* trained. Now, you are a sentinel, and I will eat my gym shorts if you do not reach archon. Not every high-level vampire teaches, but *all* high-level vampires are role models. You are very likely to mentor someone. Perhaps even Miss Lamarr."

"Well, now I *have* to reach archon." Elana's face twisted in an unpleasant grimace. "I don't wanna make you eat your shorts."

"I would appreciate that."

She drew a deep breath and also looked Vicky up and down. She ran her tongue over her teeth and eventually shrugged. "I have to admit I don't know enough about how Vicky moves to recommend starting with any specific style. I know she's resilient and already has practice with physical activity. I think she used to do spin classes and biking. And we did Zumba in lockdown."

Vicky snickered and covered her face with her hands. "Oh, God. The framing on my webcam was the *worst*."

"Yeah, everyone on the video call became intimately familiar with which sports bras actually functioned..."

Gustav cleared his throat. "Your intuition is good, as usual. You do not know enough to make a solid recommendation. Therefore..."

Elana blinked, then smacked her forehead. "Basics. Basics, basics, basics. *Duh.* We do more of what she and I just did. Calisthenics, aerobics, fitness training, and testing. Bring the obstacle courses out and see how she does. You need to gather information. Otherwise, you're shooting in the dark."

Gustav applauded. "*Good.* Yes! That is exactly what you

do." He grinned and clapped Elana on the back again. "See? I knew you would be a good teacher."

Vicky bounced on the balls of her feet and shook out her arms. "I haven't done an obstacle course since high school. Those are fun. Set me up with one of those, coach."

Gustav headed for the console built into the wall by the door, but Elana bit her lip. "Are you sure? They're nasty. I got so tangled in the ropes one time that Gustav laughed at me for ten minutes before climbing up and setting me free."

Vicky grinned. "Sounds like a challenge. Race you?"

"Are you kidding? I'll leave you in the dust! I'm a sentinel!"

Panels on the ceiling opened in sequence, and a series of ropes on frames descended, tied in nets, ladders, and tightropes with the occasional platform thrown in to give you a false sense of security. One knotted rope dangled a foot off the floor as though enticing them to draw nearer and shinny into the jungle above.

Gustav informed them as he approached, "This course is built for one, but a little healthy competition never hurt. May I make a suggestion?"

"Please do," Elana invited.

"Miss Lamarr goes first, so she learns the course. You watch. Then, when she finishes, you take your turn while she watches." He laid a finger on the side of his nose. "Do you remember how you felt watching Arbiter Draven spar when you first arrived in Haven?"

"Do I ever. God, she was amazing. Still is. Seriously inspiring."

"Then you understand the exercise."

"But she's an *archon!*" Elana protested. "I'm not that good!"

Gustav shook his head, then wagged his finger at her, and when he spoke, he used the tone that indicated Elana had better listen up or else. "Elana. It is not good to be prideful. Why?"

She frowned. "Overconfidence means you underestimate your enemies' abilities. Bad plan. Gets you killed."

"Correct. It is not good to be self-effacing. Why?"

Elana's frown deepened, but Vicky answered before Elana could. "Because if you don't trust what you're capable of, you'll underestimate *yourself* when you need to perform at your best. Negative self-talk is the mind-killer. No room for that!"

Gustav clicked his tongue approvingly. "Correct, Miss Lamarr. Very good. *You,* Miss Bishop, need to be objective about your skills. Have you watched any footage of yourself fighting or training lately?"

"Uh, no. I haven't really had the chance."

"Make time. Also, I recommend asking your mentors for honest opinions about your strengths and weaknesses. Self-reflection is a vital part of ascending in the Nexus without going mad. I like you. Please don't go crazy."

Elana couldn't help but laugh. "You got it, Gustav. Thanks."

"Any time. Miss Lamarr?"

"Ready, coach!"

He chuckled. "No, you're not. But you will be. Go!"

Vicky took off running for the dangling rope. She leaped, snagged it, and got her feet onto the first knot with only a small slip. Then she worked her way up hand over hand, "jumping" her feet to each successive knot.

"I would have dead-jumped it," Elana murmured to Gustav. "More efficient that way, and you don't have to counterbalance for the momentum of the running jump."

Gustav nodded. "Humans typically leverage the forces of nature to give themselves the advantage. Swinging as Miss Lamarr is doing might help her gather the impetus to propel herself up the next step.

"On the other hand, you are already capable of delivering a great amount of kinetic energy from a static position. It will take time before Miss Lamarr discovers and develops that ability, but perhaps not *very* long. You said she does spin?"

"Yeah, and she bikes wherever she can, too. Says she prefers it to renting a car, especially when she's on assignment in bike-friendly cities in Europe and Asia."

The Russian nodded thoughtfully while watching Vicky gather momentum at the top of the rope to leap into the netting. "Then I *suspect* we might start with a martial art that emphasizes the legs since she already has the foundation of that kinesthetic awareness, but we shall see. She is doing quite well for a newly turned human."

Elana grinned, proud of her best friend, but the moment was broken by her phone going off in her gear bag beside the wall.

She frowned and jogged over. That was her priority ringtone, which was never a good sign.

Elana retrieved the phone from the bag's depths, grimaced at the name on the screen—double bad news— and swiped to answer the call. "Elana here."

Valeria's reply was curt, which ratcheted Elana's nerves up by several degrees. "Whatever you're doing, get out of it. I need you at the Citadel as soon as possible."

Elana's gaze flicked up to Vicky, still working through the course. "I'll be right there."

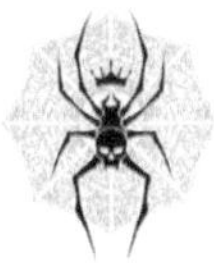

CHAPTER FIVE

"I have to go," Elana called up to Vicky as she put her phone away. "Sorry, Vick."

Vicky hooked her legs in a net, let herself dangle upside-down, and crossed her arms. "Everything okay?"

"Definitely not, but I have no idea what's happening, so don't bother asking."

"Be safe. I'll figure out a way home if I don't hear from you."

"Please don't take a glider unless Gustav clears you for it."

Vicky chuckled. "Go save the world, Lana. I'll be fine."

Elana smiled weakly, then turned her worried gaze on Gustav. "You okay if I abandon you with Vicky?"

Gustav snorted and shooed her toward the door. "We will be fine. You heard Miss Lamarr. Go save the world."

Elana nodded and dashed out, swinging her bag over her shoulder as she ran. She didn't shower or change out of her workout clothes. Valeria's tone had been sharp and urgent enough that Elana didn't think she had time.

She sprinted through the corridors back to the lobby, then through the parking lot to her Emeya. She skidded on a patch of snow but righted herself with the next step and kept running. *Thank God vampires are resistant to cold. I'm no shrinking violet, but this would be unpleasant otherwise.*

Elana slammed the car door shut behind her, jabbed the ignition button, and peeled out of the parking lot like a bat out of hell. Whatever was happening was bad and urgent, which was a deeply concerning combination. Elana could only think of a few situations that would warrant a call like this, and all of them made her stomach churn.

She screeched to a halt in the first Citadel ring parking lot she could find, grabbed her dimensional handbag off the front seat, and ran through the gate. She passed the Rebels' Memorial on her way through and gave Sarah Goldin a wide berth as she did so. Sarah was almost as much of a landmark as the monument, and she was bitchy enough in general that Elana had no desire to irk her by impinging on her personal space.

That'd be just what I need today. Elana burst through the consulate's doors and sprinted up the stairs of the Tower of Shadows. *Piss off the vampire Mafia by accidentally hip-checking their mom.*

She paused halfway up the tower, not to catch her breath but to focus. The arbiter hadn't specified where to meet in the Citadel. It was a safe bet that Valeria was in the Tower of Shadows, but *where* in the Tower was an open question.

Elana grumbled silently. *I should have checked on the ground floor, not halfway up. If I have to go back down the stairs, I'll be grumpy.*

"Elana?"

Matt's voice brought her out of her focus and around on the stairs. He also looked like he'd been running. His tie was askew, his suit jacket had come unbuttoned, and his hair wasn't perfect.

She greeted him with a wave. "Valeria called you too? Now I'm *really* worried." In fact, she felt both more *and* less worried than she had a moment earlier. Matt being there too meant the situation was truly dire, but it also meant Elana wouldn't face it alone.

Matt grimaced. "Ditto. Did she say where she was?"

"No. I was trying to figure that out." Elana gestured at the stairwell, then closed her eyes and let her focus drift outward, searching for the sense of presence she associated with the Arbiter of Shadows.

When she discovered her ability to track high-powered vampires by instinct, Elana had thought it a very strange and magical skill. Now she knew it was simply nanocytes calling to nanocytes. High concentrations of nanocytes naturally pulled to one another, something like magnets. Elana's insight power gave her the extra ability to discern more specifically between those concentrations, a skill she likened to being a super-taster or a super-smeller.

She opened her eyes when she zeroed in on Valeria's unique signature, which always made Elana think of a thin, sharp dagger. "She's upstairs."

"Then let's not keep her waiting. You and I both know this can't be good."

"No kidding."

They ascended the stairs three or four at a time. Matt was a sentinel, like Elana, and a well-trained one at that, so they kept pace to the top of the tower. When they stopped on the highest landing, Elana lifted a hand to ask Matt to pause while she caught her breath.

She doubled over and panted for a few seconds. "Nice to finally find an upper limit. Jesus. Guess I need to do some cardio."

Matt's answering chuckle also sounded a touch out of breath. "I haven't done a full-tilt sprint like that in a while, especially not up stairs. You good?"

Elana drew one more deep breath and straightened. "I'm good."

Matt knocked twice on Valeria's office door, then pressed his palm against it. The built-in scanner glowed under his hand, verified his biometrics, and went dark as the door swung open into the Arbiter of Shadows' least-used office space.

The topmost rooms of the arbiters' towers were identical in shape and size and were the eight points of the consulate's cloud-piercing crown. Its architecture supported the greatest part of Haven's climate-control canopy, too. The combined effect of the imposing spires and the swooping "leaves" placed the consulate among the most identifiable buildings in Haven.

These offices were the arbiters' private spaces. Elana had been up here a few times, most notably during her first meeting with Valeria when the arbiter informed her of her status as a vampire. Otherwise, the Arbiter of Shadows tended to do her business in less rarefied locations.

This was Valeria's sanctum, and the monochrome décor reflected that. The furniture was simple and elegant, tending toward Scandinavian minimalism. A tall, spindly white orchid sat beside the window. Its green leaves provided the only splash of color in the room, apart from the two shell-shocked individuals huddled in the Spartan chairs at the low white coffee table.

Their clothes had been brightly colored at one point, a cavalcade of reds and golds, but now they were dingy and tattered. They added color to the space, but certainly not life.

Valeria turned from her desk as Matt and Elana entered. She hadn't changed out of the outfit she'd worn for the walk-and-talk that morning. Her unblemished, snow-white figure cut a sharp contrast to the pair of desolate souls also inhabiting her office.

The arbiter nodded at Matt and Elana, then approached the silent visitors and gestured for Matt and Elana to do the same. "Thank you for coming so quickly."

"At the king's pleasure," Matt promptly replied. Elana echoed the formality, recognizing in Matt's tone that he was opting for "default" responses until they had more information.

As she sat across from the hard-done-by pair, Elana dialed her insight power up to eleven and took in every detail. One was a man, the other a woman. The woman's clothes didn't fit as well as the man's, and based on the cut, Elana wondered whether the woman wore clothes she'd *borrowed* from him.

Both appeared to be in the same physical and mental state of exhaustion. Their heads were bowed and their shoulders curved with fatigue. Their hands were clean, but the crescents of their nails were dirty and slightly ragged. Their thick, black, wavy hair was very similar, and while they'd tried to run a brush through it, the attempt had failed thanks to the myriad tangles.

Their olive skin was caked in dust, indicating they'd had a chance to wash their hands but nothing more. They shared similar noses, but their jawlines and cheekbones differed. The woman was considerably petite in comparison to the man's broad-shouldered frame. Siblings, Elana guessed, in their twenties or maybe early thirties. Interestingly, she felt a faint aura of active nanocytes coming from the man but not from the woman.

Valeria coughed once, under her breath, and Elana snapped her gaze over to meet the arbiter's. Valeria side-eyed the pair, then raised an eyebrow at Elana as if asking a question.

She knows what I'm doing. To answer the question, she gave a subtle thumbs-up. *Got my first impression. We're good to go.*

Valeria inclined her head a degree, then audibly shifted in her chair and cleared her throat properly. Elana hid a smile. Valeria handled criminals and her employees well, but the austere attitude didn't quite jive with the downtrodden and exhausted. It was almost *cute* seeing Valeria slightly out of her element.

"Francesco, Ginevra, I'd like you to meet Mathieu Richelieu, Haven's head guardian, and Elana Bishop, our Consort of External Affairs and Diplomacy," Valeria stated. "Matt, Elana, meet Francesco and Ginevra Leone. They are refugees from Il Giardino."

"Welcome to Haven," Matt offered.

Elana sucked a breath in through her teeth. *Refugees*

from Il Giardino? Holy crap. They look like they've gone through hell.

"*Grazie,*" Francesco replied. He did his best to straighten, but his movements were slow and halting. He didn't appear to favor any particular body part as though he were injured, but he was fatigued beyond measure. "We are glad to have made it safely. *Signorina* Bishop, we owe you our freedom."

Elana's eyebrows drew together in confusion. "I'm sorry, I don't follow. We haven't heard anything out of Il Giardino since shortly after I left. Honestly, the radio silence has been concerning. Can you explain?"

Francesco looked at Ginevra instead of answering. "*Vuoi raccontare la storia, oppure...*" He watched the woman until she minutely shook her head. "*Va bene. Lo farò.*"

He returned his attention to Elana and Matt, drew a deep breath, and let it out in a weary sigh. "I have been an attendant in the Vincenzis' court for thirty years. I made an impression as a young man—possibly thanks to my command of many languages, possibly because *la marchesa* liked the way I looked. *Dio lo sa.*" He shrugged, and the movement held the weight of the world.

"Whatever the reason, they liked me enough to offer me the Rights." He grimaced. "To be clear, this was not so much an offer as a requirement for continued employment. Despite having a wife and a baby daughter, I consented. Now, thirty years later, my adult daughter works with me. I in the court, she in the kitchens."

Francesco put his hand on Ginevra's shoulder. "We did not know any other way of living. My parents came to Il

Giardino after the great war, drawn by the promise of steady employment and a place to live. Not so long before that, my family knew what it was to serve kings and queens.

"The *marchese* and *marchesa* were no different, even in their proclivities. We knew the way—avert your eyes, grit your teeth, move on. Be grateful to remain out of their sights, and do what you can in the background to help those who were not so lucky.

"Your arrival changed everything. Being castle servants, we were not in the lower city when you visited that night, but we certainly heard the rumors. Our colleagues had met your companion, *Signorina* Lamarr." He rolled the final sound of Vicky's surname, turning it into a musical trill.

"It was common knowledge that if you were chosen to be a *volontaro*, your survival was unlikely in the long run. Not that the *volontari* have short lifespans—as long as only the interior court uses them, they are usually safe. It is when the Vincenzis have guests that they fear for their lives.

"For this reason, Clarissa's death was not a surprise. It disappointed many of us 'in the wings' because we had seen you, *Signorina* Lamarr, and *Signora* Lucia. You did not seem like those pigs who typically availed themselves of the Vincenzis' hospitality. Still, we had seen many virtuous nobles overtaken by the rush of fresh blood. These things happen. They should not, but they do.

"But the details that came from your visit to the lower city..." Francesco shook his head again. His gaze glossed over Elana and settled somewhere over her right shoulder.

"Indiscretions are commonplace among the nobility. They believe they are untouchable and that God or the

Nexus—or both—has ordained their superiority over the rest of the world. Mass murder, however, was not the Vincenzis' style. One or two deaths, here and there. To these, we pretended to turn a blind eye. But *hundreds* of bodies… No. Unacceptable.

"The townsfolk came with torches and pitchforks." His voice flattened, becoming a two-dimensional representation of the trauma Elana saw replaying in his gaze. "And, of course, more modern implements. Molotov cocktails. Improvised bombs made of cleaning chemicals and spare hardware. Glass bottles that mixed ammonia into bleach when broken. These sorts of things.

"It will not shock you to hear that this turned into a massacre. Even vampires living off the fat of their people and reveling in their leisure are still powerful killers. The *volontari* were summoned to the temple. I doubt any of them lived beyond a night or two, but I have no proof. Perhaps Lady Margareta exercised moderation in consuming her food supply.

"The rebel front broke in the face of the vampires' power. They were many, but the court was too strong and too well-defended. The castle was built against attack, and the Vincenzis had the high ground. The revolution was over as quickly as it began, although the fires burned for several days.

"Silence for a day. Those of us within the castle held our breath that whole day. Would we be told to march forth and slaughter our families? Would we be allowed to bury our dead?

"Then, as though nothing had happened, Lord Giovanni emerged from the inner sanctum and decreed that business would go on. The destruction would be cleared, and work would continue. Nothing would change."

Francesco swallowed. Ginevra shuddered, and he moved his hand to her other shoulder and squeezed her close.

Father and daughter, not siblings. That's...actually kind of fucked up to think about. He'd watch her grow while he didn't age. I bet he wouldn't be allowed to give her the Rights, either, or if he did, she'd be taken away from him. God.

Francesco continued. "For a time, nothing did—at least, nothing on the outside. In truth, the rumors never stopped. Thanks to you, for the first time in as long as anyone could remember, the civilians of Il Giardino tasted freedom. It would not be easily relinquished.

"Then people started disappearing." He heaved a sigh, briefly closed his eyes, and kissed the top of his daughter's head. "This, again, was not unheard of—but the scale was. We were used to one person disappearing in a year, perhaps two if the lord and lady were displeased. But soon the count exceeded twelve, and it had only been three weeks.

"No one could find a pattern in the disappearances. All servants and serfs, naturally, but beyond that? *Pfft!*" He snapped his fingers. "A mystery. A baker, a grocer, a mason, a student. Old, young, male, female. It did not matter.

"More rumors were spreading by this time. If we could have made wine from that grapevine, it would have been fruitful indeed." The corner of Francesco's mouth turned up in a ghastly smile, then back down in a horrible grimace.

"Chamber servants to the highest nobles spoke of an

army being raised. A fighting force that would not retreat and would not flinch. These men and women, in their great gilded finery, bragged of the atrocities they would commit in the name of the Nexus. They boasted that the blood they spilled would fuel a new age of vampirism, where all humans would know their place.

"With these whispers on the wind, many civilians tried to escape into the hills, leaving on foot to find the Italian border. Many, if not most, were dragged back to the castle and disappeared into the lowest levels, which had been declared off-limits to humans and vampires below guardian.

"Ginevra and I had intended to do the same," he added. "We planned to sneak out at midday, find my beloved Letizia, and do our best to escape when the vampires would be most vulnerable. We set aside as much food as we dared and prepared to leave in the fourth week, when we had nearly lost count of the disappearances.

"When dawn broke on the day we had chosen, Lord Giovanni announced that the castle would be closed."

Ginevra stifled a sob and turned to bury her face in her father's chest. He wrapped both arms around her and held her tight, hiding his face in her dusty, tangled hair before surfacing and continuing.

"All gates were locked. No humans and no vampires below the level of guardian were allowed to pass between the upper and lower cities. Civilians gathered at the main gate almost immediately, clamoring to be told what had become of their loved ones. The *marchese's* guard led a sortie that killed dozens, and those they did not kill, they dragged into the castle."

"The dead bodies were, too," Ginevra whispered. Her accent was stronger than her father's, and her voice was hoarse. Elana hoped that was from dehydration rather than overuse from, say, screaming.

Francesco closed his eyes again and held his daughter closer. "It is as she says. The bodies were brought in as well, although we do not know for what purpose.

"We could not leave the castle. We could not reach Letizia. I bribed a vampire whom I had served for twenty-five years to take her a message that read, 'Stay safe,' but I do not trust it arrived in her hands. They have no reason to be true to their word. But I had no choice. I had to try to let her know we were alive."

Tears welled in Francesco's eyes, and when he opened his mouth to continue, no sound came. He swallowed convulsively, tried again, and shook his head.

At the sudden end to the torrent of words, Ginevra looked up, and her brow creased as she took in the pain on her father's face. She straightened, kissed his forehead, and brought his head to her shoulder as she took up the tale.

"We hid," she told them. "There are passages in the castle that are only known to the servants. Several lead to the caves under the mountain because they were used as food storage in the old times. We took whatever we could and disappeared as far into the caves as we dared. We did not know what would come next, only that the air was tense like the hour before a great thunderstorm, and we did not want to be struck by lightning.

"We snuck back into the castle to steal food when we could. One time, we had to stop and hide because three vampires were bringing bodies down, wrapped in sheets.

We followed them after they passed us and discovered an underground lake with hundreds of bodies lined up on the shore. The bodies were being fed into the lake one at a time, and the lake glowed a sickly green. My stomach wanted to tear itself from my throat. The smell was horrific.

"After that, we stayed in our nook for as long as possible. Three weeks later, our choices were to find food or starve. We crept to the lake first to see if they were still bringing bodies down, but no one was there, and the shore was empty.

"We encountered no one on the way back into the castle and no one *in* the castle." Ginevra's voice became hollow, and her empty gaze settled on Elana's. "The torches were lit, and the cupboards were full, but we did not see a soul, and the halls were quiet as the grave.

"We did not search for survivors. We packed as much food as we could carry, used the servants' passages to travel as far as we could toward the lower city, then kept to the shadows to avoid being seen. The main gate was open and unguarded. We met no other humans or vampires. No bodies, no smells, no destruction. Only silence.

"We reached the Italian border after walking for several days and begged for asylum. Since my father is a vampire, they brought us to a vampiric embassy. The woman on staff told us that only Haven was accepting refugee claimants—otherwise, we would have to apply to my father's House."

"Not an option. We will never set foot in Il Giardino again," Francesco spat. "*Mostri.* I will renounce my House in an instant. I never wanted it to begin with."

This declaration hung in the air for several seconds. Francesco bent his head to his daughter's hair again and closed his eyes. Ginevra's gaze settled briefly on Valeria, Matt, and Elana in turn, and she embraced her father again.

The three Havenites let them have a moment of silence while they processed the huge amount of information they'd just received. Elana felt as though the pit of her stomach had been hollowed out, and judging by the look on Matt's face, he felt similarly. Valeria's expression was inscrutable, but Elana read the tension in her jaw muscles and around her eyes. She was *angry*.

At length, Elana caught Valeria's eye. "I can speak to Arbiters Mélissand and Gow and start the refugee process."

The corner of Valeria's mouth turned down. "It will be more difficult than usual, so yes, you should start it right away."

Elana frowned. "Why? It's not like we need the okay from House Vincenzi for a *refugee* claim." Valeria motioned at Ginevra and raised an eyebrow, and Elana inhaled sharply. "Oh. Right."

She drew a deep breath and mentally steeled herself. "That's okay. This is my circus, and these are my monkeys. I will fight for a joint human-vampire refugee claim until I run out of breath."

"It could be made much easier," Matt pointed out. "That is, if Ginevra and Francesco are willing."

Ginevra had been listening intently to their exchange. She looked Matt square in the eye. "I am willing. I have been willing for years, but it was not permitted. I will gladly accept the Rights. Then I will train to become the strongest I can be, and I will rescue my mother."

"We can discuss that as a possibility after you both have time to recuperate," Valeria firmly interrupted. "Right now, you likely wouldn't survive. Don't throw away that spark. You'll need it."

Ginevra grumbled, but her father pulled her in for another hug and kissed the top of her head. "I could not stand to lose both of you," he murmured into her hair. "We are safe, *carina*. Let us rest for now. We will fight again soon. *Lo prometto.*"

CHAPTER SIX

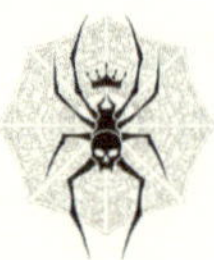

Valeria stood and subtly motioned for Matt and Elana to follow her. She led them out into the hall, closed the door behind them, then turned and crossed her arms. "Your assessments?"

Elana bit her lip. "They're telling the truth about what they saw and heard. I didn't get any hint of duplicity."

"Agreed, although my judgment isn't quite as enhanced as Elana's." Matt drew a deep breath and exhaled forcefully through his nose. "I also think we can pretty safely assume a lot about what was going on in the background based on what we already know."

"Yeah. The rumors about the Vincenzis creating an army? I did *not* like that." Elana shuddered. "Especially the bit about the dead bodies being brought back. If they hadn't seen hundreds of corpses being tossed in the lake, I'd be worried we were suddenly facing zombies."

Valeria's mouth set in a grim line. "We still might. I wouldn't count that possibility out just yet."

"Goddammit." Elana pinched the bridge of her nose.

"Great. Okay. I'm gonna set that aside for a second until I'm ready to contemplate the likelihood that my action-movie life has turned into a zombie apocalypse movie. What do we do? Infiltrate Il Giardino? From the sounds of it, it might *be* the zombie apocalypse. Also, what the hell is that lake about?"

"They were—or are—using it as a nanocyte reservoir," Valeria replied. "The natural mineral levels and composition of the water create an environment where decomposition is slow but steady, and they feed it with engineered nanocytes so the nanocytes in the bodily tissues are fully harvested."

"It's like nanocyte soup," Matt offered.

Throughout Valeria's explanation, Elana's grimace deepened until she could imagine her father telling her, "Careful, it might freeze like that." Her stomach rolled over, and she swallowed hard. "That's horrific."

"Especially since it sounds like something went awry," Valeria added. "When I was there, it didn't smell particularly bad, and it wasn't glowing. Both of those are signs that the balance is off or a contaminant's been introduced."

"Synthetic nanocytes?" Elana guessed.

"Could be, or they overloaded it with too much organic tissue too fast. Hard to say without seeing it."

"So, we *are* going."

Valeria's lips stretched into a thin line as she thought, then she shook her head. "I don't think that's where you'd be most useful. I might send a team of Chimeras. But you... No. No, I think you need to go to Scotland."

Elana blinked. "To visit Lucia? Why?"

Matt raised his index finger. "I can answer that. Thanks

to the alliance you formalized last year and your friendship with Lucia, House Stormhaven has invested significant resources into intelligence-gathering on our behalf. Lucia and I have corresponded heavily on the subject since she's been back on the radar. Unless I miss my mark, Valeria thinks these new revelations about Il Giardino might help Lucia put some of the puzzle pieces together."

Valeria nodded.

"Okay, fair enough, but I could just *call* her," Elana pointed out, then hissed a breath in through her teeth. "Never mind. I just heard Colonel Webber in my head yelling at me about secure lines never being as secure as you think they are. Face-to-face is always safest."

Valeria nodded again. "When can you be ready to leave?"

"By tonight?"

"Acceptable."

"I'll contact Lucia and make arrangements," Matt offered. "I already have a call scheduled with her later."

"Very good." Valeria's gaze flicked toward her office door. "Elana, would it throw too many wrenches in your preparations if I put you in charge of getting them settled? They need to be somewhere safe—probably here in the tower—and I'm already double-booked at several points today."

Elana considered, then shook her head. "I can manage it."

"Thank you. Use my console to make the arrangements since it's the most secure access point you'll find. Don't snoop. I *will* know, and you *will* regret it."

Elana's eyes widened, and she crossed her heart. "That

would be supremely stupid, and I make a habit of *not* being supremely stupid. You have my word."

"Good. In that case, I'll touch base with you both later. Good luck." The arbiter strode past them down the hall, leaving Matt and Elana outside her office door.

Matt watched her for a second, then shook his head. "God, what a mess."

"I'm just glad they made it out," Elana remarked. "I can't imagine how terrifying that must have been."

"I don't doubt it. Hey—you might not be aware, but the guardians' office liaises with multiple organizations in Quarto and Zevenda that can provide support to people who don't have resources. If you loop my secretary in, he can get you in touch with the right ones. Don't feel like you have to do everything yourself."

Elana's eyebrows rose. "Really? I kind of expected that vampire society would have been the ultimate in bootstrap culture."

"In a lot of ways, it is, but that's not how the SpiderKing does things. We have plenty of resources we can share. Most Havenites don't have the same existential stressors as the general populace.

"It's much easier for those initiatives to fly under the radar of the people who would get pissed off if they thought someone was getting something they didn't deserve. It's way less of a slice of the pie than it has to be in human cities."

"Fair enough. Thank you. Something tells me Francesco and Ginevra will need as much support as they can get, so I will definitely use those resources."

"Good. I'll text you when I have everything set up with Lucia."

"Appreciate it."

Matt departed the same way Valeria had, and Elana faced the office door. *I hope the few minutes of quiet were nice and not panic-inducing. In their shoes, I'd be hard-pressed to believe anyone could be nice to me ever again.*

She pressed her hand to the scanner and waited for it to verify her identity as it had Matt's. After it had done so, she pushed the door open and quietly announced, "I'm coming back in, and it's just me this time."

Francesco and Ginevra hadn't moved far from where they'd been when she, Matt, and Valeria had left to discuss the situation. They'd relaxed against the couch's backrest but still had their arms wrapped around each other. Francesco looked as though he was falling asleep, but he roused at Elana's voice and lifted his head from atop his daughter's.

"Is everything all right?" he wearily asked.

Elana smiled and sat across from them. "As all right as it was when we stepped out. You're safe here. We'll do our best to take care of you. Thank you for telling us what you've been through. I'm sorry you had to endure it."

"We can endure anything as long as we have each other." Francesco squeezed his daughter hard enough that Ginevra's eyes widened and she had to tap his arm to get him to loosen up. "*Scusa, carina.*"

"*Va bene, papà.*" She patted his forearm, then met Elana's gaze again. "Where will we go?"

"You'll stay here in this tower for now. Not in this office. That would hardly be comfortable, and besides,

Arbiter Draven has to work." She winked and was gratified to see them both smile faintly.

"I'll get you set up with a secure suite right away. I'm also going to bring in a healer to look you both over and make sure you get any medical attention you need. Does either of you have dietary restrictions?" They shook their heads. "Good, that makes it easy. Any favorite foods you missed while you were on the road? I don't imagine you had much cash on you. You're probably starving."

"We were before we reached the embassy in Italy," Ginevra admitted. "But since then, we've been fed well." She blushed and averted her eyes. "Would it be too much to ask for a cheeseburger? They were very *out of style* in Il Giardino, so I have only ever had one…"

Elana laughed, then quickly stopped herself and waved off their surprised looks. "I'm not laughing at you. The thought of cheeseburgers being out of style just caught me by surprise. That's an easy yes. I'll have some sent up ASAP while I sort out where you'll stay."

"*Mille grazie.*" Ginevra hid her continued blush by ducking her head and playing with the hem of her disheveled shirt.

Elana clicked her tongue. "We'll also get you some new clothes while we're at it. I have a friend who can make that happen. I'll call her right now."

She fished in her dimensional handbag for her phone, then did a quick mental calculation. *Vicky should be finishing up with Gustav soon if she hasn't already. If she doesn't pick up, I'll leave a message.*

Elana tapped the button to call her best friend, then waited. Vicky picked up after a couple of rings.

"Hey, Lana. Anybody dying?"

"Nobody we know, although you sound kind of dead. How'd your session go?" Based on the data her insight power was giving her, Vicky sounded tired but not pissed or disappointed. *A good training session, then.* Elana hoped so, anyway.

Vicky laughed breathlessly. "I am gonna be sore for a week, but god*damn*, that was fun."

Elana's smile grew. "You're still doing better than me. I was cranky as fuck after my first session. Congratulations. Also, you won't be sore for a week—probably until morning. You'll be fine in time for your next session with Gustav."

"Hallelujah. So, what's up?"

Elana eyed Francesco and Ginevra. Francesco had slumped back on the couch and closed his eyes again, but Ginevra watched Elana with interest. *Interesting that the vampire seems more tired than the human. I'll have to chat with the healer about that. My bet is Francesco hasn't had any blood since leaving Il Giardino. I doubt he'd feed off Ginevra if you held a gun to his head, even if she offered—and that's a big if, considering the culture they came from.*

"I have two wonderful people here who just arrived from one hell of a sticky Italian situation," she told Vicky. "They have nothing but the clothes on their backs, and I suspect they'd like to burn said clothes. You up for some shopping?"

"*Hell*, yes." Vicky's tone was already brightening, faced with the prospect of doing something she loved. "Do I get measurements or am I eyeballing and returning what doesn't fit?"

"Six of one, half a dozen of the other. I'll send a car for you. It should arrive by the time you're done in the locker room. It'll bring you to the Citadel. You remember which building is the consulate, yeah?"

"Definitely not, because I didn't have artists' renditions of all the coolest architecture in Haven plastered all over my bedroom wall in high school," Vicky deadpanned.

Elana snorted. "Great. I'll meet you in the atrium and bring you up to meet your buyers."

Ginevra lifted a finger. "Ah—*Signorina* Bishop—I hate to interrupt, but we do not have any money..."

Elana waved this off. "Figure of speech. I have the tab."

Ginevra sagged with relief. "*Grazie ancora.*"

"My pleasure." Elana returned her attention to the other end of the phone line. "Sorry I don't get to be there for your first experience in the Training Grounds showers."

"I've been dreaming about them since we got here," Vicky admitted. "The prospect of soaking in one of those baths became more tempting every time I hit the mats."

"Amen to that. If you want my advice, spend ten minutes in the sauna, dunk yourself in the ice bath, *then* shower. The ice bath is brutal, but the hot and cold combo will mean you might stop being sore by this evening. Also, the hair dryer is magic, and so is the two-in-one washer-dryer. You won't be frizzy, and your clothes will be clean before you're done in the shower."

"Vampires are the best," Vicky proclaimed. "I'm gonna go scrape this grime off. Tell my new friends I'll be there soon."

"Will do. Thanks, Vick. You're a gem."

Vicky snorted. "Oh, yeah, because it's so hard to convince me to go *shopping*..."

Vicky ended the call. Elana quickly brought up her favorite meal-delivery app and ordered a trio of cheeseburgers with all the fixings. It was lunchtime, and she was starving too.

"Okay, lunch is on its way, and you'll have new clothes in a couple of hours," she told Francesco and Ginevra, who both visibly brightened. "Next, you need a place to stay and people to take care of you. Elana Bishop is on the case."

She stood and stepped toward Valeria's desk, but Ginevra stopped her with a hand on her elbow. "Yeah? Can I get you something else?"

Ginevra shook her head. "No, it is not that. You are already doing more than anyone has ever done for us in our entire lives. I...I only wanted to thank you."

Elana smiled. "You're welcome. It's the least I can—"

"No," Ginevra interrupted.

Elana's insight power flared, and she knelt beside the father-daughter pair and clasped Ginevra's hand. "Talk to me."

Ginevra drew a slow, shaky breath and stared at the floor next to Elana while she gathered her thoughts. Francesco put his arm around her shoulders and squeezed her.

Eventually, Ginevra spoke in a halting voice. "You saw more of what Il Giardino was like than anyone who had ever visited. No, that is still not right. Many people saw. Many vampires saw. None of them ever did anything. They left us to suffer. They might even have thought it right. You did not."

Ginevra locked gazes with Elana. The bags under her eyes only emphasized the fire within them. "I worked in the kitchens. We knew everything that happened in the castle. *Everything.* And you? You were only there for a few days, but you saw and *understood* the horrible things they did to us, and you said, 'No more.'

"You put yourself in harm's way to try to help us. You inspired us to fight for ourselves in a way we had not done...*ever.* It is thanks to you that anyone in Il Giardino tasted freedom before they died. Even if we are the last, if everyone else is already dead or will be soon, I want you to know that it was worth it, and we are grateful."

She gripped Elana's hand hard enough to hurt. "That is what I mean when I say thank you. You brought life and hope back to hundreds of thousands of people. You are different from all the vampires I have ever met, and I will do whatever I can to help you bring that hope to the rest of the world."

Elana stared into the exhausted woman's eyes and felt the core of steel in her words. She put her other hand on top of Ginevra's and held her gaze steadily, even though her heart was racing. "And I will do everything I can to be worthy of that trust and gratitude."

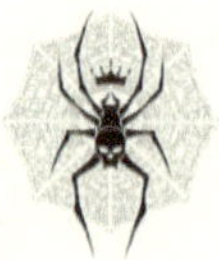

Comfortably squaring Francesco and Ginevra away took longer than Elana hoped, but less than she'd expected. Haven's social services functioned better than most cities', but they still involved more paperwork than anyone wanted to deal with.

Fortunately, Elana had leveled up in her paperwork abilities over the past year, so the gauntlet of bureaucracy did not give her pause. She buckled down and got to it, and by suppertime, Francesco and Ginevra were settled in a comfortable pair of rooms on a lower floor of the Tower of Shadows.

These rooms were designed to be prison cells, much like Edward Korynchuk's, but in this case the disappearing door was a comfort to the Leones rather than a reminder of their forced isolation. After devouring their cheeseburgers and fries, they gratefully and with many tears accepted Vicky's coaxing to try on all the new clothing and find what they liked and what fit best. She left with a phone full of notes and a promise to return with more tomorrow.

Elana ordered them dinner as well, at their request. The giant tureen of spaghetti and meatballs couldn't measure up to their home cooking, but they assured her it tasted marvelous because, as Francesco kept muttering, they were free.

She bid them goodnight after they'd polished the dish clean with the ends of the garlic bread. "Remember, you can ask for help with *anything* with this panel." She tapped the hand-sized intercom panel beside the door, which the guardians had set up to be visible on the inside but not the outside. "Don't get too sucked down the rabbit hole of the Internet, either. I'll be back in a couple of days, and if I'm not, I'll call. Okay?"

"Okay," Ginevra echoed, then grinned like a kid in a candy shop. She was well into the giddy stage of freedom while her father was still working his way through being stunned. "Thank you again, *Signorina* Bishop, a thousand *thousand* times."

Elana smiled and tapped in the command to open the door. "You're most welcome. Sleep well."

She waved on her way out, then checked in with the guardians posted on either side of the door after it shut. "You two need anything?"

"No, ma'am," the woman on the left replied. "We have strict orders from Arbiter Draven not to let anyone in who isn't on the list, and the Leones' comm is linked directly to our headsets. They need anything, we'll get it."

"Good. Thank you. Any problem, you know where to find me."

"Actually, we don't," the man on the right joked, only to

straighten up and avert his eyes when the woman glared at him. "Sorry, ma'am. Yes, ma'am."

Elana snorted. "Carry on."

Both guardians snapped a respectful consorts' salute—right arms up to forty-five degrees with their palms down, index and middle fingers touching their temple, and their ring and little fingers curled over to touch their thumb.

This was an area of etiquette Elana had only learned in recent months when she'd increased her work with the guardians. She still caught herself failing to salute on occasion. The arbiters' salute included the ring finger, in a sort of militarized Scouts' salute, and to salute the SpiderKing, all fingers would be straight. Since the king never showed his face, this one was only practiced in drills.

Her phone buzzed in her pocket before she made it down two flights of stairs. She fished it out while continuing to jog, and seeing it was Matt, lodged the phone between her shoulder and ear. "Talk to me."

"I've chartered a jet for you. It'll be waiting at the airstrip in three hours. Is that enough time?"

"Plenty. Any news?"

"Nothing I can repeat over the phone, and nothing Lucia won't tell you herself. Nothing you need to know before you arrive in Scotland, either."

"Okay." Elana plastered herself to the wall to let another consort by while still dashing down the stairs. She nodded at them as they passed. "Are deputy consorts a thing?"

"Sure. Why? Do you want a concubine?"

Elana grumbled, "We *really* have to work on our internal titles, but yes, essentially. I'm living a double life and it's driving me up the wall. Zilmann's trying to fuck me over left, right, and center, and any time I disappear on assignment she doubles down. I need a proxy. Preferably someone who isn't already swamped with their own workload. How many consorts have a second parallel career in covert operations?"

"Not many. Typically, the political sphere doesn't overlap so pointedly with the espionage one. *Well…*not in one person, anyway. Haven's ambassadors all have Shadow agents in their retinue. It's about reducing the need to multitask… You know, I see your point."

"Thank you. How do I get a concubine? *God*, that's weird. Couldn't we call them anything else? *Language has changed.*"

"Not my call. Actually, I'm pretty sure that's *Zilmann's* call."

Elana pushed open the consulate's doors and groaned. "Of *course*, it is. Domain of Legacy. *Fuck.* Okay, shelving the outdated language issue. How do I do it? Do I put up a job description and hire someone?"

"No, you submit an application to your arbiter, and if it's approved, you receive a shortlist of candidates."

"All right, that's not so bad." She trotted across the courtyard, noting in the back of her mind that Sarah Goldin had gone home, and exited the Citadel. "I might fill that out on the plane, honestly. Anything else before I go?"

"Dress warmly. There's a wicked storm in Scotland right now."

"Oh, joy."

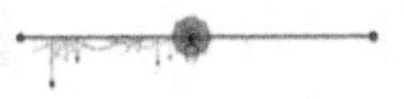

Elana parked outside the small, private terminal that serviced Haven's airstrip. Some vampires flew commercial because they felt they had all the time in the world, but most chose to charter a vampire-made jet for their global travels. Nanocyte technology made for a far lower carbon footprint than any human-made planes were capable of. It also allowed vampire-made jets to indulge in the luxuries of air travel that hadn't been present in human society for decades.

Elana shouldered her dimensional handbag and headed into the quiet terminal, where they would check her biometrics before she boarded the plane waiting on the tarmac.

This was among the examples of vampire technology Elana wanted *most* to bring to the human world. Making air travel environmentally friendly and more comfortable simultaneously was a win-win in her books, no matter how you spun it. Unfortunately, it turned out that the specialized nanocytes responsible for the high-efficiency fuel weren't as abundant as needed to increase production on a scale that would service the globe.

Elana had her sights set on changing that as soon as the House Veridian bullshit was done. She'd joined the vampire world with the goal of bringing its advanced technology to humanity. She understood the necessity of doing it carefully so nobody blew up the planet before they could engineer the equitable existence Elana dreamed of. Still, part of her wanted to rip the Band-Aid off.

She sighed, then smiled and shook her head at the flight attendant who caught her sigh and looked at her with concern. "Not you. Head's still in work mode."

The woman smiled and bowed politely. "Of course, Consort Bishop. Please, have a seat wherever you'd like. Can I get you something to drink after we take off?"

Elana considered how her day had gone and how her meeting with Madame Lucia would undoubtedly result in more unthinkable drama. "A hot toddy, please. How long will the flight be?"

"About four hours."

"Great. Enough for a nap. Thanks." Elana selected one of the comfortable seating pods in the last row near the front and settled in. She cinched her seatbelt, let her head drop back to the headrest, and closed her eyes.

The aroma of hot honey and whiskey roused her a few minutes later, and she opened her eyes to see the elegant glass mug of orangey-brown goodness sitting on her tray table.

The flight attendant bobbed a quick curtsy. "Apologies, Consort Bishop. I hope I didn't startle you."

"No, it's fine. Thank you again." She yawned. "I assume we're underway?"

"As of about ten minutes ago."

"Perfect." Elana wrapped her hands around the warm mug, smiled, and exhaled so her shoulders relaxed. "Time for a break."

"Would you like me to dim the lights?"

"Please."

Elana opened her eyes again almost four hours later when the gentle chime of the PA system alerted her to an imminent message from the captain. Sure enough, the speaker above her head crackled briefly, then the captain's calm voice piped out.

"We'll be landing in Scotland in a few minutes, Consort Bishop," he informed her. "The weather is less than ideal, so you might experience light turbulence. You'll be on the ground soon."

"Thank you," Elana replied in the direction of the speaker. She wasn't sure whether he could hear her, but it was polite to thank him anyway. The flight attendant would pass on her thanks if he hadn't.

Her empty mug was long gone, whisked away during her nap. Elana stowed her tray table and stretched, then slid open the cover over the window beside her pod and grimaced at the roiling black clouds and lashing rain outside. A flash of lightning made her flinch, and she shut the cover.

It was the kind of storm that would have diverted a human jet long before landing, but it posed little difficulty for a vampire jet. Apart from a few subtle bumps and a touch more pressure on her ears, Elana would have thought they were gliding through a clear, blue sky.

The landing gear hit the tarmac with a faint jolt. Elana slid the window shade open and frowned when she spied a rocky coastline within walking distance of the plane. This didn't resemble the private strip she'd landed at either of the times she crossed the Atlantic to see Madame Lucia.

Matt wouldn't send her to the wrong place, so Lucia Lambra Mor was out in that dismal storm somewhere. Elana hid a smirk. *Maybe we're at her secret spy base she keeps hidden under the sea. Perhaps the flight attendant will have to put a bag over my head before I leave the plane.*

No such indignity was imposed upon her, although the attendant offered her an umbrella. This time, Elana had come prepared. She gripped the handle of her heavy-duty umbrella firmly against the gale-force winds with one hand and the guardrail of the debarkation stairs with the other.

Madame Lucia was not on the tarmac to meet her. Instead, a tall, broad-shouldered man in a huge coat awaited Elana on the wet asphalt. A black SUV that gleamed with rainwater stood a few yards behind him.

He tipped the brim of his hat as she approached. He didn't seem bothered by the rain, although he'd flipped his coat collar up against the wind. He had a whiskery beard and keen, deep-set eyes set close to his bulbous nose. He wasn't a looker by Elana's standards, but she would trust him in a heartbeat to have harsh words for troublemakers and a swift fist if they didn't listen the first time.

"Mornin'," he greeted her. "I'm t' take yeh t' Madam L. Name's Colin."

"Hi, Colin." Elana glanced from side to side and burrowed into her coat. "This is morning? How can you tell?"

Colin laughed, appreciating the jab, and nodded sagely. "Only way anyone does in storm season. Yer watch and yer gut. Mine says it's almost breakfast. Are y' hungry?"

"Starving, actually." Elana's stomach rumbled to prove the point.

"Aye. We'll pick up kippers on our way t' the missus. Best breakfast in the islands."

"I'll take your word for it."

Colin shepherded Elana into the big SUV and closed the door behind her after she managed to fold her umbrella. Then he lumbered into the front seat and started the engine. "Y' ever been t' the Shetland Islands, miss?"

"Oh, is *that* where we are?" Elana peered out the tinted window. "No, I haven't. Isn't House Stormhaven situated in the Highlands?"

"The manor house, aye, but the madam keeps a safe house up here where nobody likes t' look. Discourages the unfriendlies."

"Fair enough."

A long drive and one surprisingly pleasant breakfast of smoked fish and bread later, Colin pulled up to a deserted bit of coastline pummeled with waves and rain. "Here we are," he announced. "Mind yer footin'."

Elana appreciated the warning since she hadn't opted for hiking boots. She wasn't picking her way across the slippery rocks in stiletto heels, but her winter boots were for snow, not wet stone. The wind made it even less pleasant.

"No wonder Madame Lucia hides up here," she muttered. "*I* wouldn't want to come."

She looked around the empty stretch of beach, then raised an eyebrow in Colin's direction. "Is she just gonna... appear? Or is there a door I'm not seeing?"

Colin laughed heartily. "No, miss. The madam will be

here soon enough. Our arrival will have sent her a message, and—Oh! There she be."

"Beach" was somewhat of a misnomer for the landscape around them. "Coastline" would be more apt, and a wicked one at that. Huge, craggy boulders were strewn across the waterline like a giant's marbles, casually tossed aside at the end of a game. At Colin's cue, the largest of these boulders, easily twice Elana's height and wide enough she couldn't get her arms around it, cracked in two and silently levered open to reveal a hollow space within.

Standing at the top of a staircase descending into the rock was Lucia Lambra Mor. She waved at Elana, then beckoned to her. "Come on in out of the wet!" she called over the wind and rain.

Elana started forward, then paused and looked back at Colin. "Aren't you coming?"

Colin shook his head, sending raindrops flying off the brim of his hat. "I got work t' do for the missus yet. Yer go on. Nice t' meet yeh, Miss Bishop."

"You too."

Elana stuck her hands in her pockets and hurried to join Lucia, eager to get out of the rain. Even after the rock had closed around them, her inner ear refused to believe she wasn't hearing the constant assault of raindrops anymore.

Lucia nudged her elbow. "Let's get you warm and dry. The North Sea's pitching a right fit today. Come on."

Elana followed Lucia down a long staircase, hewn from the rock and lit by warm sconces every few feet. It reminded Elana of how she'd imagine a secret underground tunnel from medieval times, except the steps were even and well-swept and nothing reeked of torch tar and open sewage.

This impression was borne out when they emerged from the tunnel into a cozy cavern. Vintage wooden furniture filled the short-ceilinged space. All the seats were cushioned and upholstered in rich red and blue brocade rendered all the brighter by the firelight flickering in the hearth. More hewn passages led out of the sitting room, each with curtains drawn on either side of their entrances.

"This hardly looks like the safe room for the world's most powerful information broker," Elana quipped as she shook her umbrella before the roaring flames. Drops of water spattered and hissed on the hearthstones. "This looks more like the place you'd get away for a night to yourself."

Lucia chuckled, then rested her palm on the solid wood desk in the far curve of the room. Its polished surface glowed under her hand, then erupted into an array of windows and documents. "Looks can be deceiving."

Elana facepalmed. "Duh. The hobbit-hole vibe threw me off. Of course everything in here is laden with nanotech."

"Of course," Lucia agreed. "Take off your coat. I'll hang it by the fire. Then, if you go down the left passage, you'll find a washroom with all the amenities *and* a set of clean, dry clothes that ought to fit you just fine. I'll be here with tea when you get back."

Elana gratefully relinquished her sodden coat and disappeared down the hall. The wall sconces lit at her approach like candles and led her to another cozy chamber carved from the rock. Fresh jeans and a T-shirt sat on the vanity beside the sink…and an enormous stone bathtub set into the wall called her name, with a basket full of salts, fizzy tablets, and vials of gleaming soaps on the rim.

Elana considered indulging in a bubble bath. She imagined the heat seeping into her limbs and leeching away the stress.

Then she remembered she was here to get information about the sudden and precipitous fall of Il Giardino, possibly including the rise of the vampire zombie apocalypse. *Bubble baths do not solve global crises. You can have one after you save the world.*

She washed her face and brushed her teeth before changing. The kippers had been remarkably tasty, but they hung around in the back of her throat. In a small, warm room *with a vampire*, bad breath was a big faux pas.

Elana returned to the main room a few minutes later, refreshed and dry. Lucia was working at the desk, and a tray of tea sat on the high wooden table between the pair of armchairs that faced the fire.

Lucia looked up from her many windows, closed them all with a swish of her hand, then joined Elana at the fire and poured tea into the two waiting mugs.

"Make yours how you like," she instructed, then plunked into an armchair and did the same, adding two cubes of sugar and a splash of milk to the dark brown liquid.

"Thanks." Elana sat, doctored her tea, and stared into the fire with her hands wrapped around the mug. "It never rains but it pours."

"Amen to that."

"I gotta say, this wasn't what I expected when Valeria

recommended I come get an update from you. Even knowing the desk is a console, I expected… I don't know, holographic projections and a James Bond-style scene, not tea and a cozy fire."

Lucia smiled and sipped her tea. "We spend enough time in mortal danger as it is, so why not talk shop over a cuppa? Everyone needs a bit more R&R in their lives, if you ask me."

Elana side-eyed her Scottish friend. "You really *have* mellowed out."

"Survival mechanism. That, and somebody's been shaking all the Old World Houses to their cores over the last year and a half, and it's been a right *delight* to watch and laugh."

Elana's eyebrows rose. "You're not talking about me, are you?"

"Sure I am. They all thought they were safe as houses when they offed your mother. Then, a few years later, who shows up but Tessa Hart's secret daughter!" Lucia cackled.

"The looks on those barmy ol' codgers' faces when news broke in the House of Cardinals—brought by House Richelieu, no less—that the person making waves in that eternally shit-disturbing, whirling dervish of a city was none other than *Tessa Hart's daughter!*"

Elana's cheeks warmed, and she hid behind her tea. "I knew I had big shoes to fill, but… Wow. I didn't know they reacted like *that*."

"White as ghosts, the lot of them. Fucking *hilarious*. Made my day." Lucia gulped more tea and set the cup on the table between them. "But I suppose we *should* get down to business. I figured you might appreciate a few minutes of calm before I send you into the lions' den."

Elana's eyebrow rose again. "What does *that* mean? Valeria told me she didn't think it would be worth it for me to go back to Il Giardino. Has that changed since I got on the plane?"

"It hasn't. I agree with her assessment in that regard. No, my dear, I'm sending you somewhere entirely different and arguably even more dangerous. I'm sending you to New York City."

CHAPTER EIGHT

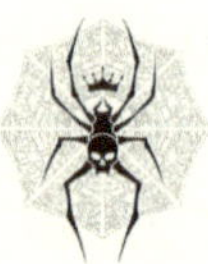

Elana blinked a few times, then her eyebrows drew together and she tilted her head. "New York City?"

"New York City," Lucia confirmed, this time in a ridiculous parody of a Brooklyn drawl that had made stops in several Scottish shires before taking a day trip in the West Midlands.

Elana stared. "You had a perfect Latina accent the entire time I was in Winnipeg. Are you telling me you can't do a New York accent?"

Lucia snickered. Back in her normal brogue, she replied, "You'll never know. Luckily for us, it won't matter if you're similarly *dialectically inclined*. You're being contracted to the Mafia, and unlike what the movies would have you believe, organized criminals aren't walking stereotypes unless they deliberately *choose* to be."

Elana choked, coughed, and sputtered on her mouthful of tea. After wiping her face with a handkerchief the smirking Lucia handed her, Elana glared and protested, "This is the *real* reason you invited me in here for tea—so you could get the spit-take! What do you *mean* I'm being contracted to the Mafia?"

"The vampire Mafia," Lucia clarified as if that explained anything. "Tell me what you know about them."

Elana huffed, settled back in her chair, and shifted her glare to the fire while she dug around in her brain for tidbits on the vampire Mafia. Truth be told, she'd mostly avoided the subject since her mother had been killed in a drive-by shooting that investigators chalked up to some organized crime syndicate.

She eventually stated, "They're officially Houseless since no House worth their salt could bear to be *formally* associated with crime. It's all well and good if it's white-collar, acceptable crime, of course, but when you get into the gutter, it has to be all hush-hush.

"However, it's an open secret that the overwhelming majority of organized crime in the vampire world—and that's worldwide—is executed by House Viverri." The mental image of Sarah Goldin wearing her black gown that draped elegantly on the ground of the Citadel's courtyard flashed through Elana's mind. The woman had class, but she stank like a dead fish. Figuratively, that is.

"Their head of House keeps the family tree squeaky clean," Elana continued, remembering Sarah's open contempt for her son, one of the rebels who had prompted Haven's refounding. She'd disowned him not because he'd betrayed his king but because he got caught. "House Viverri *looks* small, but that's because it's an iceberg. Anyone with even a hint of impropriety is nixed from the official line...but kept on the books to do the shadow work."

Lucia nodded. "Well done. I suppose I shouldn't be surprised you know as much as you do, given your mother's history with them."

"Thanks." Elana refilled her mug and added more milk and sugar. "What do they have to do with Il Giardino?"

"Nothing *directly*—or at least, not that I know of *yet*, but I've been drilling into Edward Korynchuk's communications and financials. It's been a hell of a job. The man employed a crack cybersecurity team, and I had to wheedle my way into a few House Scarapha databases to get the good stuff. Little Eddie was smart. He slipped some of his riskier communiqués under the radar by innocently asking his beloved Ali to send them."

"And the trail leads back to House Viverri?"

"Indirectly, which is the only way Viverri does anything." Lucia sounded impressed, almost respectful. Elana supposed it was only healthy to understand and respect your opponents' strengths and abilities. Still, listening to Lucia sound like she *approved* of Viverri's business practices was a touch unnerving.

"I have confidential informants in just about every criminal organization in the world," Lucia explained. "I have *several* in the vampire Mafia. None of them know about each other, naturally, since that would undoubtedly end in disaster.

"I had only explicitly asked one—the most trustworthy —to keep an ear to the ground about anything related to House Veridian. With informants, I find it's best to mainly let them come to you, only call them when you need something, and not let them run around with information that might hurt *you* if it gets into the wrong hands. This situation falls into the latter category, so it requires extra caution."

"But it paid off, I take it, from what you're saying."

Lucia drained her mug and set it on the table. "I received word from a *different* informant within the Viverri *familia*. I'd inquired with my lass in London, but it was my lad in New York who contacted me a few days ago. Let me give you some context.

"You'll recall that we discovered Edward Korynchuk was working with information that could only have come from House Veridian's experiments?" Lucia waited for Elana's nod, then continued. "However, there was no straight line of communication from one to the other. Not surprising. Whoever's at the heart of all this nonsense hasn't managed to keep it undetected for so long by not being good at covering their tracks.

"As I said, it took plenty of digging and coaxing, but in the end, I traced the information to a contact that looked familiar. I checked my records and found the name Kristoff Rosenfeld buried in my notes from decades ago. A sometime contact for the Viverris, but mostly a mercenary on his own dime. Cropped up here and there, but very rarely. I'd left a note for myself in the '80s suggesting that the name might be a shared alias.

"I started hunting for Rosenfeld but didn't suspect it would come to anything. The Viverris are good enough at their clandestine business that it's nigh impossible to get ahead of them, try as I might. I'm usually picking up their puzzle pieces well after the fact."

"Sometimes I wish bad guys in the real world acted like

bad guys in the movies," Elana commented. "It's annoying when they're competent."

"You can say that again." Lucia rolled her eyes and shook her head. "I *didn't* find anything, but I kept the name on my radar. If Veridian used Rosenfeld to make contact with Korynchuk, it stood to reason they might use him again elsewhere. No guarantees, but worth keeping an eye on."

"Sure."

"You can imagine my surprise, then, when my man in New York contacted me, unsolicited, with a report mentioning Rosenfeld *by name.*"

Elana frowned. "That doesn't seem suspicious to you? They could have figured out you were keeping tabs on Rosenfeld and are using your guy to feed you false information."

Lucia lifted a hand, palm up in acquiescence. "You're absolutely right. It *does* strike me as suspicious. However, I have a strict policy with my informants of only contacting me first in situations of grave danger, with the under-standing that betraying me is likely to lead to reprisal...and I pay them *very* well. It's not in their best interest to try to pull the wool over my eyes."

"Doesn't mean they won't try anyway if they're between a rock and a hard place."

"Certainly, which is why I'm maintaining a healthy level of suspicion instead of tossing the information outright."

Lucia shifted in her chair to face Elana. "My informant is a hardened criminal who's been working for the Viverri *familia* for the better part of a century. He was the second son of a second son, which all but guarantees him a position in the *familia,* and he's the type who found out about his family history early on and decided to embrace it. The schoolyard bully type who doesn't much care whether anyone likes him."

Elana grimaced. "Sounds like a real charmer."

"Oh, yes. I'm told he cleans up nice, but to be honest, I think that would be *more* frightening to the average citizen. Anyway—my point is, he doesn't scare easy. He's been tossing people off piers with concrete shoes for decades, has few morals if any, and generally doesn't see anyone else as human unless they're giving him money. And even then, I wouldn't bet on his loyalty.

"For him to contact me with an indication that he was *scared* is a big deal." Lucia sucked her lower lip between her teeth. "So, I took a chance and got in contact directly. As I said, his loyalty is generally given to the highest bidder, and it's not unfathomable that someone might pay him a chunk of change to flip on me. I needed more information.

"Long story short, I believe him. He told me that Kristoff Rosenfeld has been running errands for somebody higher up the chain that coincide with a lot of people disappearing. He was quick to clarify that people disappear all the time, and that wasn't the issue—but he'd 'never seen anything like this before,' and he 'didn't want to become one of the puppets.'"

Elana's frown deepened. "Puppets. He used that specific word?"

"He did. I tried to press him for more details, but he cut the connection. No way for me to tell why, but the simplest assumption is that he was in danger of being overheard— which suggests to me the disappearances are *internal.*"

"Meaning...someone's cleaning house?"

Lucia shook her head. "The easiest way to unsettle a criminal organization is to introduce internal fear that the rules don't apply anymore. My informant wouldn't have given two shits if the Viverris were disappearing more targets than usual. He would have shrugged and chalked it up to the bosses' plans. Above his paygrade.

"The same thing would happen if it made *sense* who was disappearing. Every criminal organization has factions, and if you piss off the big boss, you'll find yourself on the other end of the knife. Comes with the territory, you might say. If there was an internal war, or someone new had ascended into a position of power and was replacing operatives with their people, that would be understandable.

"For him to be scared means none of those things are happening. It tells me he's afraid for his survival, and more importantly, *he doesn't think he can handle it himself.* That, more than anything else, sounds the alarm bells for me."

"And combined with the reference to 'puppets...'" Elana tried to put the pieces together. "You think Veridian is collecting subjects from the Viverri Mafia?"

"I think there's a distinct possibility that's the case. That, or I *have* been found or bought out. My instinct says it's the former, but I have been wrong before. Seldom, mind." Lucia winked.

Elana chuckled. "No doubt." She sobered just as quickly. "So, if I'm hearing you right, you want me to find out whether he's telling the truth."

"Aye. I spoke with Matt at length, and the timelines agree based on what I could get from my informant. The disappearances among the Viverri *familia* began in earnest at about the same time as your two refugees left Il Giardino. If we follow that trail of breadcrumbs..."

"Then it's possible the experiments continued at Il Giardino until they ran out of subjects, and now those subjects are coming from the Mafia." Elana bit her lip. "That seems like a big leap of logic to me. There could be a million other explanations."

"There could," Lucia readily agreed. "But not paying attention to things that *seem* like coincidences is how the East Coast Staker operated with impunity for decades. It wouldn't be wise to go in guns blazing, certainly. But sending a single undercover agent to check an informant's story and dig up more information is, if you ask me, precisely the right amount of verification this situation requires. And *you*, my dear, are the most suited to the task."

Elana's eyebrows drew together in puzzlement. "What makes you say *that*? I've only been training for a year. I *know* you have a Rolodex full of agents with a hundred times my experience."

Lucia laughed. "I do, yes, but none of them have your level of familiarity with the case. Nor are any of them blessed with the power of insight! Elana, you can intuit in minutes what would take the rest of us hours or days to piece together. No one is better equipped to handle a mission this dangerous and this vital."

Elana gnawed on her lower lip for several seconds while she considered this. "I see your reasoning, but I'd be lying if I said it didn't scare the hell out of me. *I* don't want to become 'one of the puppets,' either."

"Nor do I want you to. And it *should* scare you. It's risky in the extreme, and I can't give you anywhere near the intel

I'd like to before you infiltrate. I expect you to use your best judgment on pulling the rip cord. Your life comes before the mission objective."

Elana drew a deep breath, then let it out in a slow sigh. "Matt and Valeria both think this is the best way forward?"

"It's the closest lead we have at the moment. It's kind of the *only* way forward. You up for the challenge?"

"I damn well hope so. Am I leaving from here?"

Lucia shook her head. "I suggest you catch a few more hours of sleep before heading back to Haven. As I understand it, Valeria's making sure you're kitted out with all the best before you go, and Matt is working on making the final connections with the Viverris—or rather, the 'not-Viverris'—so you aren't shot on sight."

Elana winced. "I'd appreciate that. I take it the vampire Mafia doesn't adhere to the same code of honor that everyone else does?"

Lucia snorted. "Hell, no. They have no compunctions about using firearms, nor anything else that's typically considered 'inferior.' Have you been training with guns?"

"Not as much as I'd like, knowing that. I'll schedule a session with Webber before I go."

"Very wise."

Lucia showed Elana to the bedroom of the safe house not long after, and Elana curled up in the handmade quilts and passed out for several hours. She woke feeling refreshed, had a light lunch with Lucia, then hopped in the SUV with Colin at the wheel and headed to the airstrip.

It had stopped raining at some point while she'd been asleep, but the world was no less wet. "Is it ever *dry* here?" she asked Colin.

Colin chortled. "Only in the worst droughts and only well inland. If y' live here, y' best lay in several pairs of good wellies."

"No kidding."

The return flight was uneventful, although Elana's mind was anything but. Plots and plans, each more outlandish than the last, chased themselves around her mind. She would infiltrate the mob, be picked up immediately, and be presented with a *Godfather*-style ultimatum where Sarah Goldin played the role of the patriarch. She would infiltrate, and Sarah Goldin would stab her in the back in the first five minutes. She wouldn't even *reach* New York. Instead, Sarah would disguise herself as a flight attendant and poison Elana's drink.

As such, Elana felt distinctly *less* rested when she touched down in Haven than when she left a little over twelve hours earlier. Judging by Matt's raised eyebrows as she descended the steps to the tarmac and approached his blacked-out official guardian sedan, her hastily applied makeup hadn't hidden the evidence.

"I told Lucia to keep you there so you'd get some sleep," he admonished her. "What did you do instead, go swimming in the North Sea?"

Elana glared at him. "I spent the flight back imagining all the things that could go wrong. This is a one-person plan with a *brutal* amount of responsibility. If I fuck up, or worse, if I'm *captured*, all of this goes up in smoke."

Matt waited until they were both in the car before

responding. "At the risk of you biting off my head, don't give yourself too much credit."

"The hell does that mean?"

"It means a few things. One, Valeria and I have planned a million operations. We know how to build contingencies into plans that don't seem like they could *have* contingencies. You might be in the mob's den alone, but you won't be without backup.

"Two, there are always more irons in the fire than you're privy to. Yes, this is our best shot at finding useful information, but it's not our *only* option. If you get in there and your gut says you need out, pronto, you pull the plug. We can find another source, but we can't find another Elana Bishop.

"And three, I know from experience how hard this is to wrap your head around, but you have *got* to start thinking like a vampire." Matt paused to signal, then turned onto the ring road surrounding Haven. "Vampires typically fight wars quietly over decades. The Cold War has nothing on some inter-House wars that have simmered over the last millennia. If this operation doesn't go according to plan, another occasion will present itself."

He tilted his head to catch her eye. "You move at the speed of light compared to the rest of the vampire world. So far, that has worked to your advantage, but Elana...you scare people. I wouldn't be surprised if Veridian has scaled up their operations so much and so quickly because they're terrified of you catching up."

"That just means they're even more likely to make mistakes," Elana argued. "If they're not used to working quickly, but I am, it means we have *another* advantage."

Matt lifted a hand from the steering wheel in acquiescence. "That may be. Or it may lead us to overconfidence and our own mistakes."

He braked to turn into the entrance between Quarto and Senkyem—the Gate of Secrets—and fully turned his head to hold Elana's gaze. "Not *everything* vampires do is bad, you know. It might serve you well to spend some time considering what you can learn from this half of your life beyond the powers afforded you by the nanocytes."

Before Elana could respond with the surge of frustration that threatened to overwhelm her, Matt turned into the gate and rolled down the window to speak to the guard on duty. She bit her tongue and grumbled silently instead.

I've learned plenty from vampires. Most of that has been arrogance and selfishness.

Elana caught her reflection in Matt's window as he rolled it up and was surprised by how bitter she looked.

Hm. Maybe I do *need to engage in a little self-reflection.*

CHAPTER NINE

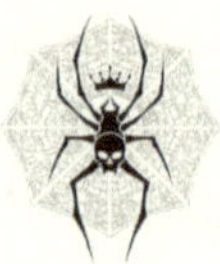

"Would you mind dropping me off at the Consorts' Gallery?" Elana inquired as they drove into Haven. "Or is our timeline so tight that we have to get moving?"

Matt glanced at the dashboard clock and nodded. "You have time for a stop. I'm still waiting for one piece to fall into place. Why the Consorts' Gallery?"

"I need to chat with my mom."

Matt's eyebrows rose a fraction of an inch, but he turned into Quarto at the next intersection.

It was still relatively early in the day since Elana had only been away for twelve hours. Vampire jets cut travel time to a fraction of commercial air travel. As such, the sidewalks bristled with activity. While most low-level vampires reacted poorly to sunlight, which like everything else had to do with nanocytes, specifically immature nanocytes reacting strongly to ultraviolet light, Haven remained on a "standard" diurnal cycle for the most part. This was thanks to the climate canopy that floated over the city, draped from the towers of the

Citadel and hanging from every skyscraper in every district.

Looking out the window, if it weren't for the floating stop signs and the other supernatural signatures of the architecture around her, Elana could have believed she was in any other bustling metropolis. *Vampires came from humans, and we aren't as different as some think. On the other hand, the ways we are different can make the chasm feel pretty damn wide sometimes.*

Matt pulled up alongside the Consorts' Gallery in a loading zone. He put on his four-way flashers and turned to Elana. "When you're done, come to guardian headquarters. I don't know for sure where Valeria will want to prep you, otherwise I'd give you a more specific destination. You'll have time to pack afterward."

Elana nodded. "Better to know what I have to take with me before packing. Thanks, Matt. And thanks for getting me out of my head."

"Any time."

Elana let herself out of the sedan, grabbed her handbag, and closed the door behind her. Then she hurried into the Consorts' Gallery.

For once, the place was open while she was visiting. Usually, she came around after hours, let herself in, and talked openly with her mother's oil portrait until she'd gotten her head around whatever was bothering her. Today was one of the few days the gallery had staff on duty, and a couple of patrons were wandering the halls under the cathedral ceilings.

Elana briefly considered invoking her status as a consort and kicking them all out. Then she realized that would be a very Zilmann thing to do and decided it wasn't her style. Her mother's portrait wasn't so far off the floor that she could whisper without being heard, thanks to everyone in the building having enhanced senses, so this would have to be a silent conversation.

Elana politely nodded at everyone she passed. She recognized a consort who worked for Arbiter Mélissand and a concubine who worked for the Domain of Creation, and they recognized her in turn. They each looked like they were on a mission, presumably sent by their bosses to look up some artifact kept in the gallery.

That was the thing about the Consorts' Gallery. It wasn't solely a repository of portraits of civil servants. If it were, it would have been in Octava, the Domain that housed Haven's arts and culture scene.

No, the Consorts' Gallery was a subsidiary of the King's Archives. The walls were covered with the likenesses of all the arbiters and consorts who had served the SpiderKing since the founding of Haven. Still, the niches and plinths scattered through the tower held more artifacts and curiosities than any museum in the city.

This was the true purpose of the Consorts' Gallery. Those artifacts told a story, hidden in plain sight, about the history of vampirekind and the founding of Haven. Elana understood many more of them now than the first time Valeria brought her here to introduce her to her mother's portrait, but some were still beyond her comprehension.

The Consorts' Gallery was a history of nanocyte technology, and thus a history of the evolution of vampirekind. Fragments of the first devices that harnessed nanocyte power outside of a vampire's body sat on pedestals beside patented applications that had broken barriers only decades ago.

Elana did *not* understand why it was open to the public at *all*. She suspected many of the items on display were replicas, and the real ones were safely hidden away in the sublevels of the King's Archives. To do otherwise would have been tantamount to inviting nuclear destruction. However, apart from a handful of edge cases, no one below sentinel was allowed in, and absolutely nothing *left* the building. That raised the security somewhat.

Still, Elana's insight powers always twinged whenever she visited the Consorts' Gallery, and she had yet to pin why.

Her train of thought pulled into the station as the platform under her feet lifted into the air, prompted by her gentle tap on the hidden panel in the wall. Directed by her gaze, she rose until she was eye-to-eye with the larger-than-life portrait of Tessa Hart, previous Consort of External Affairs and Diplomacy and Arbiter of Sanctuary.

Elana sank to a cross-legged seat on the platform, once again wished the floating disk had a backrest, and gazed at her mother's kind face for a very long moment.

I turned my first vampire last week. She stared at the brushstrokes that formed Tessa's dark eyes. *It was Vicky. Did you know who Vicky was before you died? I know you came to visit me before I was old enough to remember, but you never said whether you checked up on me when I was older. Did you watch me grow up?*

Elana closed her eyes and bowed her head. *Did you give anyone the Rights other than me? And did you ever truly forgive yourself for giving the Rights to a toddler?*

I can barely forgive myself for giving Vicky the Rights, and she's a fully grown, consenting adult. It just... It feels so weird and wrong, Mom. Like I took life away from her rather than giving it. Is that fair, or am I feeling guilty for no reason?

She sighed gently, opened her eyes again, and peeked at Tessa. *It also feels like things are coming to a head. I can't tell what's giving me that impression, so it must be my insight power working overtime on what's happening around me.*

This operation in New York has me on edge. I have no idea what to expect, and it's so risky. I know Matt said I can pull the plug, and we'll find our information other ways if I do, but it's hardly fair to cop out before even giving it the good old college try. This could be a huge break if I play my cards right.

Elana glanced over the edge of her floating disk. A pair of patrons meandered across the floor, many feet below, murmuring to each other about the portrait they had examined and about the artifact they were there to find. *I suppose I should get going.* She looked at her mother again. *Just wanted to say hi, I guess. Sometimes I really wish you could say hi back.*

She stood and directed her attention down, and the floating platform reached the floor within a minute.

Elana grabbed a glider outside the King's Archives to get to Guardian HQ. This method of individual public transit wasn't used quite so often in the winter months, but that was more because nobody liked the wind in their face. Elana didn't mind. The chill was a nice distraction from the persistent, nagging worry in her gut.

The worry wasn't specifically about New York. It was bigger than that, *broader* than that. It felt like packing for a trip and knowing you'd forgotten *something*, but no matter how many times you went over your packing list, you couldn't figure out what you'd forgotten.

Anxiety, Cathy would say. *Just anxiety. Breathe deep and release it into the universe. The clouds will part, and you'll either relax, or you'll figure out what you're missing.*

Elana tried to breathe deeply all the way to Guardian HQ. Her thoughts slowed and ceased their swirling muddle, but the knot in her stomach didn't go away, and neither did the twinge between her eyebrows that meant her insight power was hard at work.

It's onto something. I've realized something's not adding up, but I don't have the information to solve the puzzle yet.

She sat up on the hovering bicycle-like glider in the parking lot of Guardian HQ, put her feet on the snowy asphalt, and crossed her arms. She closed her eyes and let her enhanced senses reach out to detect the concentrations of nanocytes she was looking for.

After a moment, she lifted her feet again, leaned over the front end of the glider, and shot off toward the snow-laced fields of outer Senkyem. Neither Matt nor Valeria had been in the headquarters building. They were farther afield, no pun intended.

Elana stopped in the middle of a field and waited. "Guardian HQ" was the *public* face of law enforcement in Haven. Plenty of administrative work went on in the pagoda-esque building that dominated Senkyem's skyline. The real work happened in their subterranean complex hidden beneath Senkyem's carefully tended agricultural land.

The entrances to that complex were unmarked, as far as Elana had seen. She only found them by feel, like dowsing for water.

I wonder if dowsing is nanocyte-based, too, she pondered as the snowy ground beneath her and the glider shifted, then gradually descended. *Humans have nanocytes too. Maybe if someone almost has vampire genes, or has off-the-scale nanocyte numbers, they could sense the nanocytes in water?*

She would most likely find the answer in Quarto, either in the King's Archives or by asking someone like Arbiter Tarsin. Right now, Elana was glad her intuition had not led her astray and that she'd found an entrance to accommodate the glider. Leaving it in the field or on the road would have looked strange.

When Elana reached the bottom of the shaft, a door slid open in front of her. It was also wide enough to admit the glider, so she pushed it out of the entrance shaft and into the spacious tunnel.

Matt was standing inside. He smiled in greeting, but his lips were tight. "I knew you'd find the place. This way. Leave the glider."

Elana swung her leg over the glider and tucked it against the wall. She brushed stray snowflakes off her coat, straightened it, and fell into step beside Matt. "How do *you* feel about cooperating with the Mafia?"

Matt snorted. "We're using an informant to gain access to information they probably don't want to see the light of day. I'm not sure I'd say we're *cooperating.* But I get what you're asking, and the answer is 'nervous.'"

"Honestly, it's usually easier to run *long* undercover ops with the Viverris. Sending someone in for only a couple of days means it's a blip, not a gradual fade-in and fade-out. That's more likely to be noticed."

"Do you think it's too risky?"

"I think it's *risky*, but I don't think it's *too* risky. Not for you. Valeria has a few tricks up her sleeve that I think will help, too. Turn left."

Elana followed him at the T-junction. Matt stopped only a few steps beyond and knocked on, then opened, one of the hundreds of unmarked doors.

Beyond was one of the hundreds of unadorned rooms that made up the underground complex. Black walls, basic furniture if any, lit from above by hidden lights, and otherwise entirely unremarkable. Being down here always felt like being in a rabbit's warren to Elana. She felt certain rooms existed within the complex that did *not* look the same, but she'd never seen them.

Valeria and Colonel Webber were inside waiting for them, as was another Shadowguard operative. Valeria sat at the large black table that dominated the room's center, and Colonel Webber stood beside her. The third person stood by the wall, and the shadows obscured their face. *Extra security?* This wasn't standard procedure.

A black and silver briefcase sat closed on the table, facing Valeria. With Webber in his black Shadowguard uniform, Valeria's snow-white suit was the only blinding spot of non-black in the room.

Matt closed and locked the door behind them, then sat at the table a few feet away from Valeria. Elana walked up to the table, faced Valeria across it, and laid her palms on its smooth black surface. Without a focused command, the nanotechnology within remained still.

"Your flight to New York leaves tomorrow morning," Valeria informed her. "We have a very short time to get you prepared. Your requested shooting range session with Colonel Webber will occur this evening after completing the other preparations."

Elana raised an eyebrow. "What's left to do? I assume you're gonna kit me out with whatever's in that box, then I'll go practice my marksmanship with the colonel, and I'll review whatever intel we have tonight before the flight in the morning."

Valeria patted the briefcase. "You're mostly correct, but the preparation method for this operation is far more involved. We're not just handing you a set of armor and a stun baton and saying *Go* like we did when you went to Winnipeg."

"The Agoracor infiltration was comparatively low-risk," Webber chimed in. "Immediate danger wasn't likely, so we could get away with nano-implants for your disguise. When you're rubbing elbows with the Mafia, you gotta step up your game."

Elana frowned. "I have no idea what you're talking about."

Valeria pressed both thumbs to the latches of the briefcase. They glowed bright blue, then unlocked with a *click*. She flipped them open before raising the lid and spinning the briefcase to face Elana.

Inside, two syringes and two vials lay nestled in thick black foam. The vials were opaque, and a bag with a pair of hypodermic needles sat beside the syringes.

Elana's stomach did a nervous little squeeze. "I didn't know I needed special shots to go to New York," she weakly joked. "It hasn't been that long since my last measles booster."

Valeria cracked a smile but shook her head. "This is a preventative of another type. As the colonel mentioned, the nano-implants were sufficient for you to pass under the radar in Winnipeg, especially paired with your impressive interpersonal skills. Also, nano-implants last longer before degrading, so there's very little fear of being caught like Cinderella on the palace steps."

Elana's heart flip-flopped, but she stayed quiet and waited for Valeria to finish her explanation. This was a situation where she did not want to chance being caught out when her coach turned back into a pumpkin.

"You might have heard that some criminals use DNA screening to attempt to fool guardians or other vampire law enforcement agencies," Valeria continued. "I assume you have extrapolated that we use it, too. That's what this is."

Elana frowned. "Sure. I had a DNA screen backup while I was in Winnipeg in case I needed to fool a biometric scanner into thinking I *was* my cover identity. They didn't look like that."

"This is a *full* screen," Valeria clarified. "This vial is full of specialized nanocytes primed with a DNA profile we've designed from the ground up to be your ideal cover. Upon injection, they'll begin interacting with your nanocytes, then every cell in your body. Within twenty-four hours, you will essentially *become* the cover profile."

Elana's eyes widened. "That is *incredible* technology. I

gotta ask, though. How do I go back to being *me?* I am not a hundred percent certain I'm comfortable signing up to become someone else for the rest of my life. Is that what the second vial is for?"

"It's time-limited. This one is, anyway. The replicant DNA is encoded with a time bomb virus fragment that will 'detonate' after seventy-two hours. Once it does, you'll have another twenty-four hours before the reverse transformation is complete and you look like and test as yourself again."

"So, that's *not* what the second vial is for."

"No. The second vial is to create your decoy. Sergeant?"

The fourth person in the room, the Shadowguard operative lurking in the background, came forward into the light. It was Sergeant Michelle Ferns, the Irishwoman Elana had met while searching for Cassandra Matthews, née Rhuland. She was slimmer and more petite than Elana, but her facial structure matched quite well, and Elana imagined basic traits like hair and eye color were a cinch to alter via genetics.

I wonder how closely they screen the DNA. If someone has genes with latent tendencies for stuff like breast cancer or chromosomal deficiencies, how does that work when you "turn back?" Does the damage stay? Maybe the nanocytes clean it all up.

She shook herself and returned her full focus to Sergeant Ferns. "So, you'll pretend to be me while I'm infiltrating the mob, huh?"

"Sure will, miss." Ferns smirked. "I look forward to going toe to toe with Arbiter Zilmann on your behalf."

"Oh, God. Don't do anything I wouldn't do."

"I don't think that narrows it down much, Consort."

"Fair." Elana pressed her palms harder against the table and wrenched her gaze from the briefcase with its ominous syringes and hidden potions to Valeria's face. "Okay. I turn into somebody new, then what?"

"Then you'll make contact with the operative who's bringing you into the inner circle." Valeria tapped the table and brought up a picture of a balding man who appeared to be in his late forties. "Constantin Nabkovich. He sent out an inquiry late last night looking for new blood in the far reaches of the recruiting tree to help with a job."

"The recruiting tree being the Viverri family tree?"

"Yes."

"Last time, we had to bribe two Houses to add me to their records. Those Houses were *allied* with us. How the hell are we pulling *this* off?"

Matt chuckled. "The genius of the Viverri *modus operandi* is also its weak spot. As you know, anyone who isn't in the immediate line is disowned. Not shoved into a sub-House—fully disowned, and on the spot, too. No record is kept, not even a civil one. These people are functionally ghosts in every administration on the planet. If they're born in a human hospital, someone sneaks in, destroys the paperwork, and alters memories on the way out."

Elana frowned. "Not even the House itself? There's *no* verification?"

"No identities whatsoever," Matt confirmed. "Numbers *only*. And not identifying numbers but *population* numbers. They keep track of the number of people in the family tree, but not who those people are."

Valeria added, "Most of the Viverri 'ghost scions' are

swept right into training for organized crime, but once in a while they leave someone 'on the outside.' Usually, they're sleeper agents—backup, basically—or the end of a line that hasn't shown much success for the last few decades. Those are the ones we keep careful track of for precisely these situations."

Valeria tapped the table again and brought up another picture, this time of a woman with dark auburn hair and a sharp, pointed nose. "Meet Kat Stevens. She is so far removed from the main Viverri line that she's barely even a vampire anymore. She was born the same year as you and passed over for training because her line has been dying out for a century.

"We're banking on a couple of things by turning you into her. One, she's unimportant enough that no one will check to see if there are two of her. Two, she's unimportant enough that if this job is bait, which I suspect it is, she'll be seen as expendable."

Elana narrowed her eyes. "*I* don't want to be expendable. Won't they be suspicious if this nobody from an end-of-the-line *twig* of the family tree shows up with actual skills and training? And *gear,* for that matter?"

Matt shook his head. "They will think you were a sleeper agent all along and Sarah's been downplaying your line for her own reasons. Their loyalty to their matriarch is *ironclad.*"

Elana watched the portrait of Kat Russell and bit her lip. "Well, I always wanted to see what I'd look like as a redhead."

CHAPTER TEN

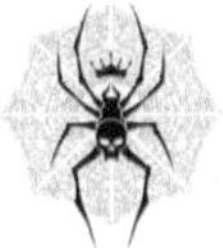

The injection made her dizzy enough that she swayed in her chair and Matt had to steady her. Sergeant Ferns' injection had no such effect, so Matt brought Elana to the healers before sending her to pack.

"The last thing we need is for you to have an allergic reaction to your cover identity," he teased, but Elana heard the concern behind the lighthearted tone.

Luckily, the healer told them after a quick blood test that Elana wasn't having a negative reaction. "Quite the opposite, in fact. Your preponderance of stem nanocytes and high nanocyte count in general are resulting in a faster uptake than usual." She pointed out several markers on a projected screen of the blood test results, none of which meant anything to Elana. She supposed she should fix that.

"Does that mean it will wear off faster?" Matt asked.

"If anything, it might last *longer*," the healer replied. "Hard to know for sure since I've never seen results like this. Based on a theoretical examination of the data, I'd guess she might have an extra six to twelve hours before the viral fragment kicks in."

The healer, a round-faced woman with curly blond hair, noticed Elana's blank look and smiled. "Think of it this way, dear. The only cells the DNA screen *doesn't* override are your bones. We include a suppressant to keep your body from attacking itself, but it's only safe to have it last a certain time. Too long, and you'll essentially have runaway cancer."

Elana's eyes widened. "That was *not* included in the original brief. Matt?"

Matt shrugged. "It's carefully calibrated so that *doesn't* happen. Trust me. We've been doing this long enough to know how to keep people alive and healthy. It's counter-productive to warn people of side effects that won't happen."

She glared. "Ever heard of informed consent?"

"Vampires. Not humans. Informed consent works a *little* differently."

Elana grumbled.

Twelve hours later, the process of turning into Kat Stevens was well underway. It was bizarre, to say the least. Elana had enough to do to prepare, so she couldn't spend the entire time staring at herself in the mirror. This was a good thing because every time she *did* check the mirror, she peered at herself, trying to detect what had changed since the last time she'd looked.

Her shooting range session with Webber had gone well.

She had remembered her form, and now she carried a small, easily concealable pistol that packed a hell of a lot more punch than any human firearm. Vampires might turn their noses up at guns, but that hadn't stopped them from creating far more deadly models.

She'd packed with Vicky's help, using pictures of Kat Stevens Matt had provided to do basic color matching. "If you show up wearing the wrong colors for your skin tone, people *will* notice something's off," Vicky had flatly told her. "I don't care if you're walking into the filthiest den of iniquity on the planet. When it comes to vampires, style *matters,* even if it's unconscious."

Vicky had also promised her she'd look after Francesco and Ginevra in Elana's absence. "Have no fear. Vicky Justine Lamarr is on the case. It'll give me something to do instead of biting my nails down to the quick worrying about you rubbing shoulders with mobsters."

Elana was waiting on tenterhooks for Matt to text or call with a time for her flight. She'd never been to New York, and part of her wanted to go early and sightsee before she had to get down to business. Unfortunately, she was at the point in the transformation where she looked like a chimera of two people. New York was a progressive place full of strange folk, but even that might turn some heads.

Elana turned over in bed. *An hour of sleep. Come on. One hour. Please. I'll even deal with Matt waking me up with flight info. Just give me a break from the nerves.*

The moon outside her window was unsympathetic, and she grumbled and buried her face in her pillow.

Elana's phone buzzed, and she sat straight up, instantly awake like she'd had a pot of coffee spiked with Red Bull.

Flight's leaving in two hours. Last call for prep.

She glanced at the carry-on suitcase by her bedroom door, wryly chuckled under her breath, and texted back a confirmation.

When she pulled up to the airstrip, Elana was surprised to see Colonel Webber in plain clothes standing outside the terminal and smoking a cigarette.

"I hear that's bad for your health," she ribbed him as she hauled her suitcase from her trunk and locked her Emeya with a wave.

He snorted. "I'm a vampire. Cancer can try." He took the last puff, stubbed out the butt, and incinerated it with a tiny flame between his thumb and forefinger. "You look good, Stevens."

Elana flipped her auburn hair over her shoulder and put a hand on her hip. "Thanks. Why're you here? You don't seem the type to see people off."

"Coming with you."

Her eyebrows drew together. "Don't get me wrong, I appreciate the backup, but I thought this was a solo mission."

Webber nodded. "Functionally, you're right. I won't infil with you. I'm your getaway driver and your outside intel if you *really* get stuck. We want this to work."

"Me too."

They said nothing more on their way through the terminal and onto the plane. There was no need. Webber wasn't the talkative type, and Elana's nerves were still sufficiently frayed that she wanted to go back to bed and pretend none of this was happening. The tiny refrain of "something's wrong" was still on repeat in the back of her mind. All she could do was reassure it that she was doing her best to find the missing information.

The plane took off. They flew northeast along the coast and landed at another small airstrip well outside the city proper. A blacked-out sedan was waiting for them. Webber produced the keys from his coat pocket, and they drove off into the slow, gray dawn.

Elana fell asleep on the drive into the city. Something about car travel had always been able to knock her out. When she woke to Webber's hand on her elbow, she was grateful she'd slept and disappointed she'd missed the sights. They were deep in the metropolis of New York with cars and pedestrians choking the streets and slowing traffic to a crawl.

"Ready?" Webber asked.

Elana swallowed her knee-jerk snarky reaction and checked in on herself. She could pull the plug while inside, but this was the last opportunity to do so before she would have to cover her tracks.

With a few deep breaths, her nerves settled into a leaden puddle in her stomach. *Good enough.* She nodded at Webber. "Ready."

He drove another block and a half, then turned into an alley and stopped. It had started raining while Elana was asleep, and small rivulets ran down the alley toward the street. "See you in three days."

"See you in three days," Elana echoed. She let herself out, grabbed her carry-on from the back seat, then hunched her shoulders and trudged into the rain.

Kat Stevens hadn't been picked to learn her House's criminal trade, but she'd ended up in the same field anyway. Her "official" skills included a diploma from a temp agency in administrative office work, but she paid her bills by cooking the books for anyone who needed to fleece the IRS.

She was good with numbers, had taken a few self-defense courses, and could handle a gun. She hated rain. She lived in Texas. Right now, she was on a week-long trip to Cuba with her girlfriends.

Elana's target was a basement pub two blocks from her drop-off point. They were constantly hiring. Its entrance was also in a back alley, and the rest of the building was cheap apartments. Elana figured it was the type of place everyone in the neighborhood *knew* was a mob front, but nobody cared. In some ways, knowing your neighbors were mobsters meant you might be *safer*. After all, most people weren't stupid enough to pick a fight with the mob. Better the devil you knew, right?

Elana hitched her carry-on over a bump in the sidewalk and turned into the grimy alley that was her destination. An unlit neon sign announcing The Lock and Key Pub hung at waist level, just above the railing of the stairs that led down to the basement door.

She stowed the telescoping handle of her carry-on and lifted it by its fabric handle. Puddles had formed in the bowls worn into the concrete stairs. Elana splashed through them carelessly. Kat Stevens was the opposite of high maintenance.

In some ways, it was a nice change to wear jeans, sneakers, and ratty T-shirts again. Haven's high fashion was nice, but Elana missed the days of working construction sites, where she didn't have to think about what she wore.

She knocked in the code pattern Constantin Nabkovich had sent to "Kat Stevens." Three short, one long, repeat. Morse Code for VV—Viverri—and coincidentally the opening to Beethoven's Fifth Symphony. "Definitely not why they picked it," Matt had told her. "They're *not* that classy. Well, maybe Sarah Goldin is, but none of the rest of them."

The door opened thirty seconds later, when Elana thought she would have to knock again. A mousy woman a head shorter than Elana stood on the threshold. She wore a stained apron that had been white at one point, and her hair was up in a messy bun. She appeared to be in her sixties, with wrinkles in her jowls, a couple of stray whiskers on her chin, and a mole above her right eyebrow. Her blue eyes were sharp like the points of icicles.

The woman didn't say anything. She looked "Kat" up and down, then stepped back to let her in. As soon as Elana's suitcase cleared the door frame, the woman slammed the door shut behind her and thrust a small black box into Elana's hand. Elana could barely see what it was. The only light came from a grimy wall sconce twenty feet down the hall.

"What do you want me to do with this?" Elana brusquely asked. This was the first test. She'd spent several hours practicing a mild Southern drawl like she'd heard from her great-aunts on her dad's side. It was more Georgia than Texas, so she was banking on no one here ever having listened to Kat Stevens speak.

"Stick your finger in it," the woman snapped. "What are you, stupid? Or did Constantin not tell you shit?"

"Constantin didn't tell me shit," Elana retorted. "He gave me the pattern to knock and said show up here." She wiggled the box. "What's this crap?"

"Gotta prove you are who you say you are."

Ah. A bioscanner. Elana scoffed. "Jesus Christ. I come all the way from Texas to help you guys out with a job, and this is how you greet me?"

The woman put a hand on her hip and stepped into Elana's space. "You sayin' you got somethin' to hide?"

Elana rolled her eyes and stuck her finger in the opening she'd found in the box. As she expected, it warmed briefly while it scanned her fingerprint, then pierced her fingertip to draw a drop of blood. "No. Just commentin' on a distinct lack of trust. What the fuck happened to 'blood is thicker than water?'"

The woman snatched the box back and turned it over. She peered at the faint orange markings that appeared on the back, then stuck the box in the deep pocket of her apron. "Gotta be careful," she admonished Elana. "Must be nice in Texas, not havin' to worry about anyone stabbing you in the back."

Elana laughed harshly. "Amen. In Texas, if you got a problem with somebody, you say it straight, and you have it out. Out of curiosity, what would have happened if I *wasn't* who I said I was?"

The woman shrugged. "Ben woulda shot you in the head, we'd have dumped you in the river, and we'd get the next nobody on the list. I'm Sandy. Bring your shit."

Elana looked up to see a hulking man squeezed into a nook on the other side of the hallway. He grinned when Elana met his gaze, showing two black teeth and one gold, and he patted his hip, where the butt of a gun showed, hanging in a holster on his belt.

Elana smiled, then sedately followed Sandy. *Ben looks altogether too happy about the prospect of having a body to dump in the river. These people do not fuck around.*

"You're only here for the job, so you'll bunk in the common beds on the third floor," Sandy sharply told her as they traversed the hall. It was dark but clean. The paint was chipping on the walls, but no stray trash or stains marred the floor. "You're lucky. I don't think we have many guests in the ladies' room at the moment.

"If you're not out working, you can get nosh three times a day in the pub kitchen," she continued. Some of the doors they passed in the corridor were open, and some were closed. Sandy was keeping a quick pace, but Elana still caught glimpses of people in suits and casual clothes either quietly talking or, in one case, playing cards. "If you help clean up, the girls won't spit in your food next time."

"I'll keep that in mind."

"See that you do. Carolyn's on housekeeping this week and she *will* put rats in your bed if you're a shit."

"Noted."

"Constantin's coming back tomorrow to pick you up. He got delayed in Amsterdam. You've got a day to kill. Use it however you want. There's a library on the second floor.

Pub opens to the public at five PM. Don't do business during business hours or—"

"Or Ben will shoot me?"

"Now you're getting the idea."

Sandy slammed open a rusty fire door with her hip and ushered Elana into a concrete stairwell. "Make yourself at home. Lunch is at noon. Borscht and dill buns."

"Tasty." Elana had no idea what borscht was, and she'd never heard of putting dill in buns, but turning her nose up at hospitality seemed like an extremely dumb idea. "See you at lunch."

"No, you won't. I do the books and make sure this place runs like a well-oiled machine. You don't *want* to see me."

"Yes, ma'am."

"That's better. Get out of my sight."

Elana trotted up the stairs until she reached the landing with a big "3" painted on the wall. She let herself through the door, which announced her arrival with a creak loud enough to wake the dead. Nothing stirred in the corridor, so everyone here must be used to the noise.

This level of the building reminded Elana of the shitty apartment Vicky had rented the first year after high school. She'd been on an independence kick, refusing to stay at home, so she'd gotten a bachelor pad in a three-story walk-up in downtown Ashford.

The walls were dingy, the carpet was so beaten down it could have been linoleum, and cigarette burns marred the rubber on the handrail in the stairwell. Elana's suspicion that the walls were thinner than tissue paper was borne out when she heard snoring, loud television, and a heated conversation within twelve steps.

She found a door marked *Ladies' Commons* written in surprisingly elegant handwriting on a laminated paper tacked to the door. The string of vulgar graffiti scratched into the wood underneath destroyed the note of sophistication.

Elana rolled her eyes and tried the handle. Sandy hadn't given her a key or a code, so she assumed it was biometric or unlocked. The knob warmed in her hand, then the lock clicked, and she swung the door open.

She swallowed the urge to grimace. The place was clean, but that was about all it had going for it. The room was like a barracks, full of metal bunk bed frames and thin mattresses that wouldn't have made good firestarter. Two dozen beds, all told, in two rows stretching away from the door. Flimsy curtains covered the windows at the room's far end.

Someone was sitting on the bed closest to the window on the right. Their back was turned, and their shoulders were hunched. Elana considered saying hi, but judged by the level of friendliness displayed so far that extending a hand in friendship might get her shanked.

Instead, she let her suitcase thump onto the lower bunk closest to the door on the right. It was the second-most defensible position in the room, the first being the bed already taken. The door opened to the right, meaning Elana would have a heartbeat or two to get into cover, but she wouldn't immediately be visible from the door.

Webber would be proud of me. I'm almost as paranoid as him.

"Welcome to hell," the woman at the other end of the room called. "What're you in for?"

"A job," Elana blandly replied. "You?"

"Just passing through. Doing a job in Paris next week, needed a place to lie low for a few days. What're you called?"

"Kat."

"Cat, like kitten, or cat, like cougar?"

"Kat, like Katrina."

The woman bounced off her bed and strode down the aisle of bunk beds. She stopped beside Elana's and leaned heavily on the frame across the aisle, making it creak in protest, then crossed her arms. "You're new."

"Maybe." Elana eyed the other woman warily. She was a *tank*, broad-shouldered and broad-hipped, a couple of inches shorter than Elana but about a hundred and fifty pounds heavier. Judging by the biceps, a good portion of it was muscle, but she would float if you tossed her in a pool.

Her head was shaved apart from a flop of bright purple hair over her left eye, and she'd had geometric designs shaved into the fade on the rest of her skull. These patterns connected to intricate tattoos that covered the side of her head, and as far as Elana could tell, continued down her neck to the rest of her. She wore a studded leather jacket, had huge rings in her earlobes, and a string of piercings in her right eyebrow. She wore lipstick that matched her hair, and her boots could have been army surplus if they hadn't had leather straps that went to her thighs.

"Yeah, you're new. Here's your freebie, new girl. Nobody gets your name. You get a nickname. I'm calling you Kitten. Nobody's gonna argue with me, so you're stuck with it."

Elana made a face. "Thanks."

"Could be worse. I coulda called you Pussy."

"Fair. What're you called?"

The woman cracked an ear-to-ear smile. "They call me Dust."

"Hi, Dust. Nice to meet you."

"Same. You got money?"

Elana narrowed her eyes. "That seems like an *incredibly* stupid question to answer."

Dust clapped Elana on the back hard enough to make her stumble. "There's hope for you yet. You're here for Constantin's job, yeah?"

"I thought nobody got names."

"Stan hires, he doesn't do jobs. He gets a name. Come on, it's almost time for the next round of poker. I'll introduce you to the boys."

Dust steered Elana out of the room before she could protest and locked the door behind them with a snap of her fingers.

CHAPTER ELEVEN

Elana trailed in Dust's wake because what else would she do? The woman was built like a brick house, and she didn't take no for an answer.

The mission-aware part of Elana's brain chimed in that riding Dust's coattails was likely to get Kat in with the "in" crowd, which was useful in a time-limited operation. The pure survival part of her brain suggested Elana wanted to get as far away from Dust as possible. She was *clearly* heavily involved in House Viverri's under-the-table operations, and proximity to that could only be dangerous.

Elana swallowed her fear and reminded herself that she was Kat Stevens, in New York City to do her birth House a favor and get the fuck out. Elana Bishop desperately needed information, but Kat Stevens had no skin in the game and could walk any time she wanted.

The Viverri *familia* functioned on a razor's edge. Since nothing was documented, they didn't truly have leverage over their operatives beyond the threat of death. Granted, that was enough for most, but it would be easy for a snubbed family member to whisper in a few ears and cause trouble for the higher-ups.

The system worked because everyone understood that no one *owed* anyone any loyalty. Everyone was there for the job, nothing more. Do your job well, and you got perks. That kind of loyalty was easy to buy, so Viverri operatives weren't likely to moonlight for anyone else. But dying for your family? They'd already disowned you. You would sooner rat them out.

Open secrets are no good for blackmail. Elana and Dust reached the end of the corridor. It opened into a large parlor decorated in the style of a luxury gentlemen's club. That is, if the gentlemen's club had bought all their furniture from Goodwill, and your cousin Vinny had done the wallpaper.

Everything in this room revolved around the card table at the center. Eight chairs were squished around it, but spectator chairs sat in haphazard "rows" radiating out from there. A retro fridge in mustard yellow sat in one corner, next to a double sink that had seen better days and probably more rinsed bloodstains than Elana cared to think about.

The cupboards had been painted a dozen times, but the doors had never been straightened, and several were missing handles. The windows were dingy and covered by threadbare curtains. Those matched the upholstery on the chaise longue, armchairs, and couch that surrounded the brick fireplace opposite the entrance.

The room stank of cigarette smoke and stale alcohol, and Elana stifled a gag as they walked in. *Jesus Christ, it reeks in here! Everyone here is a vampire—how can they stand it? Have they all cauterized their noses?*

She breathed through her mouth as Dust brought her to the table, where six *familia* members of various shapes, sizes, and cleanliness levels were deep into a poker game. Elana didn't recognize the layout of the cards, but that didn't surprise her. *Probably a house variant.*

The best word to describe the man with the most chips was *scrawny*. He reminded Elana uncomfortably of a Chihuahua turned into a man. His beady eyes bugged out, his chin receded, and he was twitchy. He convulsively glanced around the table at his opponents' hands, doubtless watching for tells while the rest relaxed and greeted the new arrivals.

A woman Elana's age with stringy brown hair, gaunt cheeks, and the second-highest number of chips eyed Elana with the evaluating look you might turn on a horse or a dog. "Who's this, Dust?" Her voice was thin and raspy.

"This is Kitten," Dust informed them. "New girl Stan brought in for the job this week."

The big guy next to the gaunt woman made a disgusted sound deep in his throat, and the guy next to him punched him in the arm. Given that the puncher wore a ratty tank top that showed off his impressive biceps and his form was impeccable, Elana suspected he was an enforcer.

"Shut up, Flint," the enforcer growled. "Shit-talk the boss, and you'll take the new girl's place."

Elana slid into one of the empty chairs and made a show of rummaging in her handbag for something to add to the pot. "Sounds like I should turn tail and go back to Dallas."

The other woman at the table, a squat, compact woman with no neck, laughed harshly. "Might serve you well, Kitten. This ain't no place for pussies."

Elana casually stretched over the back of her chair, letting her hair fall over her shoulders. She yawned in the most bored manner possible before casually tossing the fifty she'd dug out of her purse onto the table. "Kittens have claws. What's your call sign? Sow?"

The rest of the table burst out laughing, except for the man who was currently winning. The puncher chortled. "She's got your number, Gnash."

The woman with no neck grinned after briefly narrowing her eyes. "She does indeed, Billy Joe." She leaned over, plucked Elana's fifty off the table, and tucked it into a satchel strapped to her hip. Then, she opened a box beside her on the table and counted out Elana's chips. "I'm Gnash. Like gnashing teeth…like a boar sow on the hunt."

"Pleasure."

Dust took the last empty seat and handed Gnash a fifty as well. "Gnash is the treasurer for this branch of the business. When you and whoever Stan sends with you finish your job, you'll see her for your payment. You've met Billy Joe. He's dumber than a sack of bricks but punches twice as hard. The rest of these idiots are Polar, Flint, Franklin, and Lead Pipe."

Elana nodded. The introductions had done nothing to tell her who was who, but she'd figure that out herself. "What's the game?"

The game leader caught her gaze a moment before he spoke. His eyes were chips of glittering granite, and his voice was soft and mellifluous. "Aces are wild. Standard poker hands otherwise. You get four cards, and you'll hand one to your left-hand neighbor. After the first round of betting, dealer adds two to the table. One more round of betting, then lay. Clear?"

"Crystal."

Elana readied herself to lose before she won. She had little doubt she could do reasonably well right out of the gate, thanks to her insight power, but she wanted them to underestimate her. Depending on how obvious their tells were, a round of beginner's luck wouldn't go amiss, but they would be suspicious if she won too many times in a row.

She hid a smile as she remembered the last time she'd played poker with the Bishop's construction boys. She'd cleaned them all out and treated herself to a steak dinner after. Only Jerry had been smart enough not to play.

Even then, my intuition was good. Thanks, Mom.

Elana played the first round with all the tells of an over-confident beginner. Too snarky, too clever, and too much smirking interspersed with stupid questions and silly mistakes. She hemmed and hawed. She folded at the last second, even though she likely had the second-best hand at the table, and with some bluffing, could have won the round.

"Bad luck," Lead Pipe crowed as he raked his winnings over. Elana had bet a little higher than she normally would and now sat at thirty-five of her original fifty dollars.

"I'll get the next one," Elana promised. She put on her "game face" and was gratified to hear a couple of hastily stifled guffaws. *That's it. Peg me as the newbie. I'm not interesting enough to pry into, just new enough to hassle.*

She folded early in the second round since she'd been dealt unsalvageable crap. The draws would have had to be phenomenal. Elana wasn't bothered by the early out because it gave her more time to study the others.

Gnash was easy to read in the way of those who prided themselves on being hard to read. Her face and hands were still, but her gaze flitted around, and her crow's feet tightened when she wasn't happy.

Flint was a stone and played like one. He leaned in when he was excited and leaned back when he wasn't. Billy Joe did the exact opposite, plus he grinned when he thought no one was looking. *Dumber than a sack of bricks, indeed.*

She'd figured out in the first round that Franklin was the game leader. No idea where his nickname came from, but he was incredibly hard to read, which was probably why he was winning. Elana's best theory right now was a specific twitch in his left eyebrow, but she hadn't decided whether it was deliberate or involuntary.

Polar was the gaunt woman who'd been disgusted by her. She had constantly downturned lips, which initially suggested she was good at bluffing. It didn't take long for Elana's insight power to catch that she had an involuntary tic that moved her left ear when she thought she had a chance.

Lead Pipe was either an idiot in the same league as Billy Joe or clever enough to rival Franklin. Elana wasn't sure whether Franklin had let Lead Pipe have the first hand as a pity round or whether Lead Pipe was brilliant at bluffing.

All that said, the best poker face at the table was Dust's. Elana was not a whit surprised. The punk woman played hard and fast, and it wasn't lost on Elana that Franklin sat up a little straighter and played a little tougher in return on the second hand.

Franklin took the second hand, but when he laid his cards after Dust had folded, she swore with enough conviction that even Billy Joe and Lead Pipe blushed. After she'd finished her blue streak, she collected her cards, tapped them square, then slid them across the table with an amicable, "*Damn* you, Franklin."

"I aim to please," he laconically replied.

Elana decided to test her theories on the third hand after being dealt decent cards. Judging by her first impression, Polar and Flint thought they had a chance, Billy Joe would fold at the first opportunity, and God only knew what Dust, Franklin, and Lead Pipe were thinking.

Elana tossed a question into the circle as she slid five bucks' worth of chips into the center. "Anybody want to bet on who Stan's sendin' with me?"

"Depends," Dust replied with the tip of her tongue between her teeth. "What's your specialty?"

"She don't look like a bruiser," Billy Joe opined while leering at Elana.

Elana casually flipped him off and smirked at his answering chortle. "I can hold my own in a fight, but I specialize in... Let's call it, 'gettin' into places where I shouldn't be.'"

Polar eyed Elana over her cards. "With tools or sweet talk?"

"Sweet talk." Elana slipped her cards into one hand and did a silly little wave with the other. "You want to let me in there, sir. Not lettin' me in might be *dangerous to your health.*"

As she gestured, she exerted a tiny bit of nanocytic influence over the room. This was the swaying power all vampires held over humans, and it scaled as one ascended in the Nexus. Elana had no idea what level any of these guys were, but she'd have put decent money on a couple of them being savant or below.

Franklin's gaze jumped from his cards to Elana's eyes, and Dust shifted in her seat. Polar flinched. Gnash rolled her eyes. The rest only chuckled in amused agreement. *So, those four are advanced enough to notice it, which means they're probably guardians or above. Fascinating.*

Franklin cleared his throat. "In that case, my bet would be on some muscle for you to order around. Someone like Billy Joe here."

"Hey!"

Flint elbowed the boxer. "Dude, he's complimenting you. Saying you're strong."

"He's also saying I'm dumb!"

"Aren't you?" Dust asked in a fake *sotto voce*, triggering another round of snickers.

"Let's face it, Billy Joe. You've never been the brightest bulb in the box. I'm out." Polar folded, leaving Elana in with Franklin and Dust before the last card was drawn.

An ace of spades was pulled, which was no help to Elana. She hadn't bet high while chatting, so she could still stand to lose this round without it hurting too badly.

Flint sat back in his chair and crossed his arms. "I'm just glad it ain't *me* goin', I'll tell you that much. I'll stick to knockin' down people's doors what owe us money. This creepy shit's too much for me. Turns my stomach."

"You are the most cowardly mobster I have ever had the displeasure of meeting, Flint," Franklin serenely stated.

"Downright lily-livered," Billy Joe agreed. "I'll go wherever the boss sends me. Ain't my call to make. I'm just the muscle."

Dust rolled her eyes as Billy Joe flexed his biceps. "Provin' Franklin's point, Billy Joe." She eyed Franklin and Elana, then glared at her cards. "I fold."

Elana gazed at Franklin, who calmly stared back. "Raise you five."

"I'll meet," Franklin easily agreed, and after they'd slid the respective chips into the center, they laid their cards on the table. "Well played."

"Thank you. I thought you had me for sure. I'm sure it won't last." Elana winked, then gathered her chips in and flicked her cards into the pile to be reshuffled. "What's so creepy about this job? Constantin's—sorry, *Stan's* message wasn't very detailed. I mean, *duh*, but now that I'm here, anybody wanna shed some light on what shitstorm I'm walking into?"

Lead Pipe, Billy Joe, and Flint grimaced and averted their eyes. Uncomfortable glances flicked between Polar, Franklin, and Dust. Then Dust cracked her neck, sighed, and tapped the deck of cards on the table. "You sure you wanna know?"

Elana raised an eyebrow but dropped her tone to match. "Seems stupid to send someone in without knowin' what they're up against. Unless I'm cannon fodder, in which case I'd like to know so I can get my affairs in order."

Lead Pipe snorted, but Flint elbowed him hard, and he shut up with a baleful glare at the other man.

"You won't die unless you play your cards very poorly," Franklin calmly told Elana. "Dust, you might as well deal while we talk."

Dust grunted in agreement and flicked cards across the felt. "You're body-snatching, essentially. Stan's been given a target by the big boss. It's your job to pick them up."

"Kidnappin'. Seems simple enough. Or—grave-robbin'?" Elana didn't give the question any more weight than the rest of her words. *Dead or alive, it doesn't matter to me.* And it didn't, in truth, because both options presented terrible implications.

"Kidnapping," Flint clarified. "Although it's never kids. Well…"

"It's not kids," Polar snapped.

An uncomfortable ripple went through the circle. Dust let it pass, then added, "It *is* usually simple. You're right. Get in, snag your target, get out."

"What's the catch? Why *usually*, and why's everyone bein' so weird about it?"

Gnash laughed. "Because of what happens if you fuck up. Christ, Dust, what kind of hand is this? I fold."

"Sorry." Dust didn't sound very sorry. She regarded her cards, then slid twenty bucks' worth of tokens into the center.

Elana side-eyed her, then let her gaze slip around the table. Satisfied with what she saw and the cards she'd been dealt, she matched Dust's bet. "If this is a job straight from the big boss, I know my head's on the line. You fuck up a job, you get what's comin' to you. That's nothin' new. That's just business."

Billy Joe grimaced. "It ain't like that. Yeah, if you screw up a good job like this, straight from Mama, you might get your head handed to you on a silver platter. Tell you the truth, I'd prefer that. Clean and quick."

Dust flipped the first table card. Polar and Flint folded. Franklin raised them ten, Lead Pipe folded, Billy Joe met Franklin's bet, and Dust and Elana did as well.

"Didn't know Mama was in the habit of internin' flunkies who didn't hold up their end of the bargain," Elana casually ventured. "I'm with Billy Joe. Waste of resources, if you ask me."

Dust dealt the final card, grimaced, and folded. Franklin raised another twenty. Billy Joe hemmed and hawed, then folded as well.

Elana stared Franklin down, looking between his eyes and her cards. "It's not internment, is it?" It wasn't really a question.

Franklin shook his head. "It's an honor to do a job that comes right from Mama…but fuck this one up, and you're the one on the slab."

"We've lost more people to these jobs than we have in the last decade," Gnash muttered. "Talk about a waste of resources. You in or out, Kitten?"

Elana held Franklin's gaze for another half a second, then pushed the rest of her chips in. "In. Let's see how my luck holds."

The right side of Franklin's mouth curved up in a joyless smile as he and Elana laid their cards on the table.

Billy Joe leaped to his feet and whooped the second they were down. "Kitten's got balls!"

Elana snorted, then swept the pile of chips into her corner. "Kitten got lucky."

Gnash checked her watch, then coughed. "Time for nosh. Everybody cash in your chips."

Franklin hadn't dropped her gaze yet. He was mildly impressed, and rightly so. The table cards had been shit. The whole hand had been a bluff-fest, and Elana had correctly called his. It wasn't an astonishing display of insight, but it was enough to demonstrate that Elana was no fool.

"You'd best hope that luck *does* hold," he told Elana with quiet gravitas.

Elana inclined her head. "I intend to stick around. Thanks for the intel."

"I like you. Don't waste it."

"Never crossed my mind. Now, what the hell is borscht?"

The table erupted in laughter, and Elana smiled. It didn't take much to convince a room full of criminals you were on their side. Getting in the door had been the hardest part, although from the sounds of it, this job wouldn't be a cakewalk, either.

Two and a half days. Just gotta make it two and a half days.

CHAPTER TWELVE

Elana spent the rest of day one solidifying her connections with the denizens of this particular Viverri safe house. After lunch, where she discovered borscht was a tangy, beet-based soup she was surprised to enjoy, she played another round of poker. She won a couple of hands but lost in the end by a smidge.

Then everyone scattered to do their own thing. Gnash and Sandy spread a pile of papers over the card table and gabbed while doing the books. Dust, Lead Pipe, and Billy Joe all went to work out at a gym down the street. Polar and Flint went in the same direction but at slightly different times, and everyone rolled their eyes, obviously knowing exactly what they were up to. Franklin straight-up disappeared.

Elana opted to join the gym crew. She worked up a sweat, then returned to the bunk house with the others, where they devoured an entire ring of garlic sausage, much to Sandy's dismay. Then she flopped in the barracks and stared at the ceiling while Dust read the latest Danielle Steel.

So far, Elana hadn't picked up on a single suspicion pointed in her direction. Her impression after the first poker game had been correct. The hardest part had been getting in. Her cover was holding perfectly. She'd fully convinced them that she was who she said she was. Kat Stevens was well-embedded.

All that remained was to do the actual job, which nagged at the back of Elana's mind like a woodpecker. From the sounds of it, the *familia* was kidnapping targets for House Veridian's experiments—and if the snatch didn't go to plan, the Viverri operative was on the hook.

Veridian must be desperate if they're picking up so many subjects in such a short time, and there's so little margin for loss that if a job fails, they take the mobster in question. That means they're being less picky about subjects, too.

Elana grimaced. *And if it's not about desperation, they're not worried about* quality, *and they've started focusing on* quantity. *That doesn't bode well.*

She wondered who her target was. Hopefully, she would find out soon.

The next morning dawned grimy and gray. If not for the clock on her phone, Elana wouldn't have been able to tell any time had passed. She dressed, bid a groggy Dust good morning—the other woman had gone out drinking the night before—and headed for the pub's kitchen.

Elana greeted the cooks on duty and gratefully accepted a plate of hash browns and scrambled eggs, then slid into a booth in the empty pub and squirted ketchup over the lot. Three mouthfuls in, someone thumped onto the bench across from her with a cup of coffee that almost sloshed over her plate.

She instinctively covered her eggs with her hand. "Watch it, fucker. Get your own damn booth, there's plenty —Oh. Mornin', Stan." Elana looked up to glare at her intruder after ensuring her plate remained unmolested by coffee and immediately recognized her guest as Constantin Nabkovich.

The bald-pated man grinned toothily. He didn't seem offended. He knocked back half the cup of coffee and slammed it on the table again. "I hear you fit in good. I'm surprised. I expected you to walk in with cowboy boots and a Stetson and look down on all us *Yanks*."

She gave him an unimpressed look. "I know how to fit in with a crew. Just because this is my first job for *you* doesn't mean it's my first job."

"Your record said otherwise."

"My record's bullshit, just like yours."

Stan accepted this with a wave of his empty hand. "Franklin says you won more than you lost yesterday, and Sandy says you haven't caused any trouble. You're lead on this job, then."

"Got it. Who's my backup?"

"You'll take Billy Joe."

Elana could work with that. "Understood. Who's our target?"

Stan fished a Polaroid out of his weathered leather jacket and slid it across the table. A thin-faced, pale-skinned man with a thick head of even paler hair, looking utterly out of place in a military dress uniform, looked nervously over his shoulder. The picture had been taken surreptitiously.

Stan tapped the photo with a thick finger. The crescent of his nail was encrusted in dirt. "Brunetto Marconi. He's staying at the Chateau Montblanc under the name Amerizio Bellagio. As if that would keep us from finding him."

Elana considered the picture of Marconi while chewing her mouthful of potato and egg. After she swallowed, she gestured at the photo with her fork. "He looks like a strong gust of wind could blow him over. You sure we need two of us to take him out?"

Stan snorted. "A fair question. He's at least guardian-level, possibly sentinel. I've been keeping him on the run, so he probably hasn't fed recently, but when he's on top of his game he has a nasty way with fabric. Can tie you in knots without touching you."

"So, Velcro and leather then," she quipped.

"You're getting the idea." Stan downed the rest of his coffee. "Unfortunately, you'll have to blend into hotel security, so you'd better hope he hasn't snacked on a maid. Sandy's tailoring your stolen uniforms now. I've got the blueprints of the hotel if you want 'em. No idea what Marconi's up to, but my guess is hiding in his room because he knows we're on his tail."

Elana scraped the last of her breakfast onto her fork and slid the plate aside. "Plans never hurt. You got 'em here or downstairs?"

Stan retrieved a data crystal from the same pocket as the Polaroid and spun it over the polished tabletop. "He's planning to move tomorrow, so you only have today. Better move."

Elana caught the crystal and held it between her thumb and forefinger. "Drop-off point here or elsewhere? And how much can we rough him up?"

"Here's fine. Rough him up if you want, but the big boss wants him breathing."

"You got it, boss."

Elana rapped on the boys' room with three sharp knocks before shoving the door open. "Billy Joe!"

"Aw, c'mon, Kitten, let a guy have his privacy!" Lead Pipe groaned as he dove under his blankets. A magazine flapped to the floor.

Elana snorted and stalked in. "First thing in the mornin', Lead Pipe? God, you're pathetic."

"Not like I can put a sock on the door!" he retorted from under the thin quilt.

She ignored him and banged on the bedframe where Billy Joe was still snoring away. "Billy Joe!" she repeated, louder this time. "Wake the fuck up, we got work to do!"

He jolted awake and sat up straight, feet hitting the floor before his eyes were all the way open. "*Sir, yes, sir!*" he yelped, then blearily blinked as everyone else in the room roared with laughter. "The fuck? Kitten?"

"Get dressed and put some food in you," Elana snapped. "I've got a target, and you're my backup. I want to move in half an hour. Let's *go.*"

The atmosphere tensed, then sharpened. "Yes, ma'am." Billy Joe grabbed a pair of boxers from under the bed. "How much kit? What do I need?"

"You'll get a uniform. Bring something quiet. We're in and out. If I have my way, we're back by lunch."

He crouched beside the bed and reached underneath it. First, he pulled out a sawed-off shotgun, which he shoved aside with a grunt. Next came a silenced pistol, which he held up to Elana. "That what you had in mind?"

"As long as it fits under your uniform. I'd bring a knife too."

"Got a special spot in my boot."

"Perfect. See you in twenty."

"You said half an hour!"

"Better hurry, then."

She left him scrambling to haul on clothing. Flint caught her eye on the way out and grinned. Franklin met her at the door, peered past her to see the chaos within, and nodded before continuing down the hall.

Elana retreated to her room and retrieved her tablet from her carry-on. While on assignment in Winnipeg, she'd used a tablet with the sigil of Haven etched into the back. The one she held now was blank, but it would still upload to the Domain of Shadows' servers if she told it to, with a fully secured and encrypted connection.

She sat on her bed, leaning on the wall at the head with her knees up and the tablet resting on her thighs. She attached the data crystal and opened it in safe mode. If it had any malware or trackers attached, they would report back that the tablet was air-gapped and had no data stored on it.

Elana loaded the blueprints and studied them. They were basic, although the building was old enough to have basement tunnels and back-door corridors only used by staff if they weren't boarded off altogether. She would case those first to determine their escape route.

If the modern staff didn't use them, that would be where she and Billy Joe took Marconi, but if the staff did, she would have to get creative. Maybe frogmarch him out the front door—if you looked like you were supposed to be there, no one argued—or toss him in a bucket of laundry and go out the service elevator.

When she was satisfied she had the blueprints sufficiently memorized, she stashed the data crystal and tablet in the inner pocket of her slim, low-profile protective suit, which she changed into. Valeria had given it to her for her trip to Winnipeg, and the black bodysuit hid perfectly under whatever else she wore. It included gloves, boots, and a hood that could extend over her face. It would stop almost anything.

Then she donned the stolen hotel uniform she'd picked up from Sandy after waking Billy Joe. The navy and cream paired with her auburn hair made her look a bit like a sailor, in her opinion, but that hardly mattered.

She twisted her hair into a bun and fastened it in place with a pair of pins that doubled as nanocyte-powered lockpicks. Then she donned her coat and shoved her uniform cap in her pocket.

"Wonder if Billy Joe's ready," she mused. Dust had disappeared to do something else, and Polar had her own room. "Guess I'll find out."

Elana was pleasantly surprised to see Billy Joe waiting by the back door in uniform. She sniffed the air as she approached and raised an impressed eyebrow. "You even managed to shave."

He saluted. "Did forty years in the Army, Kitten. When your sergeant says move, you fuckin' *move*."

"How old *are* you, Billy Joe?"

"Eh, eighty-something. I got out during Vietnam. Not my kind of war. According to the US government, I died in the jungle. Fine by me."

"Fair enough." *And now you're in organized crime. How do you square that, Billy Joe? Is this really more honorable? I guess it must be.*

They took the subway to the Chateau Montblanc, getting into their characters as hotel employees on the way. Elana had to hand it to Billy Joe. He was smarter than he looked and had a knack for undercover work.

"What's the plan, ma'am?" he asked Elana once they got off the train, murmuring so no one else would hear him in the crowd of commuters.

"These are housekeepin' uniforms," she whispered. "This is gonna be the easiest fuckin' job in the world. We waltz in and say we heard a fuss about Mister Bellagio wreckin' his room when we got in. The front desk will roll their eyes at another rich asshole and send us up to clean it."

Billy Joe's eyebrows raised. "You think that'll work?"

"I'd be stunned if it didn't. I did my research on the Chateau Montblanc. It's not a standard stop for vampires, just the four-star version of a flophouse. They're gonna be used to people trashin' their rooms, and there'll be too many staff for the front desk to know everyone."

"And if they do?"

Elana winked. "Nothin' a little bit of mental encouragement can't fix."

Billy Joe chuckled under his breath. "Amen to that. All right, boss, lead the way."

They walked up to the Chateau Montblanc and around back to the staff entrance. As Elana expected, she barely had to exude the thinnest veil of "we're supposed to be here" to get past the all-human staff. One person asked if they were new, and Elana said they'd started last week. The guy quickly accepted this, wished them a good shift, and headed off to do his job.

They stashed their coats in the back, wiped their boots to get rid of the road salt, put on their caps and smiles, and headed into the lobby.

The front desk clerk, a young woman with frizzy red hair, had bags like oversized suitcases under her eyes. Her nametag announced her as Jessica, which she told them in far too chipper a tone before realizing they were staff and visibly holding back her tears. Elana knew shift change for the front desk didn't happen for another hour, so Jessica was running on no sleep...*and* she also happened to know that Jessica *was* new.

"Sorry. *Sorry.*" Jessica blinked furiously and rolled her shoulders. "It has been a *hell* of a shift. What floor are you guys on today?"

"We gotta do Bellagio's room first," Elana told her. "I hate to deliver bad news at the end of a crappy night, but word has it that he left it a disaster."

Jessica moaned and put her head in her hands. "God*dammit.* I knew he was gonna be trouble as soon as he checked in. He has that *look* about him."

She fished in her desk drawer for a keycard and slid it

across the counter to Elana. "Seven-fifteen. It figures he trashes *that* room. We originally had him in five-twenty-five, but he asked to change it when he got here. Something about the way the window was facing. The presidential suite was the only one we had available. Dammit, dammit, *dammit.*"

Elana took the card and smiled gently. "Hey. It's gonna be okay. We'll make it all go away before you even get off shift. Take a breath, hon."

Jessica hauled in a shaky breath and let it out in a sob. "End of shift can't come fast enough. Thanks. Call down if you need any more supplies."

"You know we will."

Elana traded a victorious glance with Billy Joe as they headed for the back corridors again to pick up their cleaning carts. As soon as they were ensconced in the service elevator, Billy Joe let out a whoop that wouldn't have been out of place in the jungles of Southeast Asia.

"You were right!" He punched the air. "Fuck, that was easy!"

Elana winked. "What can I say? I know my shit."

"I could work with you on *every* job. This is like taking candy from a baby!"

The service elevator rose smoothly, then *clanked* as it settled into place on the seventh floor. Elana and Billy Joe strode down the corridor, matching the navy carpet and cream walls as though they belonged. Elana tucked a stray strand of auburn hair under her cap and politely nodded at a guest who passed them without looking.

They arrived at the end of the hall. Elana slipped the Do Not Disturb sign off the handle of room seven-fifteen, added it to the stack on the cleaning cart, and knocked. "Housekeeping."

An annoyed, high tenor complained within, quietly enough that they wouldn't have been able to hear if they hadn't been vampires. "*Cazzo! A cosa serve un segno se...*" Marconi subsided into grumbling, then called, "No, thank you!"

Elana knocked again. "Sorry, sir, but we received reports of a mess that needed cleaning. I'm afraid we'll have to insist."

She caught Billy Joe's eye, nodded to the side of the door, and mimed a punch. Billy Joe sidled into position with a nasty smirk.

The *sotto voce* grumbling in Italian got closer, then much clearer as Marconi opened the door. He was taller than Elana had guessed from the picture, but that was no problem for Billy Joe. The boxer switched from the right hook he'd set up and delivered an uppercut to the man's jaw that lifted him off the floor and into the doorframe.

Marconi stumbled back, but not nearly fast enough to avoid Billy Joe grabbing him by the lapels of his burgundy dressing gown and shoving him to the floor. Elana followed the men in, closed the door behind them, and shoved the housekeeping cart under the lever handle.

To her surprise, Marconi wasn't fighting.

She crossed her arms and shifted her weight to her back foot. "Leave off."

Billy Joe had delivered another pair of sucker punches to Marconi's head. He bounced back on his heels with his fists up. "Aw, boss, I was just getting started."

"I'd like to talk to him before you break his teeth," Elana countered. "Tie him up."

"Yes, ma'am."

Billy Joe tore a spare flat sheet into strips, tied Marconi's ankles together, and tied his wrists to the bedpost. "All yours, boss. You want me on lookout?"

"That'd be perfect."

Billy Joe retreated to the door, and Elana squatted beside Marconi. The Italian already sported a split and swollen lip, and he would have a black eye in the morning if he survived that long. Regardless, he fixed Elana with a baleful stare.

"*Dite alla marchesa che non giocherò ai suoi giochi,*" he told her.

Elana shook her head. "Sorry, my Italian's not that good. What do you want me to tell Margareta?"

Marconi's eyebrows flicked upward. "You are not Italian."

"Nope. Texan, born and bred. Sent to come and get you. Don't know who you pissed off, but I do what I'm told."

Marconi scoffed. "*La puttana* won't even do her own dirty work."

"Okay, that word I *did* learn. I agree wholeheartedly that Margareta Vincenzi is a bitch. Why's she after you?"

"You don't know?"

"Humor me. You're not exactly in a position to negotiate."

The blond Italian sighed and hung his head. "I knew she would find me eventually. They find everyone. No one is safe."

Elana narrowed her eyes. "You were at Il Giardino? Before…whatever happened?"

Marconi raised his head an inch and peered at Elana. "You are different."

"Boss?" Billy Joe chimed in from the door. "There a reason you're not just knocking him out and bringing him home?"

Elana whirled and glared at Billy Joe. "You mouthin' off, punk?"

"No, ma'am!"

He straightened and snapped his mouth shut, but Elana saw the doubt in his eyes. *Fuck. I need to get this back under control* now.

"Big boss wants intel," she snapped at Billy Joe. "This guy knows more than the last ones. We need him to talk before we throw him to the wolves. But the next time you question me, you'll be joinin' him. *Capisce?*"

The hesitation melted away as Billy Joe accepted the explanation. "Yes, *ma'am!*"

"That's better." Elana turned back to Marconi. "Tell me what happened at Il Giardino."

His gaze settled over her shoulder, and his lips tightened. "*La marchesa* went mad after that American vampire turned everything upside down. The townsfolk rebelled, and she started by putting them down in the normal way. Kill them, drain them, toss them in the lake, all while bitching about how humans get worse with every generation.

"Eventually that shifted to raving about needing to protect vampires from 'humanity's rot,' whatever the hell *that* means, and that's when she stopped throwing bodies in the lake. I don't know what she did with them, but Giovanni became uncomfortable.

"One of his servants was the one who told me to get out as fast as I could. Said his master was packing to go too, and he couldn't guarantee my safety. I didn't know what that meant, and I delayed too long… When Giovanni came to tell me that all was well and I could stay, he wasn't himself. His eyes were dead, like fish."

Marconi sagged against the bedframe. "That is what will happen to me too, isn't it? *Dio.* As soon as that woman showed up, I knew something was wrong."

Elana frowned. "What woman? The American woman?"

Marconi shook his head. "No. Before that. The woman who came with the helicopters full of people, all the ones who were sent to the caves *before* the American woman showed up."

Billy Joe huffed. "Ungrateful son of a bitch. Do you know how damn lucky you were to meet the Necromancer?"

Marconi spat on the floor. "My only stroke of luck was escaping for as long as I have. Evidently, my luck has run out."

I wouldn't be so sure about that. Puzzle pieces were falling into place at an alarming rate. This was exactly the type of intel she'd come to New York for.

Now she had to get the intel back *out.*

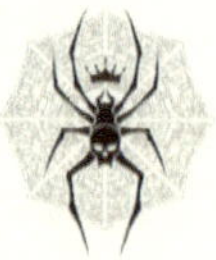

CHAPTER THIRTEEN

Elana drew a long, slow breath and hoped to God she was projecting the "I'm deciding how best to put the screws to this guy" attitude she wanted. She needed to figure out how to handle Billy Joe so she could get Marconi to Haven, *stat*. No way was she letting any of this precious intel fall into House Viverri's hands, let alone the Necromancer's.

She silently scoffed. *What kind of pretentious nickname is that, anyway? The Necromancer...you sound like a* Magic: The Gathering *card, lady.*

"Everything okay, boss?" Billy Joe inquired from the door. "You want my help making him talk? I know a coupla places to punch that hurt real good but don't leave marks."

Elana clenched her teeth to keep herself from groaning aloud. Then she deliberately relaxed her jaw, turned up the manipulation levels on her nanocyte aura, and put on her sweetest "I'd like to speak to the manager" voice.

"We're gonna take him somewhere else for interrogation," she announced while smiling ever-so-sweetly at

Marconi. "I've decided this location is too insecure. I don't want to chance anyone overhearing."

Billy Joe had been susceptible to her manipulation last night at the card table. *Please say he's* very *susceptible,* she begged the universe.

She sagged in relief when Billy Joe's mood shifted from expectant and a touch nervous to calm and chill. The gamble had paid off. Billy Joe's nanocytes were easy to convince. Somewhere between adept and savant, she guessed.

"Oh, sure," the boxer easily replied. "You got it, boss. You want me to knock him out and carry him? He looks like he weighs about fifty pounds soaking wet."

"That depends." Elana pinned Marconi with a glare. "You gonna try to run if we let you walk? This gets much more painful if you do, and I *will* have Billy Joe put you to sleep. You walk out of here with us, and all of this gets so much easier."

You want to obey, she silently told him. *You really,* really *want to obey.*

Marconi narrowed his eyes. Elana wasn't getting a strong vibe from him nanocyte-wise. Maybe a regular diet of fresh human blood obscured a vampire's baseline aura, thanks to the frequent highs and crashes, or perhaps he was weaker in the Nexus than his presumed status would suggest. Still, he wasn't convinced.

Elana *didn't* want Billy Joe to knock him out. It would be too easy for the mobster to take off with her witness if Elana's manipulation failed. She had to bring Marconi around.

She took a chance and winked.

Marconi's eyebrows lifted, and he tilted his head. "I will come quietly, with the understanding that my cooperation is dependent on better treatment than I received when you arrived."

"Billy Joe won't punch you again unless I tell him to," Elana promised. "You got that, Billy Joe?"

"Loud and clear, boss."

Marconi nodded. "Then we have a deal."

Elana pulled a pocketknife from her uniform jacket and sliced through Marconi's bonds. While he got to his feet, she stashed the ruined sheets in the otherwise empty garbage bag on the housekeeping cart and shoved the cart aside.

"We'll go out one of the side entrances," she told both men. "Keep calm and walk confidently. If anyone asks, Marconi, tell them you asked us for assistance with a delivery."

"*Va bene.* I will follow you, *signora.*"

"Billy Joe, follow Marconi so he doesn't run off."

"You got it, boss."

Elana led the way out of the hotel room and down the hall, abandoning the cart. She focused on maintaining a low-grade "we're supposed to be here" vibe, which she hoped would deter any curious guests or staff.

She had seven flights of stairs to figure out what she was doing. The fewer of those flights she had to use, the better.

They met no one on the seventh floor, but they passed another staff member on the fifth-floor landing. Elana nodded politely. The other woman returned the courtesy and went up while the trio continued down.

Elana pulled her tablet from her inside pocket between the fourth and third floor, and texted Webber.

High-value asset acquired. Need immediate extraction.

His reply scrolled in as they reached the second floor.

Planned extraction point is green.

She texted a confirmation and slid the tablet back into her pocket.

"All systems go, boss?" Billy Joe asked from behind her.

"Yep. Got a car comin' to meet us, but we're gonna need to ditch these outfits. You got something on other than your unmentionables?"

Billy Joe chuckled. "C'mon, boss, have a little faith. You know I'm ready for anything."

"Knew I could count on you. We'll strip in the alley. Good thing we're fast, eh?"

"Aw, you mean I don't get to ogle?"

"Careful, Billy Joe. You better believe I can knock you out."

"I'd like to see you try." He guffawed, but Elana sensed no real challenge in the riposte. Her manipulation field was holding strong, although the energy drain increased the longer she maintained it. She was glad she'd thought to drink a vial of blood before leaving the bunkhouse. That extra juice was making the difference.

And if I need an extra shot, I can always snack on Billy Joe or Marconi, she silently deadpanned. She had no intention of doing any such thing. The last thing she needed was an uncontrolled high while trying to reach the extraction point.

They reached the ground floor. Elana disabled the emergency alarm on the side door with a deft application of nanocyte energy through her fingertips and let them out into the alley.

"You first," she told Billy Joe after the door closed behind them. "I'll make sure nobody jumps you."

"Appreciate that, boss." Billy Joe shucked off the hotel uniform in short order. Underneath, he had on a slightly rumpled polo shirt and slacks. He looked like a frat boy attempting to look presentable and falling horrendously short.

He folded the uniform and shoved it into his pants pocket, then grinned when Elana's eyebrows rose. "Dimensional pocket. Best trick ever."

"I cannot *believe* I don't have dimensional pockets," Elana groused. "My tailor's been holdin' out on me."

Billy Joe laughed. "Stick around then, Kitten, and we'll fix you up."

"I just might do that." Elana quickly stripped off the uniform top and stuffed it in her dimensional handbag, which she'd had strapped to her chest the whole time. She left the pants on but pulled a light jacket out of her handbag and slid it over the top half of her armored bodysuit. She hated to admit it, but working with Billy Joe had taught her something. Always bring a change of clothes.

Billy Joe wolf-whistled. "Sexy suit. That ain't standard issue."

"Special order." Elana zipped up the jacket while redoubling the manipulation aura until she felt his interest smooth away. If he noticed the spiderweb pattern, she was up a creek. "Let's move out."

"On your six, boss. No funny business, Italian man." He pronounced "Italian" like "eye-talian." Elana was glad he was behind her so he didn't see her roll her eyes.

He needn't have worried. Marconi followed, docile as a sheep—so meek that Elana wondered whether he *was* lower in the Nexus than she originally thought. Convincing Billy Joe not to question anything required significant energy expenditure on her part, so much so that she was getting thirsty.

Or maybe Marconi has *figured out I don't want him dead.*

That seemed the most logical explanation. Elana hoped it was the case. The less convincing she had to do to get him into Webber's getaway vehicle, the better.

She led them through the streets of New York, deeply grateful for the crush of people and the sensible grid layout. *If I had to think too hard about where I was going, I'd lose control of Billy Joe.*

Elana swallowed against the dryness in her throat. A touch of dizziness pinged her like a pebble to the back of the head. *I can't keep this up much longer.*

She glanced over her shoulder. "We gotta pick it up. Move it."

"Yes, boss!"

Billy Joe and Marconi broke into a trot behind Elana. Elana checked her tablet as she ran. No messages from Webber alerting her to changes in the plan. She was three blocks away, the *long* way. Suddenly, she was considerably less grateful to New York's city planners.

She extended her "don't ask questions" field as wide as

she dared. New Yorkers were legendary for minding their own business—you had to, in a city of eight million—but it would be *just* her luck to find the one passerby who got curious.

They were halfway down the last block when Elana's insight screeched a warning. She whipped around, yanked Marconi behind the nearest building, and shoved him farther in before turning back to face whatever her powers had alerted her to.

As she turned, the *crack* of a gunshot rang out. Her eyes widened in horror as she saw Billy Joe standing between her and the street, facing out, with a spreading bloodstain on the back of his shirt.

"*No!*" The cry burst from her lips before she could stop it. She instinctively stepped forward, reaching for the boxer, but had to dance back as three more bullets slammed into Billy Joe's torso.

The big man jerked and twitched but only staggered once. He shot out an arm to brace himself on the brick building beside him and grabbed his hidden pistol with the other. "Get goin', boss!" he yelled and spat blood on the ground. "I'll hold 'em off! Pleasure workin' with you!"

Elana's heart hurt. She felt responsible for Billy Joe despite knowing she would come face-to-face with the consequences of betraying him in the next few minutes. Now it looked like Billy Joe would face those consequences without knowing why.

These had to be Veridian's or Viverri's enforcers. Had they hacked Elana's tablet? Overheard the conversation in the hotel room? Had Stan set a tail on them the whole time as insurance?

It didn't matter. Elana was wasting precious seconds and wasting Billy Joe's sacrifice. She didn't know how long he could hold out against gunfire. Nanocytes worked wonders when it came to healing, and all bets were off when you introduced battle adrenaline, but even the strongest vampires were still human at heart. The nanocytes couldn't create something out of nothing without enough functional body parts. Not here on the street, anyway.

"You're a mensch, Billy Joe," she called. "I owe you a beer, and I'll see you at the bunkhouse."

Billy Joe's laugh bubbled with blood. He was firing one-handed while still taking shots. He didn't turn, and his knees were beginning to tremble.

Elana wavered a second longer, then steeled herself, grabbed Marconi—who was cowering behind a dumpster—and ran.

The manipulation field would wear off in a minute or two after Elana was far enough away. Maintaining the effect at a distance was possible, but it got harder the farther you went. Elana had other things to worry about than Billy Joe realizing Kitten had betrayed him in the last moments of his life.

Although if he survives, that'll be another story. Yay.

Marconi was lagging. Telling him to hurry wouldn't have made a difference. Elana was a stronger vampire than he was. Instead, she forced herself to wait a couple of seconds until he caught up, swept him off his feet, slung him over her shoulders, and pelted down the alley again.

Elana's insight power twinged as they neared the end of the alley, and she sidestepped just in time to miss another bullet. *Cowards. Come down here and fight me like real vampires... Oh, God, I've gone native.*

She pivoted hard on the ball of her foot and pushed off, sprinting the last half-block to her planned extraction point. *Please, Webber, for the love of God, please be there already.*

Their rented sedan was not waiting for her.

Elana ran past the meeting point and into the park, cursing silently. *Why the hell did we pick a park? This was the stupidest idea. There are people around! Dollars to donuts I'm about to get jumped by a Viverri goon with biceps bigger than my head while someone sneaks up behind me with a syringe full of synthetic nanocytes to turn me into a puppet.*

She tossed Marconi at the base of the only tree she could find that didn't have decent sniping sightlines. "Stay there!" she barked, then sank into a fighting stance in front of him and waited, breathing hard.

The Italian vampire curled up at the base of the tree. His terror oozed off him like bad BO, and it made Elana's nose wrinkle.

Then the first goon dropped out of the tree in front of her, and she forgot about the stench.

Six-four, built like a truck, her brain supplied. She reacted by going low and breaking his knee from the side. He dropped, screaming, and she caved in his temple with another heel kick.

Elana spun to meet the next enforcer running up the path toward her. The slim, lithe woman whipped a pair of shuriken at her, which Elana neatly dodged before leaping into the air and slamming her heel into the woman's nose. She collapsed, spurting blood from her ruined face, and

Elana snatched the remaining two throwing stars from her belt.

The third and fourth attackers arrived together from opposite paths, one a few steps ahead of the other. Elana dispatched the first with a throwing star that sliced through his jugular and a second in his eye, then ducked the roundhouse swing from the second man and drove her elbow into his gut.

This guy was built like the first had been, but he displayed a liveliness the first had lacked. He bounced back from her solar plexus hit, grinned with a mouth full of dead teeth, and aimed another punch at Elana's head.

Elana slipped aside, noting the chunky, spiked brass knuckles on the man's fists. A mistimed dodge would mean a broken jaw or worse. Even more annoying, his footwork was *good*. She wouldn't be able to take him out at the knees, which was her go-to with big guys.

She faked her way out of a grapple attempt, then dashed around him and up the nearest tree trunk. He almost turned in time to catch her, but Elana was fast enough to leap on his back and get her legs around his neck.

Elana squeezed her thighs as hard as she could to cut off the circulation in his neck. The big man flailed and clawed at her. The sharpened spikes on the brass knuckles tore through the hotel uniform pants like tissue paper, but they did no damage to the bodysuit beneath.

A yell brought Elana's attention to Marconi. A fifth attacker was threatening him with a pistol. Marconi had gotten to his feet and bravely brandished a *dagger* at his assailant.

Oh, no, you fucking don't.

A sensation like electrified ice ran through Elana, starting from the point between her eyebrows and spreading down like lightning. Time slowed to a crawl. She would swear when she thought about this moment later that less than five heartbeats passed between her snapping the huge enforcer's neck like a twig and running the fifth attacker through with Marconi's dagger.

She followed up the backhanded stab by driving the blade up under his ribs and jerking it to the right. The wiry man twitched once before the light went out of his eyes, and blood poured from the open wound and over Elana's hands before she shoved him off the dagger and tossed him to the ground.

Elana stepped back to cover Marconi, only to spin at her insight power's behest and bury the dagger in a sixth's attacker's eye socket. The sight of the jeweled hilt protruding from the socket might have been comical if she hadn't fully driven it through the skull and into the tree. The attacker had dropped upside-down from the branches above to strangle Marconi but ended up grotesquely rotating on the dagger's blade as the dead weight brought the rest of the body down.

Marconi let out a strangled yelp and scrambled away from the warm corpse. He clung to Elana like a child to their mother's skirts, panting in primal fear. "Where are they all coming from? Why is no one helping us?" he sputtered.

The intense adrenaline spike was dulling to a roar in the back of Elana's mind. Time returned to its normal passage, but Elana's fingers still tingled with the sheer power at her command.

Elana realized with a start that several cell phones were up and recording as bystanders and pedestrians stopped to ogle. She'd been aware of the presence of humans while running, but she'd had to trust that her "don't pay attention" field would do the trick. It had not—at least, not after she turned the half-dozen assailants into so many bloody smears.

I'm gonna have to train that. The last thing I want is someone taking a human hostage in the middle of a fight. God, this will be a PR nightmare.

Luckily, it seemed the overwhelming presence of humans had shifted the balance of the battle in Elana's direction. No more attackers, whether Viverri or Veridian, were coming out of the woodwork. That, or Elana had scared them off.

The screech of brakes brought Elana's head around to the park's entrance. A battered, bullet-riddled sedan sat waiting, and the driver revved the engine as though to tell them to hurry.

Elana didn't need telling twice. She swung Marconi over her shoulders again and sprinted for the car, determinedly ignoring the dozens of cameras pointed in her direction. She yanked the back door open, threw the Italian in, then slammed it shut and leaped into the passenger seat.

Webber put the pedal to the metal the second more of Elana was in the car than out, not even waiting for the door to close. She hauled it shut with difficulty since the door had taken damage and collapsed into the seat with an explosive sigh. "They came after you too."

Webber scowled and took a turn with enough acceleration that the back tires skidded. "I got ambushed two blocks out. We almost beat them. I don't know how they heard what we were up to, but I do *not* like the implications."

"Ditto, and ditto again. You okay?"

"I'm fine. You?"

"No injuries."

"Good. Keep an eye out."

Elana sat up and turned her insight power up to eleven again, allowing her focus to slide through and over the cityscape around them as Webber careened through city streets like a New York cabbie from hell. *That might be a tautology.* A tiny giggle escaped her.

Webber's concern sharpened to a point. "What's so funny?"

"Adrenaline's coming down. Also, if any of this makes it to the news in Texas, Kat Stevens will be really, *really* confused."

CHAPTER FOURTEEN

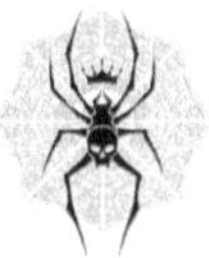

They made it to the airstrip in record time, and miraculously, without the sedan falling apart. It hissed and died moments after rolling onto the tarmac, and Webber patted the dashboard in a surprisingly compassionate gesture.

"I like cars," he told Elana in response to her curious look.

Marconi asked from the back, "*Scusi*, but may I ask what the hell is going on?"

Elana burst out laughing, then turned in her seat to face Marconi. "Hi. I'm taking you to Haven. My name is Elana Bishop."

Marconi's eyes bugged. "*Elana Bishop?* But you are a threat to all vampiredom! You are the cause of—"

"Oh, for Christ's sake," Webber muttered and cut off the panicked Italian's diatribe with a swift jab to the thigh with a syringe. He peered in from the side door, which he'd just opened, and glared at Elana. "We need to work on your prisoner communication."

"What? He was trying to get out of Il Giardino! He's a source! I didn't know he'd react like *that!*"

Webber rolled his eyes and hauled the unconscious man out of the back seat onto the tarmac while Elana got out of the car. "Exactly. You don't know how anyone will react to anything, especially when you're high on combat. Keep your mouth shut until you're in a controlled environment. Also, your carry-on's in the trunk."

Elana popped the trunk open and retrieved her suitcase, as well as Webber's. "How'd you manage that? I deliberately packed so I wouldn't miss anything if I had to abandon it, and it was in the bunkhouse when I left."

"Broke a window. Couldn't risk DNA evidence."

Elana winced. "I really *do* need to work on my soft skills, don't I. That didn't even occur to me."

To her surprise, Webber smiled, and after flopping Marconi's unconscious body over his shoulder, clapped Elana on the back. "This is only, what, your third mission?"

"Something like that."

"You're still learning. Most of us get a decade or two of training, at *least,* before we're sent on a mission. You got tossed in the deep end almost immediately."

"True. Unfortunately, the universe doesn't make allowances for 'I need to save the world but don't know what I'm doing,'" Elana grumbled.

Webber grunted in agreement, hefted Marconi higher on his shoulder, and jerked his head toward the jet waiting for them. "Let's get out of here. Just because they didn't follow us here doesn't mean they're not on our tail."

Elana grabbed both suitcases and hightailed it for the plane.

Upon landing in Haven, Marconi was whisked away by a team of blue-clad healers flanked by guardians in forest green. Valeria emerged from the crush of the welcoming party to meet Elana and Webber. "Welcome back."

"Thanks." Elana stretched and cracked her neck. She had availed herself of the excellent facilities on board the Haven Air jet to shower and clean the blood and guts from under her nails. Nothing she could do for the clothes, but she'd had spares in her carry-on. "I can only imagine the shitstorm this has kicked up, though."

The corner of Valeria's mouth tightened. "Have you determined how the *familia* knew you betrayed them?"

"I haven't. It's been eating away at me since the first gunshot. Billy Joe didn't betray me. He was fully under my control. If he managed to survive, he might have spilled the beans, but… I doubt he did."

Webber interjected, "The Viverris aren't known for caring about collateral damage, but if he *did* survive, you can bet they'll grill him for all he's worth."

Elana winced again. "Oh, God. Sorry, Billy Joe."

"We're handling the media as we always do," Valeria told her. "No innocents were harmed in the shooting or the altercation in the park, so it will be relatively easy to write this off as a vampire-on-vampire incident. It'll likely result in an uptick in anti-vampire sentiment, but those die down. All in all, you honestly got lucky."

"Except for how pissed off Viverri and Veridian are gonna be," Elana pointed out.

Valeria acquiesced with a tilt of her head. "You have a talent for making friends *and* enemies alike."

"Sure, we'll go with that."

"Matt is already picking apart the situation to see what went wrong. Good job bringing Marconi back. I read the report you sent from the plane before coming to meet you. He'll be an excellent resource."

Elana nodded. "I can't believe how lucky we got. He's terrified and on the run, so he will squeal like a pig."

Valeria rubbed her hands together and smiled. "I've no doubt. On the subject of sources, however, another has just presented itself."

"Oh?"

"Cassandra Matthews is fully lucid and taking visitors."

Elana's heart leaped. An echo of the battle adrenaline surged from her feet up, and her grip on the handle of her carry-on tightened to the point that the plastic creaked. "Really? Can I go see her?"

"I believe that's what 'taking visitors' implies."

Elana glared. "I meant more along the lines of 'do you need me for anything else?'"

"I do not."

Elana sprinted to the terminal without saying goodbye.

Cassandra Matthews had been convalescing in a subterranean medical facility in Senkyem typically reserved for Guardians of sentinel level and above despite only having reached the level of guardian before her impromptu self-internment. Trios of guards had been posted outside her door, at each hall intersection, and at every entrance and exit since her arrival.

The reason for the extreme security measures was simple. Cassandra was the only person in Haven, and possibly the only person living, who had survived an encounter with the East Coast Staker intended to end in death.

She had followed the trail of a disappearance during the course of her work as a guardian and had disappeared herself. Decades later, Elana had tracked her with the help of Sergeant Michelle Ferns to an empty field outside of Ashford, where they had later discovered her "hibernating" in a tiny underground bunker.

The Staker had abandoned her in the bunker with the presumption that she would starve to death and be forgotten. Cassandra had no such intention and had self-induced the state of internment to give herself a chance of surviving to tell her story.

When Elana found her, she'd been an emaciated husk clinging to life. After months of rehabilitation, she could talk to people without possibly screwing up her sense of self. Her memories had reintegrated, and she knew who she was again.

That meant she could tell her story, and Elana wanted to be the first to hear it.

Elana had called Cassandra's father, Jack Rhuland, while driving like a speed demon to the aboveground entrance of the guardians' medical center. He hadn't answered, which meant he was already there with his daughter. This didn't surprise her. Jack had spent almost every day sitting at Cassandra's side since she'd been found alive.

Elana parked the car outside the public building, impatiently waited while her credentials were verified, then rode an elevator down into the facility's sublevels. She had honestly forgotten she didn't look like herself until the receptionist asked for her physical ID since her biometrics weren't in the system. She hoped it wouldn't throw Cassandra too much. Elana didn't think she could wait another day, much less two, to hear what Cassandra had to say.

Elana's headlong rush came to an abrupt halt at the door to Cassandra's hospital room. Quiet voices, one aged and male, one hoarse and female, spoke quietly beyond the door. Cassandra was awake and talking to her father.

Elana lifted a hand to the door, then caught the word "Mom" and paused. Linda Rhuland had passed away while Cassandra had been interned. *Maybe I should wait.*

Then Jack replied, "Your ma didn't want to look, but she never let me throw anything out. That's the only reason Sergeant Ferns and Miss Bishop found you."

Elana took the opportunity and knocked.

"Who is it? Cassandra don't need nothin', thanks."

"Dad, let the healers do their job, *geez…*" Cassandra's tone was the next closest thing to an audible eyeroll.

"It's Elana Bishop, actually," Elana called through the door. "I can come back later if now's not a good time."

A few seconds of silence suggested to Elana that father and daughter were communicating with eyes and eyebrows. A moment later, Cassandra called, "Come in."

Elana nudged the door open with her elbow and

crossed into the small, private room. The warm, green walls glowed from the indirect sunlight coming through the large window. Jack's chair sat beside Cassandra's bed, which had its head raised to support Cassandra while she sat.

Cassandra Matthews had dark brown hair that fell past her shoulders. Bright brown eyes sat a touch wide on either side of her long nose, and thin lips sat above a pointed chin. She was still thin but no longer appeared emaciated. At some point, she'd graduated from hospital gowns to comfortable pajamas. A pair of crutches leaned against the wall by the bed.

"So, you're the one who found me." Cassandra searched Elana's face with the acuity of a trained detective. "You don't look like your picture. You do undercover work too?"

"Yeah. I'll look like myself tomorrow."

Jack was openly staring at Elana. He shook his head. "Will wonders never cease. I was about to call security and say someone was masqueradin' as you. Wouldn't have surprised me, neither, what with all the trouble you get up to."

Elana chuckled and pulled up another chair. "Would have been a good call, Jack." She settled into the chair and looked at Cassandra. "Sergeant Ferns did the actual finding. I figured out you were still there. I know you're sick to death of answering this question, but how are you feeling?"

Cassandra shrugged. "I've been a hell of a lot better, and I've been a hell of a lot worse. My big memories are back in order. I still swap around or forget details sometimes, but the healers tell me that's normal."

"The day I forget nothin' will be the day I meet my maker," Jack quipped. "You're doin' just fine, sweetheart."

"Thanks, Dad." Cassandra stretched her right arm across her chest, then did the same with her left. "I'm not cleared for training yet, but my physical therapist says I'm almost back to full capacity there too. I'll be honest. When the healers told me I'd been in self-internment for almost three and a half decades, I was surprised I wasn't a vegetable."

Jack gripped his daughter's hand. "You're a fighter."

Cassandra squeezed back. "You've been here every day helping. I wouldn't have made it without you."

Elana smiled. "I'm so glad they let you in, Jack. I gotta admit, I was worried someone would pitch a fit and you'd get kicked out."

Jack scowled, then grinned. "A few people tried, but every time I dropped your name, they backed off like I was threatenin' 'em with a loaded gun."

"It's true. Dad usually took the talking-tos out in the hall, but I saw it happen once or twice." Cassandra folded her hands in her lap and eyed Elana curiously. "He told me everything he knew about you, but that made me more curious, so I read up on you. You're an interesting one, Miss Bishop."

"I'll be the first to admit it. I can see the detective gears spinning," Elana teased. "You'd get along great with Matt."

Cassandra's eyebrows lifted. "Matt? As in Mathieu Richelieu? The head guardian and member of the House of Cardinals who you're close friends with, just like you're on a first-name basis with the *Arbiter of Shadows?*"

Elana blushed. "When you put it like that, I sound like I'm way more important than I am."

"Hm. Wonder why that is." Cassandra's tone was dry but not unkind. "Maybe worth thinking about, *Consort.*"

Elana tried to chuckle, but it stuck in her throat. She swallowed. "As much as I appreciate being a novelty in Haven society, I came to ask you some questions if you're up for it."

Cassandra *did* chuckle. "Oh, sure. Deflect all you want. I have questions for you too, when *you're* up for it." She winked. "But, yes, I'm ready to talk. I've been informed of your continued investigation into the East Coast Staker cases, so I figured you'd come by after the healers cleared me to discuss the past."

"And here I am." Elana drew a deep breath. "Why don't we start with what the hell happened, and I can ask for more details when they come up?"

"Sure." Cassandra settled back into her pillows. She looked over Elana's shoulder for a second, then returned to keeping eye contact. "I was looking into one of the missing persons cases. Nico Borzoi. You familiar with his file?"

Elana nodded. "One of the highest-level vampires thought to be taken by the Staker. Sentinel of House Lusiturnia. Disappeared during a business conference in Miami."

"Mm-hmm. He was known to frequent brothels, and he'd run off with women a few times before for a few weeks of fun in the Caribbean, so no one thought too much of it. Even his House barely registered more than mild annoyance with his 'latest antics.'"

Elana tilted her head. "Then why were you assigned at all?"

The corner of Cassandra's mouth quirked up. "I wasn't. I was looking into it on my off time. My supervisor wasn't thrilled, but I wasn't contravening any regulations, so he couldn't do much about it beyond glare at me."

Elana narrowed her eyes. "But *why?*"

Cassandra sighed and picked at the blanket. "Maybe it was because I was a human-born vampire and a pretty young one at that, but the blasé attitude the guardians had at the time toward missing vampire cases really bothered me. Vampires had been disappearing for decades, and Ashford was noticing more than Haven was."

"I remember the websites," Elana mused. "I was obsessed with vampires growing up. The conspiracy theories about the Staker were creepy as fuck. I couldn't read much of them."

"Me neither. They were lurid and full of speculation. But they'd noticed the patterns before we had even admitted there might *be* patterns, and I thought those patterns were worth looking into. I became convinced of that the more I dug into the cases.

"Nico's case intrigued me. One, because he was a sentinel, like you mentioned, and two, because it was the farthest out of town we knew about yet. That took my working theory from 'weirdo kinkster' to 'scarily powerful vampire with ulterior motives,' *real* fast."

Elana leaned forward on her elbows and steepled her fingers. "Did you have any other evidence yet?"

"No, just hunches. Something didn't feel right. My

vampire powers are mainly observational. My sight is extraordinary, and I've been training my pattern recognition skills since I was a kid. When you're tracking a deer in the bush, you learn to spot deviations in movement patterns a mile away."

"How did that help you with Nico's case?"

"For starters, it proved to me beyond a shadow of a doubt that Nico hadn't left of his own accord. I sweet-talked my way into his rooms in the Lusiturnia manor house, and nothing was missing that would have been if he'd taken off with a hooker to a tropical island. Yeah, he could have bought whatever he *needed*, but people take sentimental things with them—*especially* rich people.

"There were also no red flags in his financials, and any detective worth their salt knows that it's *lower-class* people who do the cash thing. Rich folks think they're untouchable. Vampires are no different.

"So, I had a missing high-level vampire, which meant someone *wanted* him missing. Tell me, if someone in Haven wants someone else dead, do they make them disappear?"

Elana snorted. "God, no. There are so many ways to get away with murder completely legally. Why would you bother?"

Jack grumbled something about "godless heathens" under his breath but didn't interrupt. Elana couldn't blame him and wasn't even sure she disagreed.

Cassandra nodded. "Exactly. There's no point. That told me if somebody had offed Nico, we'd have found a body, and it wouldn't have been difficult to trace the culprit. That meant whoever had taken Nico was working on a totally different game plan than anyone else committing crimes in vampire society.

"I started digging *hard* at that point. My first task was victimology. Looking at the vampire disappearances, a 'random' serial killer didn't fit since the likelihood of finding bodies or even just *signs* of something would have been higher. These people were being taken for a *reason*, and I needed to find out why."

Cassandra opened her mouth to continue, then stopped and glanced at her father. She bit her lip, then tapped his shoulder. "Hey, Dad? Can you do me a favor?"

Jack raised an eyebrow, then looked between the two women and rolled his eyes. "You want me to take my hearing aids out again, don't you."

Cassandra smiled sheepishly. "That, or take a walk and get us some coffee…and be gone at least ten minutes."

Jack pushed himself to his feet and shook his head as he left the room. "I'll be back. Enjoy your state secrets, girls."

Cassandra waited until the door latched behind Jack before continuing. "You're a sentinel, right?"

"I am. Are you? I thought you were a guardian."

Cassandra gave Elana a crooked smile. "The more I dug into the Nico case, then the East Coast Staker cases as a whole, the more I started to get the feeling there was a target on my back. Those observational skills make it easy to tell when you're being paranoid and when they really *are* out to get you.

"I brought my concerns to my chief, and he approved an 'undercover' op. I disappeared from the public eye, underwent my Progression to sentinel in secret, and got ready to throw myself a hundred percent into tracking this motherfucker.

"Except my plan was completely derailed almost instantly." Cassandra chuckled wryly. "My sponsor told me about nanocytes the day after my Progression. It was like having a blindfold taken off. I spent three days learning everything I possibly could. *Then* I dove headlong into the Staker victimology.

"I was still on a nanocyte kick, so I started there. Turned out to be a prescient choice. A *stunning* number of vampires who'd gone missing over the last century either had off-the-charts nanocyte counts or rare or unusual nanocyte protein ratios.

"In other words, these were precisely the kinds of vampires you'd snatch if you wanted to study the finer points of nanocytes without any oversight or regulation," Cassandra concluded. "Most of the high-level labs in Haven and around the world are actively engaged in nanocyte research, but even *vampiric* ethics get in the way of some people's ambition."

"Unsanctioned experimentation," Elana whispered. Cassandra Matthews had figured out the underlying reason for the disappearances thirty years earlier, independent of anyone else and without any support. Elana's mother hadn't even been on the scene yet. Cassandra had disappeared in 1990.

"Bingo." Cassandra rubbed her eyes. "The kind of stuff bad vampire movies are made of. The stuff we keep *out* of the public eye.

"I started digging into historical black market transactions involving medical equipment. Knocking on informers' doors, showing up to healers' offices after hours, rattling the bars. Enough was lining up that I thought I'd have a case soon, but I didn't have any hard names—only amounts, places, and types of equipment. And the scale of the operation was terrifying.

"I got a call from a tipster asking to meet where no one could overhear us. They sent coordinates with the call and specified that I should come alone." Cassandra sucked a breath in through her teeth. "I knew I shouldn't. But I was young and cocky, and honestly? I was on a roll. Pair all that with a heady mix of needing to prove myself, even though I'd just become a sentinel…"

"You were human-born, and from the sounds of it, rocketing up through the Nexus," Elana pointed out. "I get it. Same boat."

Cassandra blushed and averted her eyes. "I got a lot of flack for how fast I rose in the Nexus. My Progression to sentinel wasn't the only one I did quietly. People looked at me funny, but…it was what it was. Some people thought Allan was, like, giving me vampire steroids."

"Was he?"

"No. He was as stunned as anyone."

Elana bit her lip. "Has he come to see you?"

Cassandra's blush deepened. "Yes. Twice. Well, twice that I can remember. My dad said he came a couple more times early on."

She drew a deep breath and let it out in a slow sigh. "Dad warned me ahead of time that he'd remarried. Said he didn't know how the law worked in Haven, but he was pretty sure it was illegal. I said I didn't know either, but I would find out. Turns out his House got me declared dead so he could remarry. He wasn't happy about it, but he didn't have much choice."

"What happens now that you're alive?"

Cassandra made an unhappy sound in the back of her throat. "They forced him to serve me with divorce papers. He looked like he wanted to die when he showed up with his new wife. She served me. I signed later that day after a lot of thought. I love Allan too much to drag him through a nasty court battle. For all intents and purposes, I *did* die. He had to move on."

Elana scowled. "He could have fought for you."

Cassandra shrugged. "Maybe in another situation he would have, but from the sounds of it, he's pretty entrenched in House politics thanks to his wife. He's built a life. Who knows? Maybe it'll all come crashing down in another few decades, and we'll end up together."

She sighed again. "In any case... I should have clued in to the fact that I could have been a perfect candidate for the Staker, but I'd spent more time researching their victims' nanocytology than mine. If I had, maybe I wouldn't have gone by myself. But I did, and... Well, you saw what happened."

Elana frowned. "I saw the aftermath, sure. But what happened when you got there?"

Cassandra grimaced. "That's the only part that hasn't come back. I remember showing up and being surprised at who I met there, but I *don't* remember *who that was.* Their face is fuzzy, like a bad television signal."

Movement in the hall signaled Jack's imminent return. Cassandra reached out, and Elana met her halfway and took her hand.

"Thank you for finding me. I would have wasted away in that bunker. The minute I remember that face—and I will, because everything else has come back—I promise I'll call you."

Elana kept her gaze steady on Cassandra's as the door creaked behind her. "I know you will. And Cassandra? I *will* bring them down."

CHAPTER FIFTEEN

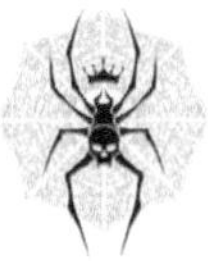

Elana left the guardians' medical center deep in thought. Foremost in her mind was the distinct possibility that Cassandra was another case like herself and her mother. The speed with which Cassandra had risen through the Nexus was eerily similar to Elana's.

What causes that? She waited for an elevator back to the surface. *I have a lot of nanocytes and a lot more* stem *nanocytes than most. I'm also human-born...but I wonder how far back the last vampire blood is in my lineage? I'm sure I read something months ago about whether vampires can have human kids... Everyone on the planet is related if you go back far enough. That includes vampires.*

Elana rubbed her temples as the lift platform rose in the shaft. She considered texting Matt or Valeria, but while both were sharp as tacks and tough as nails, neither were the nanocytology experts she needed to make sense of this.

Elana retrieved her phone from her handbag on the way from the public entrance to her car, and by the time she'd done up her seatbelt with one hand, she'd drafted the email with the other.

Arbiter Tarsin,
Could I beg a moment of your time? I have questions of a sensitive nature that I'd only trust to discuss with someone of your stature.
Courteously,
Elana Bishop

Elana sent the email and let out a heavy sigh. She and Arbiter Tarsin were on good terms, but nowhere near the friendship she enjoyed with Valeria. Over the past several months, Tarsin had usually dropped in on her unexpectedly to talk about one thing or another. It was rare that Elana took the initiative. It felt presumptuous to do so, so she respectfully maintained a professional distance.

Her email pinged.

Come by my office at your convenience.

The speed with which Arbiter Tarsin replied told Elana that the Arbiter of Knowledge held few such compunctions.

When Elana entered the consulate this time, she took the stairs to the left of those marked with the full moon. Instead of ascending into the Tower of Shadows, she passed through the arch marked with the waning crescent moon, leading to the Tower of Knowledge.

While the décor was the same—white marble with black and silver inclusions, like the rest of the consulate—the vibe was unmistakably different. Valeria's Domain *felt* quiet, like everyone working there held their breath when they weren't speaking in hushed tones. Ahura Tarsin's tower, on the other hand, felt quiet in the way a good library was quiet. You could almost hear the words in the books behind the doors, whispering about the history they held.

Elana assumed Tarsin's office was on the top floor, like Valeria's, so she headed there. She passed several staffers on the way, including some consorts with whom she was familiar from the walk-and-talks. She nodded politely, they nodded back, and both went about their business.

She extended a hand to knock on the door when she reached the top of the tower, but Tarsin's voice came through the crack before she could touch it. "Come in."

Elana nudged the door open and had to physically clench her jaw to keep it from dropping in astonishment. Ahura Tarsin's office could not have been more different from Valeria Draven's. Bookshelves stuffed full to bursting covered every wall, and stacks of books and papers teetered on chairs, desks, and every open spot on the floor. If there was paint or carpet, it was fully hidden.

A single skylight threw a perfect square of light onto Tarsin's main desk, a mahogany monstrosity that must have been built in the room. Stunned that the angle of the light would be so perfect, Elana glanced up at the ceiling. She immediately realized that the skylight was mounted on a multi-track system on the ceiling, which presumably followed the sun no matter the hour or season to provide the ideal light.

Tarsin was nowhere to be found until she popped out from behind a fortress of books and waved cheerily. "Come in, come in! Take a stack off a chair and sit down. Usually, I meet people in other rooms, but you're more than welcome to visit the lair."

"I'm honored." Elana picked her way through the literary minefield and gingerly deposited a pile of books from the chair nearest the desk onto another pile that looked sufficiently sturdy. "And I'm impressed that the desk isn't *also* covered in books."

Tarsin settled into the tall-backed, thickly upholstered armchair behind the desk and smiled. "Hard to use a console when it's covered in books, but I promise you it does happen occasionally. Now, what can I do for you? I assume it has to do with something I might find in *here*."

She motioned at the library surrounding them. While the gesture was likely meant to represent Tarsin's position as Arbiter of Knowledge, Elana more than half suspected the answer might be in this room. If anyone was likely to know about the fringe study of nanocytology, it would be the keeper and seeker of all knowledge in Haven.

Elana leaned forward on her elbows and folded her hands between her knees. "I just spoke with Cassandra Matthews—although she might be going by her maiden name again, now that I think about it. *Anyway*, that's not the point.

"She told me that before she met the East Coast Staker, she'd secretly ascended to sentinel and had been doing a *ton* of research into nanocytology related to the disappearances. She figured out that the Staker's victims were probably being kidnapped for research purposes way before anyone else, *and* she figured out they all had high nanocyte counts or specific rare nanocyte proteins."

The spark of curiosity that always lived in Tarsin's amber eyes kindled into a full flame as Elana spoke. She edged forward in her chair to get that much closer to Elana's words and leaned on her desk. "Go on."

"None of that is *new* information, not for us," Elana continued. "We figured that much out, too. What I want to ask you about is why Cassandra, my mother, and I are different from other vampires…and I want to look into the lineages of the vampires *and* humans who disappeared. Do we have nanocyte profiles for all the victims? Do we have one for my mother? Can we compare them to mine and Cassandra's?"

Tarsin drummed her fingers on the desk and held Elana's gaze for a full thirty seconds of thought before she responded. "There's no way we have genomes or nanocytology profiles for the human victims. I'll tell you that much right now. We might have been able to deduce partial profiles from the samples we found in the Zevenda complex, but they'll be suspect.

"The vampires, though… Houses keep those records, yes. It will be easier to convince some Houses to give them up to us than others. You'd have to petition each House individually, including your own.

"Once you have the information in hand, it's certainly possible to compare them to your genomic profile. Good thinking, Elana. That's probably why the Vincenzis stole your blood. House Veridian is likely thinking along the same lines. In fact…"

Tarsin tapped her desktop console. Several glowing windows sprang to life on the polished wood surface, which she glanced at in quick succession before humming thoughtfully.

"Had an idea?" Elana prompted.

"Of a sort," Tarsin muttered. She dragged a window aside to compare it to another, then flicked them into the air so Elana could see. "Does any of this make sense to you?"

Elana peered at the lines of text and frowned. "With enough time, I could puzzle it out. I see a lot of mentions of proteins, RNA, and encoding."

"These are results from tests I've been running on Edward Korynchuk." Tarsin returned the windows to her desktop, then wiped it clean with a wave. "Based on what I see in him, I think you're onto something."

Elana's gut twisted uncomfortably, and the spot between her eyebrows twinged. She exhaled gently, setting the feelings aside. Her ethical convictions about Edward Korynchuk's treatment weren't the topic of discussion. "What do you mean?"

"Mr. Korynchuk's turning has been interesting. He still had synthetic nanocytes in his system when he was given the Rights. We assumed Arbiter Draven's nanocytes would override the synthetic ones. What *actually* happened was that the synthetic and organic nanocytes adapted one to the other. As a result, Mr. Korynchuk has a surplus of 'stem-like' nanocytes that, based on his DNA, wouldn't normally be there.

"According to his genome, he should be a garden-variety vampire." Tarsin's eyes were aglow with interest. "Instead, he can access a far greater variety of proteins. He cannot make them himself, but his nanocyte RNA will create whatever proteins are introduced from external sources. I've had him test a number of different proteins, and they've all functioned as expected. That's extraordinary, given the circumstances."

Elana frowned. "That sounds like what happened at Il Giardino. The acolytes in their temple drank from the human volunteers and became far more powerful and flexible as a result. Are you saying you can do the same thing without needing a human volunteer?"

"I'm saying *precisely* that." Tarsin grinned. "This could be a *huge* breakthrough, Elana. These synthetic nanocytes could allow us to do anything we wanted with the right proteins, *without* the need for fresh human blood with a high nanocyte count."

The lead weight in the pit of Elana's stomach was inexorably pulling her toward the floor, and the twinge between her eyebrows was rapidly becoming a needle. "Something feels off about this. This doesn't feel right. You said you had Edward test these proteins. How did you do that?"

Tarsin cocked her head. "I administered the injection, waited the requisite time for the solution to propagate and the proteins to encode, then suggested he attempt the power in question. He obeyed."

Elana narrowed her eyes. "Did he have a *choice*?"

Tarsin raised an eyebrow. "I didn't *force* him. He acted

of his own accord. I told him what to do, and he did it. No coercion was involved."

"It's just…" Elana bit her lip. "It makes me think of what Veridian's been doing. Steve Kowalski. Clarissa. Turning people into mindless monsters, whether they're human or vampire. If that's what these synthetic nanocytes do, I don't think we should use them. That's what the Necromancer does."

Tarsin's expression froze for a heartbeat, then softened into gentle reassurance, although Elana's instincts told her that despite the kind tone, Tarsin felt more than a hint of pity. The combination made Elana's skin crawl. She hated being talked down to.

"Anything in the world can be used for good or evil, Elana. *Anything.* Knowledge is a tool! You cannot assign morality to knowledge any more than you can assign it to a hammer or a saw. How we *use* that knowledge to affect the world, *that's* what determines how we'll be remembered.

"Ultimately, I believe even those effects are devoid of morality. Life and death, pleasure and pain, all in balance. We will all suffer, and we will all rejoice."

Tarsin gestured at the room at large again. "It is my job as the Arbiter of Knowledge to dig up as much information as I can and make sense of it. Then the people who *do* things in the world, like yourself, can make of it what you will. My work and my tools are neither good nor evil. Open your mind, Elana! Don't let yourself be blinkered by these archaic, humanistic ideas of morality. You're better than that."

Elana worried the tip of her tongue between her teeth. She'd expected her visit to Tarsin to result in a greater understanding of herself and her role in this mess. Usually, she felt reassured when she understood what was happening. Right now, she felt sick.

"I'll keep that in mind," she finally told the arbiter. "Thanks for explaining things to me."

Tarsin showed her teeth in a sunny smile. "Any time. I'll get started on those genomic profile requisitions. I really do think you're onto something."

"Let me know what you find?"

"Always!"

"Thanks. I'll let you get back to work."

Elana managed to smile over her shoulder as Tarsin waved her out. She paused outside the door to decide her next move. The lead in her gut morphed into an even heavier rock when she realized that while she did and did not *want* to see Edward, seeing Edward was exactly what she *needed* to do.

Down the Tower of Knowledge she went, then up the Tower of Shadows to Korynchuk's cell, where she confirmed her altered biometrics with the guards before walking in. *Next time I do a full DNA screen, I'm asking for an emergency antidote. I don't want to be stuck looking like someone else for days when I don't have to.*

Edward wasn't at his desk. He was curled up on the cot, facing away from the door.

Elana quietly knocked on the desk to alert him to her presence. "Edward? Are you awake?"

"Yes." His voice was raspy. "You don't sound like yourself."

"I don't look like myself, either." Elana pulled his desk chair over beside the bed and sat. "Are you okay?"

"I'm fine." Edward struggled to get an arm under himself to lever himself to a sitting position.

Elana hurried to help him and was further distraught when he turned and revealed his gaunt, sunken face. "You are *not* fine."

Edward's responding smile was ghastly. "I'm not dying. Thanks, nanocytes. Therefore, I'm fine."

Elana brushed his messy hair off his forehead and ensured he was steady before letting go of his shoulder. "There is a *really big spectrum* between 'fine' and 'not dying.' You of all people should know that. What's wrong? Are you sick?"

He shook his head. "Side effects from the tests Arbiter Tarsin's been administering."

Elana's stomach swooped, and her insight power set off figurative alarm bells so loud she instinctively winced. "Did you consent to the tests? Because I'm pretty sure medical experimentation on prisoners contravenes the Geneva Conventions or something like that."

Edward wheezed with tired laughter. "Are you kidding? Haven's not bound by the Geneva Conventions. What army, let alone government, would dare try to enforce them? They can do anything they want to me."

Elana stared. "I…am so sorry, Edward."

He shrugged. "I should be fine as long as I keep up with the supplement regime. Not like I have a choice since what I consume is carefully mandated and regimented. If there's a pencil out of place when the Shadowguard check on me, they stare daggers at me until I move it back. I'd hate to see what they did if I didn't take my pills."

Elana blinked, struck speechless.

Edward smiled gently and put a hand on Elana's knee. "Tarsin's been very kind, actually—she's letting me see and help with all the research. I feel like shit, but I get to understand why.

"The data is fascinating. I'd have killed for this kind of research at Agoracor. I can't wait to see what comes of it. I can only hope some of the benefits reach humanity. I know that's a long shot, but… Yeah. I can hope, right?"

Elana tried to speak, but her voice didn't work. She swallowed against the lump in her throat. "This isn't fair, Edward."

He gave in to another wheezing laugh. "Oh, Elana. I spent the better part of two decades mired in resentment and bitterness that led me to develop a virus that would kill my lover and best friend along with a significant portion of the planet. I felt entirely justified in doing so.

"Only your intervention prevented me from accomplishing that horrific task. What I would have inflicted on the world would have outstripped what I'm going through now a thousandfold. I'm not sure 'fair' enters into the equation anymore."

"Still," Elana insisted. He waved the sentiment off, and anger surged in her gut. "No, Edward, I'm serious. This isn't okay. This isn't right."

Edward peered at her with bloodshot, exhausted eyes. "You are so young…" he murmured. His cracked lips stretched in a sad smile. "If you ask me, what's 'right' is what makes the most people safe and healthy. That's why Ali and I started Agoracor.

"I fell away from that in my anger. Now I have a chance to be part of something that could make more people safe and healthy than I could have ever dreamed. I screwed up my chance to do that on my own. I have to pay the price. I'd rather consent to these tests being performed on me than have them be performed on some other poor schmuck. I deserve a little pain."

This isn't "a little." Still, Elana could see in Edward's eyes that this was how he was atoning for his decisions. Whether she agreed with the sentiment didn't matter. It was his choice.

"Can I get you anything?" she asked him.

"I would kill for a real book. I've never liked reading on a computer."

"I'll see what I can do."

CHAPTER SIXTEEN

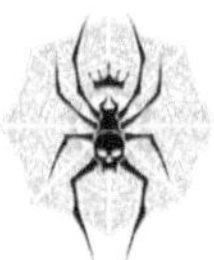

Elana ascended the rest of the way up the Tower of Shadows and knocked on Valeria's door. There was no response for several seconds, long enough that Elana thought her internal compass must have been off and Valeria was elsewhere. She was about to turn and leave when the arbiter called for her to enter.

Elana was surprised to see Marconi lying listless on the couch in Valeria's sitting area. He looked the next best thing to unconscious and was pale as a ghost. "Why is he here?"

"We were having a conversation," Valeria replied from her desk. "Do you need something?"

Elana frowned. "He needs a healer."

"He will receive medical attention when I deem it necessary and advisable. Right now, he is under the influence of a drug that is assisting our *conversation*." Valeria indicated an empty vial on her desk in response to Elana's glance. "An encouragement to speak freely."

Elana scowled. "Truth serum, in other words. Does no one in this place have any *morals?*"

Valeria's pencil-thin eyebrows rose, and her demeanor cooled further. "Excuse me, Miss Bishop?"

Elana threw her hands up in the air. "This is ridiculous! Tarsin's putting Edward through medical torture under the guise of scientific curiosity, and now you're drugging a man who ran away from one of the cruelest women I know to get him to talk to you. How is this *any* better than what House Veridian is doing?"

"We are *running out of time,*" Valeria snapped. "This man's reports indicate that Margareta Vincenzi was attempting to build an army of mindless, expendable, vampire-human supersoldiers. She might even have *succeeded*. I have operatives infiltrating Il Giardino *as we speak*. Any fragment of information I can get out of *him* might save their lives *and* the lives of everyone on the planet.

"I am the one who breaks the eggs to make the omelet in this city." The arbiter's voice was colder than ice and thinner than a razor blade. "If you don't like it, don't eat the omelet, and don't come crying to me when the can of worms *you opened* is all you've got left, *Consort*."

Elana had opened her mouth to reply with equal ire but snapped it shut again at the word "Consort." She couldn't have received a clearer dismissal.

"Understood, Arbiter." She spun and stalked out.

Elana drove her fists into the punching bag hard enough that her knuckles ached. With each hit, she tried to imagine the blows raining down on whoever was at the core of this conspiracy. Unfortunately, the lack of a face to match the name meant her mind's eye consistently supplied a substitute, usually Tarsin or Valeria.

She'd tried to bury herself in work. After the infuriating, *invalidating* exchange with Valeria, she escaped to the sublevels of the King's Archives, where she opened her mother's journals and databases again. Maybe they had missed something. None of the new tidbits of information yielded anything new, and after an hour of bashing her head against the wall, Elana had given up and chosen to bash her fists against things instead.

The receptionist at the Consorts' Training Grounds was sufficiently familiar with Elana that no words had passed between the two, only the keycard for the private room Elana favored for solo workouts. She had changed in the adjacent locker room, run laps until she lost count, then hauled the punching bag out of the storage locker.

Usually, a couple of hours of hard physical work did wonders for Elana's mood. It allowed her to work out the biochemical underpinnings of her frustration and fear while generating some exercise-induced endorphins. The combination typically resulted in her subconscious sorting through whatever disaster her prefrontal cortex was stuck on, and she *always* felt better afterward.

Today was shaping up to be the extremely frustrating exception to the rule.

Elana let out a guttural yell and a flurry of blows that tore the skin of her knuckles and the leather of the punching bag. She swore under her breath, slapped her palm over the tear, and directed the pulsing, adrenaline-fueled nanocytes to knit the torn edges back together. The bag was as good as new when she took her hand away.

Wish I could slap my hand to my forehead and do the same thing.

The twinges and stabs from her insight power were blossoming into a full-blown migraine. Elana was ready to give up on the punching bag and see if she could put a fist through the wall instead. The only reason she didn't try it was because she suspected she would break more fingers than wall.

She felt pent-up, as though someone had tossed a roll of Mentos into a bottle of Diet Coke and welded the lid on. She needed to talk to someone, she needed to figure out her shit, and she needed a *break*.

Her phone went off in her bag hanging by the door. This time, she swore loudly.

Elana yanked her phone out and put it to her ear without looking at the contact ID. "Yeah?"

"Consort Bishop." Arbiter Zilmann's dry voice sent a shock of dread through Elana's stomach. "I request your presence at your earliest convenience."

Elana leaned her sweaty forehead against the cool blocks of the training room wall. The contrast in temperature soothed her spike of anger enough to let her bite her tongue on the instinctive *fuck you*. She marshaled the customer service voice she'd used back in the Bishops Hauling days when a client got bitchy, instead.

"Arbiter Zilmann. I will of course prioritize an audience. I'm afraid I was just training, however. Is the matter sufficiently urgent that I do not have time to make myself presentable?"

"The Domain of Legacy does not make a habit of allowing matters to build to the point where immediate action is required." Zilmann delivered the veiled insult with practiced charm and serenity. "Please take whatever time you need to prepare yourself."

"You're too kind," Elana replied through gritted teeth and a forced smile. "I'll be at the consulate in forty minutes."

"I'll be waiting."

The arbiter hung up, leaving Elana with the echo of her words. Her insight power was screeching like a harpy, and Elana was ready to tear her ears out. Instead, she drew a deep breath and put the punching bag away.

Thirty-four minutes later, Elana's heels clacked authoritatively across the marble floor of the consulate toward the Tower of Legacy. She was showered, styled, and dressed in a navy pantsuit and a lace blouse. Her reflection had thrown her for a moment in the locker room. The features of Kat Stevens had begun their gradual return to those of Elana Bishop. Her hair was auburn shot through with brown, and curiously, she'd gained heterochromia.

Zilmann had forwarded a formal meeting request, which included the location where the meeting would be held. Elana hated to admit it, but she *did* appreciate the courtesy. She'd become accustomed to following her gut to find Valeria and Matt, but this required much less nanocyte power usage. Elana was almost *used* to the taste of blood now, and she wasn't sure she was happy about that.

Elana politely knocked on the meeting room's door, then opened it and walked in. This wasn't Zilmann's office, only a standard boardroom. As such, Elana expected yet another bullshit meeting full of red tape, primarily designed to piss Elana off but with the secondary goal of screwing with her plans for advancing human-vampire relations.

She was surprised to see only Zilmann and one low-level concubine in the room, who Elana presumed was functioning as a scribe for the meeting. Every room in the consulate had built-in nanotech that would record and transcribe meetings unless otherwise instructed, but Zilmann, being the Arbiter of Legacy, *really* stood on tradition.

In deference to that tradition, Elana did not immediately take the empty seat opposite Zilmann at the boardroom table. She stood behind it and to the left, waiting for Zilmann to invite her to sit. When the tall, thin, hawkish arbiter did so with a polite motion of her hand, Elana slid into the seat and clasped her hands on the table.

"To what do I owe the honor, Arbiter?"

Zilmann nodded at the scribe, who brought up a window on the tabletop and began taking notes. "I'm afraid I have bad news for you, Consort Bishop. I thought it only appropriate to inform you in person before the unfortunate incident is released to the media."

Elana's mind raced. She had *no* idea what Zilmann might be referring to. Anything occurring in Elana's life right now that was likely to cause a media stir wouldn't show up anywhere *near* the Domain of Legacy.

She cautiously ventured, "I regret to hear there is any such bad news at all, and I appreciate the arbiter's gracious recognition of any potential consequences to my person or business and her resulting notification. If you wouldn't mind elaborating…"

"Of course." Zilmann folded her hands on the table and leaned forward, catching and holding Elana's eye contact with uncomfortable intensity. Elana didn't back down. "I do regret that I have so often found myself in opposition to your innovative ideas. Your evident care about the future of Haven certainly aligns with my values."

Elana repressed the urge to roll her eyes. *Get on with it. You're making me nervous.* "I appreciate that, Arbiter. I understand and respect your devotion to your Domain."

"Sometimes I wonder if your portfolio wouldn't be more suited to the Domain of Progress."

This was the closest Zilmann ever got to a joke, and Elana acknowledged it with a light smile. "You'd have to take that up with Arbiter Mélissand."

"Of course." Zilmann's tenuous, insincere attempt at a smile disappeared. "No doubt you are concerned that this has to do with your endeavors in Thani. In this case, however, you would be incorrect. I bear news of an unfortunate incident in Zevenda."

Elana narrowed her eyes by a degree. "May I ask why you're informing me, then, instead of Arbiter Gow?"

"A fair question. The personnel side of the matter is certainly in Eleanor's purview, but the Domain of Legacy is the administrat of real estate in the entirety of Haven.

Since the most significant effect of the incident falls under my auspices, we thought it most appropriate that I break the news."

Elana did *not* like where this was going. She especially didn't like that this was the first she'd heard of *whatever* this was. That meant one of three things.

One, money had changed hands to *keep* her from knowing about it. Two, the incident was so new that it hadn't gotten to anyone but Gow and Zilmann yet. Three, Gow and Zilmann had made the whole thing up.

Elana's money was firmly on number three, primarily because nothing made it to the level of the arbiters without anyone else knowing about it. Maybe in the Domain of Shadows, where every employee trafficked in secrets, but in the Domain of Legacy? The Domain of Legacy enjoyed the questionable reputation of being the closest parallel to Old World politics in Haven. Everyone *pretended* they didn't know anything, but the grapevine was so full you could make a bumper crop of wine. Granted, they were *sour* grapes, but still.

Elana did her best to keep the edge of impatience out of her tone, but she *did* have other shit to do today. "Don't spare my sensibilities, Arbiter. What happened?"

Zilmann drew a slow breath and let it out in a painfully theatrical "repressed" sigh, and Elana again stifled the urge to roll her eyes down the stairs and across the Citadel's courtyard. *You don't fool me, you sly bitch. You are the fox in the henhouse. Everyone knows it, and you know everyone knows it. God, you're exhausting.*

"An altercation broke out between two residents of your housing complex," Zilmann *finally* told her. "The two involved were Aaron Jones and Lydia Westerland. Unfortunately, Mr. Jones succumbed to his injuries. He was declared deceased when the paramedics arrived."

Elana stared at Zilmann's dispassionate face. She felt like the bottom of the world had dropped out from underneath her, like getting air time on a never-ending rollercoaster. Her insight power abruptly took a break from driving an ice pick through her forehead and instead made her stomach roil with sudden nausea.

"What?" she whispered in horror.

"It is truly a tragedy." Zilmann's paper-thin lips turned down at the corners in a pastiche of a frown. None of her expressions reached her eyes, not even contempt. The SpiderKing couldn't have picked a better top bureaucrat. Elana had to give him that.

"Eyewitnesses at the scene reported that Mr. Jones provoked Ms. Westerland with lewd comments," the arbiter continued in the same casual tone. "Ms. Westerland maintained her composure for some time, but according to those interviewed after the fact, incidents of this kind were not uncommon between the two parties.

"Unfortunately, it seems that this was one time too many for Ms. Westerland. Despite warning Mr. Jones multiple times to cease and desist, after a great deal of verbal abuse, she attacked Mr. Jones out of self-defense. As I mentioned, he was declared deceased at the scene."

"When did this happen?" Elana asked.

"In the early hours of this morning. According to my reports, the guardians arrived soon after the paramedics. Statements are still being collated, but I'm sure you understand an incident of this magnitude is expedited to the higher authorities when it involves a probationary project. Arbiter Gow found out within an hour of the incident occurring, and she spoke with me a scant hour after.

"I, of course, waited to summon you until I was sufficiently satisfied with my own due diligence. It would be a horrible dereliction of duty to do otherwise."

Elana took a second to breathe and let the shock pass. Zilmann still hadn't told her the *real* reason she'd called Elana here. Elana didn't want her emotional reaction to the horrific news to obscure her judgment whenever Zilmann got around to dropping the other shoe. There was no way Zilmann was telling Elana this out of the goodness of her heart. The worst was yet to come.

The Zevendan housing complex and its sister complex in Ashford were the vanguard of Elana's efforts to bring rapprochement to the local human and vampire populations. In many ways, they were her pride and joy. She now employed dozens of people through Bishops LLC to manage the recruitment and application process for other "coed" housing projects in Haven and elsewhere. However, Elana had personally overseen the process for these first two complexes. She wouldn't have claimed a close friendship with either Aaron Jones or Lydia Westerland, but she had selected both from a long list of applicants to be granted suites in the Zevendan development.

Lydia Westerland was a savant of House Gravine. She specialized in the publication of children's books, with an emphasis on marginalized populations. She had sought out new experiences and perspectives throughout her two-century life.

Aaron Jones was a human carpenter who spent his days

as a general contractor for hire in the Ashford area and his evenings and weekends volunteering with Habitat for Humanity. He was in his fifties, had separated amicably from his wife, and had a son and daughter in college. He'd been nervous about living with vampires but excited about pitching in with Elana's construction-related goodwill work.

Elana *never* would have pegged Aaron as sexist or anti-vampire. It certainly hadn't come up in the extensive background checks they'd performed during the application process. The idea that he'd harassed Lydia Westerland to the extent that the gentle, compassionate woman had snapped and *killed* him sat so poorly in Elana's brain that it was like squaring a circle.

But Carlysle Zilmann was not an idiot. She could be a cruel, heartless bitch, but she wasn't *stupid*. She wouldn't lie about facts that Elana could verify. It would be a waste of time, and Carlysle Zilmann did not waste her time. Other people's, sure, but never her own.

Therefore, either Zilmann was orchestrating one *hell* of a con, or this had happened. Elana wasn't sure which hypothesis she preferred.

Elana finally broke the silence. "I'm stunned. Our vetting process was strenuous. Thank you for bringing this to my attention, Arbiter. I'll contact Mr. Jones' family and Ms. Westerland as soon as possible."

"I applaud your personal initiative." Zilmann's voice was turning silky, which raised the hair on the back of Elana's neck. It was an unmistakable sign that the hammer was about to come down. "If you don't mind my saying so, it is *such* a good sign when a consort takes full responsibility for their portfolio. Too many kick it down the line to some poor concubine."

"That's not my style. I take my responsibilities seriously."

"I'm well aware. That's why I'm certain that, as much as it will no doubt pain you to do so, you will back my royal petition that all humans be removed from Haven posthaste."

There it was. Zilmann's figurative hammer came down on the anvil and sent Elana reeling again. She'd been expecting a full shutdown of all her open projects. *Hell, I might have even agreed with the precaution. Clearly, we missed something, and until I find out what, it isn't safe to continue with business as usual. But kicking* all *humans out of Haven? That's overkill.*

"I'm sorry, Arbiter, but I must have misheard you. Did you say *all* humans?"

"I did."

"Would you be so kind as to explain your reasoning? I'd be willing to agree to a pause on all development until we get to the bottom of what happened with Mr. Jones and Ms. Westerland, but city-wide deportation strikes me as a bridge too far. The *majority* of Haven's human population lives in housing complexes run by Bishops LLC, but several Houses in excellent standing have human residents. They won't take kindly to being kicked out."

Zilmann lifted her hands, palms up, in disappointed resignation. "It is my informed opinion that this morning's incident is likely a promise of future unrest, given the state of human-vampire relations worldwide. Until the immediate global threats to vampirekind are dealt with, it is unsafe to freely house humans and vampires side by side.

"We have a Wall, Consort Bishop. It would behoove us to retreat behind it and place the humans on the other side of it for all of our safety. It would truly be a shame if more unpleasantness such as your incident with Mr. Kowalski were to occur, especially to our more fragile human friends. Wouldn't you agree?"

Elana stared at Zilmann, slack-jawed and stupefied. "You have *got* to be kidding me."

"I assure you, I most certainly am not. The level of danger in which we all find ourselves is unprecedented. We must take action. May I assume I have your backing?"

"You may not," Elana sputtered. Her shock was rapidly transmuting into rage. Zilmann was manipulating and inflating what had to be a tragic misunderstanding into a full-blown moral panic for her own political gain. If the Council of Arbiters passed this resolution, Elana would not only have to win back public opinion to continue her work, but she would also have to strike down real legislation. That could take *decades*.

A thought struck Elana, and with it came a flicker of hope. "Wait. It doesn't matter if you have my backing. A petition to the SpiderKing only goes to His Majesty if it has the support of a majority of arbiters. There is *no* way you'll get that vote, even if you *did* have my endorsement."

A terrible smile curled the corners of Zilmann's lips. "I'm afraid the only two dissenting votes are from Arbiter Draven and Arbiter Amindóttir. Unsurprising, since you're Valeria's newest pet, and Ída is allergic to anything that might impact our economic value to the human world. But the rest of them, Elana…the rest of them are on my side. Your little project is over."

Elana gripped the edges of her chair to keep from launching across the table and strangling Zilmann with her bare hands. "This *isn't* over," she ground out.

Zilmann flicked a hand out in a dismissive wave. "You may go, Consort Bishop. I'm certain you have much business to attend to with the impending deportation, not to mention the messy business of informing humans of their loved one's demise."

She clicked her tongue and continued talking as Elana stiffly stood and made her way out of the room. "It's always regrettable to see a young vampire's dreams dashed in such tragic fashion, of course, but we all have to learn which of our ideas are terrible on our own. Vampires and humans cannot coexist peacefully. I hope you see that now. All the best with your future endeavors."

Elana closed the door. Her entire body trembled with fury and shock.

To her surprise, Matt Richelieu stood in the corridor, evidently waiting for her. Without a word, he took her by the arm and steered her out of the consulate, which was just as well. Elana honestly might have doubled back to murder Zilmann otherwise.

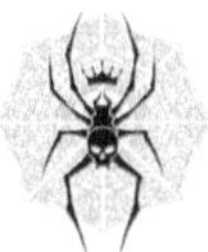

Matt didn't let go of Elana's arm until they were out of the Citadel. As soon as they crossed the threshold of the inner ring wall, he moved his hand from her arm to her lower back and gently nudged her in the direction of Senkyem.

Elana hesitated. "What are you doing?"

Matt kept his hand on her back, steady and firm, but he didn't push. "You need a distraction. Badly."

"I *need* to protect the people relying on me for a place to live."

Matt sighed. "I'm sorry Zilmann got to you first with the shitty news out of Zevenda. I promise there's more to it than she told you, which I *know* you already suspect."

"Her being a duplicitous piece of shit doesn't change the fact that she's *kicking people out of their homes.*"

"No, it doesn't, but Elana—you *have* to remember that vampires work on a different time scale than humans. Even the wheels of the fastest bureaucracy grind slow. I guarantee you no one will be on the street tonight."

Elana scowled. "She got the support for her petition real fucking fast."

"Votes don't mean action. Ída Amindóttir, for one, won't let this go down without a fight. I wouldn't be surprised if she brought Kyoi around, at *least*. Also, Zilmann can't submit a petition until the investigation is done, and you bet your ass I will be sending teams into every nook and cranny for as long as I can get away with."

He gently turned her to face him and put his other hand on her upper arm. "Elana, please come to dinner with me. Your last forty-eight hours have been a wild ride, to put it *extremely* mildly. I will be happy to continue this discussion over food, and after a movie, over drinks. Okay? You need a *break*."

Matt's warm, brotherly gaze chipped away at Elana's panic until she let her breath out in a *whoosh* and allowed her shoulders to drop away from her ears. "Fine. *Fine*. You win. Just don't look so smug about it."

He chuckled and turned them back toward Senkyem. "Wouldn't dream of it."

Elana devoured most of a platter of assorted tempura before broaching the conversation again. "I don't understand how she got so many votes so fast. How did news of this spread without mass panic?"

Matt dipped a shrimp tempura that had escaped Elana's ire into the provided sauce and crunched through it. "I'm still sorting through non-hysterical witness statements. My guess is that Zilmann has someone running to her any time anything happens around your projects so she can decide what to file away for blackmail.

"As to how she got the other arbiters to come around..." He shook his head and gazed out the window behind Elana at the sun setting over the city. "Everyone's scared, Elana. Zilmann isn't blowing that as far out of proportion as you might think, and not even the arbiters are immune."

"But *Tarsin?* Mélissand? Those surprised me the most after Kyoi. DeMarco's always a crapshoot... Amindóttir will sooner go down with her ship than agree with Zilmann, and the day Valeria doesn't have my back, I know I've *really* fucked up. But Roxanne's my boss, and she hasn't given me any hint that she isn't wholly behind me, and Tarsin wants every scrap of information she can get out of humanity. What am I missing?"

Matt reached across the table and put his hand on Elana's. "Only that Carlysle Zilmann has been playing this game for a *very* long time, and that—as I keep saying—Haven's political machinations are far more complex than even the nastiest human ones. It's chess, but on a thousand boards at once.

"You won't *stop* Zilmann, but you might be able to make her moves irrelevant before she can carry them out effectively. Focus on what you can do, not what you can't," he advised.

She pointed at him with her chopsticks. "I had every intention of doing so before you whisked me away to eat sushi."

"It's very good sushi."

"Be that as it may, it's not actively working to undermine Carlysle Zilmann's attempts to reinforce the segregation of humans and vampires."

Matt acquiesced with a nod. "Not directly, you're right, but may I remind you of the age-old axiom, 'Don't plan a revolution on an empty stomach, no sleep, and an excess of cortisol?'"

"No one said that."

"Well, maybe not in those *exact* words, but the sentiment's cropped up here and there from time to time. My point is, Elana, if you don't take time to relax, recharge, and let your brain work its magic in the background, you won't be nearly as effective as you could be."

Elana grumbled, "You sound like Vicky."

He chuckled. "I will take that compliment. Now, can I please distract you with something totally unrelated to the matter at hand?"

"Like what?"

"Did I ever tell you about the time my mother decided it was a good idea to require a dress code for my fourteenth birthday party?"

Elana clamped down on a giggle. "Oh, God."

Matt rolled his eyes. "You can say that again. Try telling a bunch of French boys who have barely hit puberty that they need to be laced into suits and ties before they're allowed to visit the fancy-ass manor and eat the ridiculously expensive food. They turned their nose up at the truffles and caviar—and to be honest, so did I. That shit was disgusting. I wanted pizza."

Elana gave up and cackled. "Didn't you get the Rights as a young adult? Did you even *have* pizza back then?"

"Of course we did! My father imported it from Italy,

and I'll have you know it was very good, straight off the boat!"

His impish grin sent Elana into another paroxysm of laughter. For a brief moment, she felt light as a feather, and her insight power relaxed enough to relieve the tension in her brow.

Maybe Matt's right. Perhaps I do need to relax.

She would let herself chill out for the evening. Maybe her brain would decompress sufficiently that she would wake up in the morning with all of the answers in a neat row. A girl could dream, right?

After dinner, Matt insisted on taking Elana to the movies. "We're not done. You need an hour and a half of cheesy romantic comedy bullshit. It's the perfect palate cleanser, especially after the story where you ended up with a mouthful of gravel because you slingshotted yourself off the swing set."

"I didn't know my own strength!" Elana protested. "I'd been a vampire since I was, like, *two*! Puberty's bad enough when you *don't* have vampiric blood sending the hormones into double overdrive!"

"Exactly why I think you need a good cry." He took her by the arm again and marched her down the sidewalk. "You are overdue for some catharsis. I'm not taking no for an answer, but I *will* bribe you with popcorn."

"Oh, my God, I am *stuffed*. I couldn't eat another bite… Actually, popcorn sounds really good. And maybe ice cream afterward?"

Matt chortled. "Your wish is my command. How's your head?"

Elana rolled her shoulders and cracked her neck. "Better. I feel like I look more like myself, too."

Matt gave her a once-over and nodded. "The screen's wearing off. You're almost back to normal. Your nose isn't quite right yet, but that's about it."

"My nose has always been weird."

"Not that weird."

"*Thanks.* That's real good for a girl's self-esteem." Elana glared at him and fished her phone out of her bag. She turned the camera on, flipped it around, examined her nose, and flipped him off. "My nose is perfectly normal!"

"Oh, so it *usually* has that awkward bump in the middle of the bridge?"

He dodged Elana's punch in the arm, then threw back his head and laughed. "*That's* the Elana I know and love. You had me worried there for a bit."

Elana sobered and fell into step beside him. "Oh?"

"Yeah. You're always serious about your work, passionate even, and that's great. But the last few days... weeks...you've been single-minded to the point of distraction. I know you're scared. I'd be lying if I said I wasn't, too. But I *also* know you're at your best when you're not tearing your hair out about what other people are doing."

Elana stuck her hands in her pockets and walked quietly for a moment. "I am scared," she finally admitted. "Scared about a lot of things. Right now, I'm most scared that while I've been trying to save the world, Zilmann's slowly been pulling the rug out from under my feet. Humans and vampires can't live together in a world that doesn't exist, but I'd also like to give them a world worth living in. It just seems unfair. Cruel."

"I can't disagree with you." They waited for a car to pass and crossed the street. "It's just like you said, though. We can't live together in a world that doesn't exist. Yes, it's frustrating that Zilmann's working against you while you're doing arguably much more important things, but you can't fix what isn't there."

"It's equally frustrating to have to do work again. I get it. But it's better than not being able to do the work at all. You have time."

"*I* do, sure. It seems like a lot of vampires forget that. We get lots of time, but the people we form relationships with don't. That's exactly what drove Edward Korynchuk to do what he did."

Matt raised an eyebrow and glanced at her. "Are you suggesting we give the entire planet the Rights?"

Elana hunched her shoulders and stared at the ground. "I won't lie and say it hasn't crossed my mind, but I know the arguments against it, and I agree with most of them. I think we'd adapt and evolve, personally. That's not what I'm pushing for, though."

"Then what *are* you pushing for?"

Elana sucked her lower lip between her teeth. "I'm not one hundred percent sure yet. Can I get back to you on it?"

"Of course. I'm not going anywhere except the movies. *Oranges in May?* The poster looks terrible. You in?"

They had arrived in front of the movie theater. Matt was contemplating one of the marquee posters, which featured a woman with unrealistically long legs wearing a bikini and holding a pair of massive oranges up to her chest. Behind her, two men threatened each other, fists up and Hawaiian shirts open to reveal their sculpted chests. The woman was winking at the camera and licking her lips, and one of the oranges had a straw stuck into it.

The longer Elana stared at the poster, the more incredulous laughter pressed against her lips. "That looks *stunningly* awful. If I'm watching that, my popcorn needs twice as much butter as is legal per FDA regulations, and I need a soda as big as my head."

"Deal."

"We're gonna regret this."

"Probably!"

They stumbled out of the theater two hours later, still wheezing with laughter. Elana drained the last drops of cream soda from her giant cup, Matt picked the last kernels out of the greasy paper bag, and they tossed both receptacles in the trash can beside the door. They leaned against the brick wall and sank to the sidewalk, wiping their hands with napkins with which they had dried their eyes.

"Oh, my *God.*" Elana let her head fall back against the cold brick and stared up at the night sky, which had a mild pink haze from Haven's lights. "That was worse than I thought *possible.*"

"Agreed. How do you think they convinced the cast to do it? I've seen Janine North's stuff before. She's a legitimately good actress."

"Honestly? A shit-ton of money and the opportunity to

do something brain-numbingly stupid and have fun with it. You could tell all three of them were camping it up, *big time*. *I* want to know if the *writers* meant for it to be shit. Hell, I wanna know if they expected the pitch to be shot down.

"Like, really? The heiress to an orange juice empire pits her two suitors against each other in a Herculean series of tasks to pick a husband. They end up in a high-stakes heist to steal the perfect orange from her father's lemonade-baroness rival who is *clearly* her long-lost mother. It's ridiculous!"

"But *hilarious*." Matt adopted a simpering, faux-British voice. "'Kenneth, you *dirty* bastard! Everyone knows your juice is from *concentrate!*'"

Elana dissolved into giggles again and slumped back against the wall. "I don't think I'll be able to buy orange juice ever again."

"Me neither. Or lemonade."

The giddiness subsided into the cold evening. Snow started to fall in tiny flakes, and Elana caught one on her fingertip and watched it melt. "Thanks for the evening."

"You're welcome. We both needed it. How are you feeling?"

"Less overwhelmed," Elana admitted. "I no longer feel like a rubber band that's been stretched too far. I'm still spitting mad at Zilmann if I think about it, but the panic is gone.

"I'm most angry that she's taking advantage of a situation where people are already in danger and hurting them more. That's not the kind of person I want to be, and I don't understand people who choose to act like that. What does she get out of it?"

"We might never know. Does it matter?"

"Not really." Elana brought her knees to her chest and wrapped her arms around them. "I won't let her distract me. I'll make sure everyone in the Bishop's LLC housing complexes knows they don't have to go anywhere until the petition receives royal assent and that there's no guarantee it will happen. I'll also get my financial department working on contingency funds to offset temporary or permanent resettlement costs. I'm responsible for them, and I take that seriously.

"I can delegate most of that, though, and I will. My priority has to be Veridian and the East Coast Staker. They are standing in the way of the world I want to build, and more importantly, they're hurting people in the process."

She bit her lip. "I'm still feeling a bit at loose ends, though. That's my priority, but how do I pursue it? Cassandra will remember when she remembers, and the Chimeras are chasing down the leads on the Necromancer. Lucia's working on how House Viverri knew what Webber and I were doing. Where do I fit?"

Matt edged closer to her and put his arm around her shoulders. "Take the day tomorrow to work on countering Zilmann. Check in on Vicky, have lunch with Cassandra, say hello to the Leones. You're so good at making connections and understanding people. Lean on *that*. We have a lot of irons in the fire, Elana. One of them will bear fruit sooner or later."

Elana snorted and leaned her head on his shoulder.

"You are really bad at mixing metaphors, but you have a point."

"I usually do."

"Smug bastard."

"Learned from the best."

"Usually that's a backhanded compliment, but I've heard the stories about your family…"

"Let's not finish the evening talking about the House of Cardinals. Can I take you home?"

"Sure. I could use some sleep. And Matt? Thanks."

"Any time."

CHAPTER EIGHTEEN

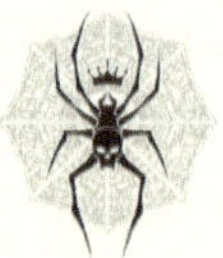

Elana dropped her keys in the bowl by the door and kicked off her boots. "Vicky? You home?"

"In here," her friend called.

Elana hung up her coat, tossed her handbag on the kitchen table, and followed Vicky's voice into the living room. "You look like shit."

Vicky cracked an eye open from her position sprawled on the couch and stuck her tongue out at Elana. "Thanks."

Elana went to flop into a chair and paused. "You need anything before I sit down?"

"Kill me?"

"No can do, boss." Elana plopped into the armchair, lifted a leg, and poked Vicky's toe with hers. "You okay?"

"Gustav promises I will be, but right now I believe him about as much as I believe people who claim the Earth is flat."

"Well, you see, something you'll learn as you progress in the Nexus is that from certain perspectives, the Earth could be *seen* as flat..."

"Count yourself lucky I'm too tired to move, or else I'd chuck a lamp at your head."

"Fair." Elana stretched and cracked her neck. "Tough training day, I take it."

Vicky groaned. "I have never been pushed so hard in my life. I've never been the most athletic, but I could hold my own! I could sprint for a bus or a taxi. I could lug groceries up stairs, I could help friends move couches. Now I feel like a teenager again, except I keep breaking things when I don't mean to. It sucks, and I want to sleep for a week."

"I hear you. I felt like that after my Progression to sentinel. I had to buy a new set of drinking glasses within a week."

Vicky snorted. "At least I'm not alone."

Elana slid further down in her chair and stared out the opposite window. "Amen to that."

Vicky narrowed her eyes. "What's wrong?"

"Who says anything's wrong?"

"I've been your best friend for twenty-three years. Your mouth gets a weird, funny line to it when you're stressed. Tell me what's wrong."

"Fine, Sherlock, geez." Vicky stuck her tongue out at Elana again. This time, Elana mirrored it. Then she gave Vicky a quick recounting of how the last couple of days had gone, glossing over the classified bits but going into plenty of detail about how much of an ass Carlysle Zilmann was.

"So yeah," she finished. "I'm trying to save the world, and Zilmann's trying to screw me over while I do it. Matt took me out to dinner, and we saw an absolutely ridiculous movie afterward, but… I dunno. I still feel off. Headache's coming back."

"*Oranges in May?*"

"How'd you know?"

"Everything else on right now looks marginally sensible. That looks like an LSD trip given a budget."

Elana snorted. "You're not wrong."

Vicky hauled herself to a sitting position, waving off Elana's help. "If I don't move, I'm gonna get stuck. Vampire regeneration is a hell of a thing, but I can still get stiff. I gotta move."

After she settled in again, she leaned an elbow on the arm of the couch and propped her chin in her hand. "Sounds like you're facing your biggest storm yet."

"Yeah, and I don't know if I can weather it."

Vicky smiled. "'Course you can. You can totally handle it."

Elana attempted to smile in return, but it turned into a grimace. "I'm not really in the mood for a pep talk, Vick."

"Too bad. You have overcome every obstacle the vampire and human worlds have thrown at you in the last year. You've built powerful alliances and shot up the Nexus in record time. You took up your mother's torch without leaving your human roots behind. You're untangling a conspiracy that took someone decades, if not centuries, to put together."

Vicky emphasized, "You have them running scared, and all you're doing is being yourself. If I've learned anything in my years dicking around, eating kick-ass food, and writing about it, it's that being yourself is the scariest fucking thing to ninety-five percent of the world's population."

Elana mirrored Vicky's posture, leaning on the arm of her chair, and gave her friend a lopsided smile. "I think 'being myself' is only gonna go so far in this instance. They're too powerful. I have to wait for an opportunity."

Vicky shrugged. "Maybe. Or maybe that's quitter talk. I *know* Jeremiah Bishop didn't raise no quitter. Find the thing that only you can do, and do *that.*

"Now, if you'll excuse me, my eyelids are dragging themselves shut of their own accord, and I don't think I have the chutzpah to get to my bed. So, whether you're gonna give yourself a kick in the pants or you're gonna keep moping, I love you, but please do it elsewhere."

Elana couldn't help but laugh. "Yeah, all right. Fair enough." She levered herself out of the chair with a grunt. "Want a blanket?"

"Wouldn't say no."

Elana grabbed a teal microfleece blanket from the back of the other armchair and tucked it in around her friend. "Is your phone dying?"

"You know it is."

"'Kay. I'll plug it in on the end table here and close the blinds. I'm gonna go for a walk. Call me if you need anything, okay?"

"Uh-huh." Vicky was already half asleep.

Elana located her friend's phone and charge cord, plugged it in, and left the phone to charge on the end table as promised. She also left Vicky a bottle of ibuprofen and a glass of water. By the time she'd done all of the above, Vicky was sound asleep and snoring.

Elana donned her coat and boots and pulled on the tuque she'd bought in the Winnipeg airport. Then she walked out into the chilly night with no destination in mind.

Neither Vicky nor Matt was wrong. Matt told her to sit back and let her brain work, and Vicky told her to use the skills only she had to get forward. Since Elana was tired but nowhere near sleepy, she didn't feel like lying in bed, tossing and turning while her insight power trundled along in the background.

Elana let her focus spread as far as she could imagine. She caught the edges of so many emotions, borne along by the stray nanocytes in the air that carried information like a game of telephone. This was something only she could do, although she suspected Michelle Ferns' power was similar. Maybe she could pick up on something that would crack the case wide open.

Those kinds of epiphanies had happened before, sometimes at the eleventh hour, sometimes after she'd gotten lucky and solved the dilemma in front of her. The only problem was that when you deliberately set out to have epiphanies, the revelations usually hung back and made faces at you.

Elana wandered aimlessly, up one road and down the next. While it was common for humans to believe that vampires were nocturnal, thanks to the sun sensitivity suffered by most low-level vampires, she was consistently surprised by how *normal* vampire cities seemed. A fraction of the population lived on a different schedule, but most lived diurnally and wore hats or sunscreen. As such, the streets were quiet and dark like any human city.

It's funny—or maybe sad—how many vampires distance themselves from their human roots. If everyone accepted that we're seriously not so different from one another, I feel like so many of our problems would go away.

She laughed as she realized she had inadvertently summed up the root of racism, sexism, ageism, ableism, and all the other -isms she could think of. *We're not different,* she repeated to herself. *We're the same. We just don't see that.*

It's like astronauts say. When you see the Earth from space, you realize we're all on the same planet, and none of the little shit matters. How do I get everyone else to see that?

Elana laughed again, but this time under her breath. She could hear her dad in her head, telling her she was trying to solve everybody else's problems again. "Elana, girl, you can't make everyone do what you want, and you can't make people accept help if they're not ready. You do you, and let everyone else handle their own business."

Elana stopped and sighed. Her breath floated away in a puff of mist, and the mental image of a soul departing on the winds of fate made her heart twinge.

For the first time in a good long while, she missed her dad.

She turned on her heel and headed back up the street.

Jeremiah Bishop was buried in the Garden of Rest Cemetery in Ashford, an unassuming plot of land in one of those massive funerary complexes that might have been golf courses if a funeral home chain hadn't bought them. It was cheap, quiet, and wholly non-denominational, all of which had been priorities for Jeremiah when he'd been wrapping up his affairs.

Elana didn't like to think about the last months of his life when he'd been wasting away in a hospital bed, his body failing because of the cancer and the treatment. He'd gone from being the strong, broad-shouldered, solid man she'd leaned on growing up to a concave husk whose skin hung loose on his frame. Esophageal cancer. Too many work sites without proper respirators early on in his career, and he'd gotten unlucky.

It had moved fast, too. Ravaged him, tore him apart from the inside out, and metastasized into his lungs and mouth. He had a feeding tube six months after the diagnosis, which was the point where Elana had stopped yelling at him for ignoring the scratchy aches and pains he'd been hiding for years.

She only found out afterward, from a great-aunt at the funeral, that his grandfather had died of the same cancer. In those years, medical science hadn't been advanced enough to do much about it, but it meant Jeremiah had known the signs, and he'd chosen not to pursue the most drastic treatments.

At first, this had stoked the flames of Elana's heartbroken anger. With time, however, she'd realized that in his way, her father had been trying to save her from the pain of watching someone linger at death's door.

"You wanted to go out on your terms," she told the headstone. "I can respect that, although I don't know if I'll ever stop being pissed at you about it."

The left half of the granite marker read **Jeremiah E. Bishop, 1959 – 2023. When we build, we build forever**. The right half read **Tessa M. Bishop, née Hart, 1960 – 1990. Let the little children come unto me.**

Only one of the urns buried in front of the headstone contained the ashes of Elana's parents. Tessa's final resting place was in her mausoleum in Haven, and she'd only been laid to rest inside it a scant couple of years before her husband had been laid to rest here.

Elana did not sit in front of the marker. The ground was too wet and cold. She wouldn't have felt the chill, but she didn't want to deal with drying her peacoat properly. It would be annoying enough to air it out from the thick snowflakes building on her shoulders.

She stared at the snowy ground and allowed the image of her father to coalesce in her mind. She tried to recall a memory of her father before his decline, but the specter of his hollow frame in the hospital bed lurked in the background.

"I miss you, Dad. I missed you like hell until all this Haven stuff started happening, and then I was too mad at you and the world to admit I missed you. Now I miss you again. So much that it hurts.

"I'm still mad at you, though. Don't get me wrong. But if it makes any difference, I'm also mad at Mom, the entire Haven hierarchy, and vampires as a whole. Humans, too."

She laughed. The sound could have been mistaken for a cough or even a sob if you squinted. "God. When I list them all, I might as well be mad at the whole damn universe. And you know what? I guess I am.

"This isn't *fair*, Dad. This isn't fucking *fair*. I swear I had this conversation with Mom's coffin months ago, but I keep getting hung up on it. You taught me to treat everyone equally and remember that everyone has a life you can't imagine. Why don't more people learn that? And why do those of us who *do* learn it end up in situations where we can't do anything about it?

"Really horrible people are doing horrible things to other people. While I'm trying to stop them, someone else is taking the opportunity to do *more* horrible things to *different* people—*just because I'm distracted.* How fucked up is that? Do you know how *mad* it makes me? I could spit nails hard enough that Jerry wouldn't need old Gertrude to frame a wall."

Elana kicked a small pile of gathering snow and grumbled when all it did was cover the toe of her boot in glittering white. "What good is being human-born if everyone ignores the unique perspective you bring? Why should I keep fighting, Dad? Why do I care so much? Why did you *teach* me to care?

"You taught me to listen. You taught me that when a customer is mad, it's usually because they're afraid they won't get what they want. It's our job to help them see that we *are* giving them what they want or *need*, even though it might not look like it at first.

"Anger hides fear. What am I afraid of? I'm afraid my failure will end up getting a lot of people hurt. What is House Veridian afraid of? Humans taking over? That'll never happen, so what's their damage? Why do all of this?

"Humans are afraid of vampires because we can manipulate them on top of all the other 'magical' stuff we can do. That's a very sensible fear, not least because nine times out of ten when a human has power over another human, they abuse it. But vampires…

"Even if every human on the planet rose up as one and rebelled against vampiredom, I don't think they'd win. They'd do a hell of a lot of damage, but I have no doubt that more than a few Houses have weapons of mass destruction in their figurative cellars. Who needs an atomic bomb when you have nanotechnology and can also change your opponents' minds?"

Elana made a disgusted noise in the back of her throat. "That's what it is. Veridian is afraid of vampires losing their stranglehold over humanity. They're trying to manufacture something that will ensure vampires' dominion over humans for the rest of existence. Since there are plenty of vampires who *aren't* assholes, they're building in a failsafe so they can threaten vampires equally effectively."

She sighed deeply, crossed her arms, and shook her head. "Again and again, Dad, I come back to the truth that vampires and humans aren't different from each other. Not at our cores. I wish you could have seen that. I don't think it would have made you *like* vampires, and I can hardly blame you. But maybe…maybe it would have been enough to mean you wouldn't kick me out of the house for being a vampire."

Elana chuckled. "God, I can only imagine how you would have reacted if you'd ever found out. Of course, that would have meant you'd also found out Mom didn't die for three more decades after you thought you lost her. That probably wouldn't have gone over well, either. Maybe it's best you didn't find out. You had enough heartbreak to deal with."

Another sigh, but this one was determined, not sad. "Okay. I think I've figured it out, Dad. They're afraid of losing their power, so they're desperate and grasping. That means they're gonna make stupid decisions. I have objective experience that lets me speak to both sides of the conflict, so it's my job to show everyone what they *actually* need.

"In this case, I think that comes back to pulling the mask off the boogeyman. If I can reveal what the hell Veridian is up to and lock them away, it'll be safe to continue with the housing projects. If Zilmann continues to fuss after that, it'll be easy to show she doesn't have a leg to stand on. Right?"

Elana bit her lip. "Seems too simple. The simplest explanation is usually right, but I still feel like I'm missing something."

She could hear her father's voice in her head. *No use dwelling on it. Don't borrow trouble from tomorrow. Today has enough.*

Elana nodded. "Yeah. Yeah, Dad, you're right. I need to focus. Letting Zilmann distract me is exactly what she wants."

She turned to leave, then stopped and turned back. She looked at the headstone squarely, drew a deep breath, and blew it out in a long *whoosh*.

"I want to believe you would have been able to look past what I am, Dad I want to believe your anger toward vampires was fear, too, and that you would have been able to set it aside and hear me out. I want to hear it wouldn't have been so shocking that we wouldn't have talked for God knows how long.

"I know you still would have loved me. I just don't know whether you would have been able to show it. Especially since discovering it would have meant you'd know Mom hadn't died. Somehow, I think that would have been an even bigger betrayal.

"You wanted to protect me from the cancer. She wanted to protect us both from the world she'd fallen into. I guess we're all just really bad at talking."

Elana drew a shaky breath and wiped a surprise tear from her eye. She laughed softly, then sniffled. "That's the crux of it. We were all really bad at not keeping secrets from each other. Isn't that just being human, though? Or being a vampire? Isn't that what I've been mad about this whole time? Nobody *tells* each other anything. Everything's a huge secret, and it's *stupid*. We'd all get along so much better if we weren't hiding from each other."

She smiled at the headstone and felt warmth in her chest for the first time. The smile was genuine. Her throat ached and her eyes stung with unshed tears, but deep in her heart, gentle waves of tranquility soothed the grief.

"I forgive you for not telling me until it was too late, Dad...and I'm sorry I didn't have the chance to share this part of my life with you. I love you. I miss you. I hope you're resting easy."

She hauled in another sniffly breath and blew it out her lips, then shook herself. "I'm gonna go save the world now, okay? Don't go anywhere. I'll be back when I'm done. Bye, Dad. See you later."

Elana crossed the new-fallen snow back to her Emeya and left the cemetery.

This time, she snuck into the house as quietly as she could. Vicky *might* have woken and moved to her bed, but Elana remembered how tired *she* was after her first days of training, so she wasn't betting on it.

Indeed, the first thing she heard upon slipping in the back door was her best friend snoring like a chainsaw. Vicky hadn't gone anywhere. *At least she's sleeping. I wonder if I can throw together something to stick in the fridge for breakfast without waking her. She'll be starving in the morning.*

Elana eased cupboards open and silently measured eggs, milk, vanilla, and cinnamon into a large casserole dish. She chopped several slices of bread and a handful of bite-size brownies, then mixed everything after giving the eggs a quick beating. Then she put plastic wrap over the casserole dish and slid it into the fridge.

She eyed the dishes, then shrugged. She'd already pushed her luck by doing the prep in the dark. Washing up would *definitely* wake Vicky.

With breakfast handled and the "conversation" with her father sitting comfortably in her mind, Elana headed for her bedroom. She tossed her clothes in the hamper, but her phone buzzed with a text from Matt before she could grab a nightshirt.

Zilmann's moving fast. Counter-petition hearing set

for two days from now. You'll want witnesses and a plan. Call me in the morning.

Elana swore under her breath, but to her surprise, a resurgence of anxiety didn't accompany the spike of frustration. *This might be a good thing. Her rushing might mean she's trying to push it through before the news spreads. That works in my favor.*

She decided she needed to think before trying to sleep, so she hopped in the ensuite shower. Standing in the stream of hot water, she could imagine she was washing away the remnants of Kat Stevens.

The memory of another shower just over a year ago came to mind—the one she'd taken after she hit the Runner. It had felt as though she was turning a page into an entirely new life.

I wasn't wrong. More has happened in the last year than I could ever have imagined, and I have a feeling the universe has no intention of stopping now.

She massaged shampoo into her hair. *A counter-petition hearing means the vote wasn't unanimous. The arbiters want more information before presenting the petition to the SpiderK-ing. I can work with that. I'll need to be at my best, though. Showing up frazzled and on a hair trigger won't help my case.*

The aroma of shea butter and honey filled the shower, borne on the billowing steam. It made Elana think of a sauna, which made her smile at the thought of Vicky enjoying the locker room baths at the Training Grounds. That, in turn, prompted her to wonder what Vicky's schedule was the next day.

Elana rinsed her hair and turned off the shower. She

grabbed a towel from the rack over the toilet, squeezed her hair out, then wrapped the towel around herself and stepped onto the plush bath mat. She examined her reflection while smoothing leave-in conditioner through her thick brown locks. No hint of Kat Stevens remained.

She smiled. *Back to being me, and there's no one I'd rather be.*

CHAPTER NINETEEN

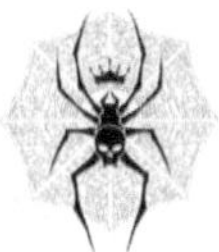

Elana woke the next morning to the heady smell of cinnamon and vanilla mixed with coffee. She catapulted out of bed and grabbed the housecoat off her chair in her mad dash to the kitchen.

"I'm supposed to be surprising *you* with breakfast, not the other way around!" she exclaimed upon skidding into the kitchen. "Go back to bed!"

Vicky threw back her head of wild, tight curls and laughed. She was contentedly sitting at the kitchen table with a steaming mug of coffee and the morning's *Haven Chronicle*. She tapped her chin with her pencil. "Guardian of House Ionescu known for winning Olympic gold before being given the Rights, seven letters."

"Anovich," Elana automatically replied, then scowled. "Hey! No distracting!"

Vicky grinned and put her pencil down. "It still counts! I barely had to do anything. I know how to cook an overnight bread pudding, and I can make coffee in a shitty hotel kitchenette while hungover and running on forty minutes of sleep. You made my morning!"

Elana grumbled while grabbing a mug from the cupboard and filling it with coffee. "Still. It's the *principle* of the thing. How long until it's done?"

Vicky checked her phone, which sat beside the newspaper. "Ten minutes. Fifteen at the outside. How'd you sleep?"

"Better than I have in a while. I went and visited my dad's grave last night after you zonked out, and it gave me some perspective."

"You do a lot of running around in cemeteries. Then again, I suppose you are a vampire."

Elana stuck her tongue out as she sat across from her best friend. "We're not *all* walking stereotypes."

"Damn. Here I was hoping you'd give me the skinny on how long I had to wait until I got my gothic gown and Helena Bonham Carter hair so I was allowed to lurk in graveyards and scare people."

Elana snorted. "You can do that whenever. Call Zizi, he'll set you up. How'd *you* sleep?"

"Like a log."

"That's funny because you were certainly sawing them."

"Very funny. Do vampires get sleep apnea?"

Elana shrugged. "Probably."

"Gross. Have you upgraded CPAP machines?"

"Also probably. You have any plans for today?"

"More reading than I've done since I was asked to judge a travel blog awards show. Never again, I swear to God."

"Wanna play hooky?"

Vicky raised an eyebrow. "Wasn't aware my attendance was being marked, but always. What do you have in mind?"

"I need a break like nobody's business, and I was thinking about a morning at the spa. There's a Nordic spa in Senkyem I've been meaning to try for ages and never made the time. You, me, Belinda, Cathy? I haven't texted them yet but I'm sure they'll be in. Could even invite Aimee. I don't think you've met her yet."

The oven *beeped*. Vicky pushed her chair back, started to stand—and groaned. "Oh, God. Every part of everything hurts. Yeah, okay, you've sold me. Spa day it is. Any chance you'd be willing to carry me there?"

Suiren was in the heart of Senkyem's agricultural district, nestled among the fields and pagoda-inspired barns that set Haven's farmlands apart from anything outside the Wall. The otherworldliness intensified when one spotted the miniature mountain beneath the canopy of climate-control nanofilament leaves, which swooped low over the spa's facilities.

"I thought you said it was a Nordic spa," Vicky remarked as the group gathered in the parking lot outside the entrance, which strongly resembled the entrance to a Shinto temple. "Looks a heck of a lot like an *onsen* in there."

"Vampires love combining traditions almost as much as they love clinging to them." Cathy chuckled. "The couple that runs Suiren is half Japanese, half Swedish. So really, it's a bit of both, but since the spa includes cold therapy, they bill it as a Nordic spa."

"Where'd they get a natural hot spring in the middle of North Carolina? That's not the kind of thing you can *make.*" Vicky glanced between her companions and rolled her eyes. "What, you can't even tell me *that?* Geez."

Elana smiled crookedly. She'd only figured out the answer recently since it was listed as "proprietary information" on Suiren's press material. As it turned out, if you prompted nanocytes in the right direction and gave them the necessary materials, you *could* make your own natural hot spring.

Aimee winked and clapped Vicky on the back. "Don't worry about it. Not all of the mysteries of the universe need to be solved in a day. Kick back and relax. You've earned it."

Vicky squinted. "You don't even know me."

"Elana's told us *all* about you," Belinda chimed in. She and Vicky could have been sisters with their matching tied-back afros and sunglasses.

"All good, I hope."

"Only the best stories," Elana promised.

Vicky groaned. "'Best' does not mean *good…*"

Cathy chivvied them all through the gate. "Come on, girls. That's enough standing around in the cold."

Elana led them in and confirmed their reservation with the woman behind the counter, which was a glittering black boulder the size of a small desk. The brunette signed them in, took Elana's black card for payment, and ushered them into the oasis.

Past the gate, Suiren's illusory world kicked in in full force. Mountain landscapes were projected at the edges of the property, and the nanofilament canopy above their heads disappeared into a blue sky peppered with cotton clouds. The faint scent of sulfur wafted on the breeze, chased by the clean smell of snow and the quiet sound of a waterfall. The air was warm enough that Elana wanted to shed her coat immediately.

They followed the cobblestone path into the mountain, which was the same stone as the receptionist's desk. Inside, candles floated on still lanes of water on either side of the path, and the light made the tunnel above their heads glitter like a million stars.

At the end of the tunnel, low stone bridges crossed the lanes of water, which curved into the center of the circular cave and created a pool strewn with more tealights. A water feature in the shape of another mountain rose from the pool. Water trickled down its side in a gentle stream edged with moss.

"Where do we put our stuff?" Vicky asked. "I don't see any lockers."

"They're hidden," Belinda explained. "Watch and learn. It's really cool."

She pressed her hand to the wall. The stone briefly glowed beneath her palm before sliding aside to reveal a small cubby. "It's keyed to your biometrics," she explained as she stripped and changed into her bathing suit. "Completely secure."

Vicky grinned and eagerly followed Belinda's lead, as did the rest. Cathy fetched robes from the hidden closet beside the next tunnel and handed them out.

"No slippers?" Elana woondered, then corrected herself. "Wait. Heated paths, am I right?"

"You're *so* right," Aimee confirmed. "In my opinion, the heated paths are the *best* part of Suiren. If I could never have cold feet again, I'd be the happiest person on the planet."

"Are you telling me vampires haven't solved *cold feet?*" Vicky scoffed. "Y'all're *slacking!*"

"Maybe that's *your* calling," Elana suggested. "Vicky Lamarr, hot foot queen of Haven?"

"That sounds like something else *entirely,*" Cathy deadpanned.

Vicky contemplated her feet, then shook her head. "Nah. My left big toe is weird. I'd never make it big."

Belinda leaned over and gave it due consideration. "I mean…people are into weird stuff."

"Oh, sure! But if you're gonna make it *big*, you gotta have *universal* appeal. Now let's stop talking about my toes and jump in a hot spring."

Their laughter echoed through the next tunnel, which brought them into the Scandinavian-slash-Japanese oasis they'd seen glimpses of from the reception area. The stone path curved between the bubbling, steaming springs and chilly pools fed by waterfalls. Seating areas with lounge chairs, ground cushions, and tables with carafes of water dotted the luxurious landscape.

They didn't *quite* have the entire spa to themselves. A handful of other patrons were scattered among the pools and chairs. Those close enough to the changing room looked up at their emergence but just as soon returned to their relaxation.

"The best spot is this way," Belinda proclaimed. "Follow me."

She led them around several curves until they arrived at a secluded area tucked in the curve of another miniature mountain. The path bordered the hot spring, and a promontory of rock with a stream of cool water hid the cold pool. The adjoining seating area enjoyed full sun.

"Everyone like green tea?" Belinda inquired. "Excellent. I'll start us a pot."

She bustled around the water table and produced a tea set from the "wall" of the mountain in the same fashion as she'd opened the cubbies in the changing room. She filled the teapot from one of the water bottles and moved the bottles aside to make space for the round metal vessel, which she placed on the tabletop.

A press of a fingertip later, the circle underneath the teapot began to glow, and Belinda nodded in satisfaction. Then she joined the rest of them in the hot spring.

Elana sank in up to her chin and leaned back against the pool's rocky edge. The heat gradually seeped into her, and she closed her eyes and focused on releasing the tension in each limb in turn. When she reached her shoulders and neck, the spot of anxiety that had taken up permanent residence between her eyes eased, and she allowed a long sigh to escape her lips.

"I'm glad you came to this idea on your own," Cathy murmured beside her. "I was getting close to collaring you and sending you off to a yurt, based on the reports I've been getting. You haven't even been to *tea* lately."

Elana cringed. "Sorry, Cathy. I swear I'm trying."

"That's the problem, dear. You need to try a little *less*, in my humble and extremely experienced opinion."

Elana cracked an eye open and rolled her head to the side. "The hell does that mean? If you're suggesting I give up on fighting for human-vampire cooperation, there's no way that's happening."

Across the pool, Aimee groaned. *"Why are we talking about work."*

"Because some of us practice engaging with our stressors rather than turning invisible and avoiding them, dear," Cathy serenely replied.

"Fuck off, you old hag." Aimee's retort was rendered toothless by her amused smile.

Cathy chuckled and returned her attention to Elana. "I'm not at all suggesting you give up. What you're doing is vital and I wouldn't for a second dream of advising you to stop. What I *mean* is that it might behoove you to seek some balance."

Vicky snorted. "The day anyone gets Elana Bishop to ascribe to work-life balance is the day I eat my own hair."

"Oh, girl, don't do that," Belinda admonished her. "You have the healthiest hair I've ever seen. What do you use?"

"A bathroom full of products I've been gathering from around the world. Want a list?"

"Hell, yes. What would you say to doing some importing? There is a *sad* lack of Black hair care shops in Haven. I've been trying to do something about it for two decades but haven't gotten *any* traction. So many suppliers want nothing to do with me!"

Vicky grinned. "I can *for sure* help you there."

Aimee splashed grumpily. "You guys are *impossible*."

"You get bored when everyone's happy, Aimee," Elana pointed out. "If we were all calmly relaxing in the hot spring, *you'd* be doing the needling. We're *helping* you relax."

Aimee huffed. "Goddamn you and your insight."

"You're welcome." Elana turned to Cathy and put her elbow up on the rock to get a better angle. "Work-life balance is all well and good when the universe *lets* you. I feel like I've been running from crisis to crisis for a solid year. I did my best while the Zevenda complex was being built, but since then everything's been go, go, go."

Cathy shook her head. "If there's anything I've learned in my many years on this planet, it's that the moment we start waiting for the universe to do something, we've already given up. Approaching life passively is the first step toward becoming a leaf in the stream. The world needs all kinds, but you are not a leaf. When you believe you have no agency, you panic."

Elana thoughtfully narrowed her eyes. "I thought releasing control was a good thing. Being Zen and all that. I swear you've recommended that to me before."

"At times, yes. There is a difference between surrendering control over things you *cannot* control, and believing you have no agency whatsoever."

"God grant me the serenity to accept the things I cannot change, courage to change the things I can, and the wisdom to know the difference," Vicky interjected. "My grandma had that up on her wall all her life. Never been much for faith myself, but I always thought it was a good life motto."

Elana sank back into the hot water. "Fair enough. That lines up with a lot of what I was thinking last night. Freaking out about what I can't change, such as Zilmann taking the first opportunity to screw me over, means I'm distracted from what I *can* change. And you're right. I asked you all to join me today because I needed a break, and I knew I'd be way more likely to *take* that break if I did it with friends."

Cathy chuckled. "Mm-hmm. Otherwise, I daresay you'd be floating here with a head full of plans for how you'll take Zilmann down tomorrow."

"Oh, I'm still thinking about that," Elana admitted. "My first stop after lunch is the archives, and I am pulling out all the stops."

Aimee opened one eye from across the pool and glared at all of them. "All right, you four. If you don't all shut up about work, I will dump buckets of ice water on your heads. Take a hot minute, no pun intended, and *be present in the moment.* I swear to the Nexus, everything will still be here when you get back."

Cathy grinned. "Well, that's me told."

Elana elbowed her mentor under the water and chuckled. "Something something, practice what you preach?"

"Something like that."

CHAPTER TWENTY

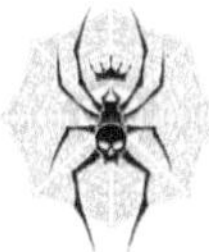

Elana woke the next morning with butterflies in her stomach, but they were born of anticipation rather than dread for the first time in weeks. She showered, styled her hair in her signature long waves, and dressed in her favorite taupe pantsuit. She accessorized with the fire opals she'd bought from Zizi for her first meeting in Haven and picked sensible wedge heels in dark brown leather.

When she looked in the mirror, she saw her mother. Her heart twinged, but her insight power rang with satisfaction. Elana had picked the hairstyle and outfit for this precise reason. Leaning into the physical resemblance between herself and her mother would, if she was lucky, rattle Zilmann's cage without Elana even trying.

Elana knew half of Zilmann's animosity toward her was born from her historical hatred of Tessa Hart. That hatred had been prompted by many of the aspects Tessa and Elana shared, the desire to bring humans and vampires closer together and an unwillingness to kowtow to tradition being the front-runners there.

While one would be excused for assuming that a woman seemingly fueled by spite would *thrive* on hatred, in reality, Carlysle Zilmann did her best work when she was calm and collected. When Zilmann knew she had the upper hand, she got shit done. When Zilmann was thrown off her game, the smallest mistake could set a snowball of errors in motion.

Elana had leftover bread pudding for breakfast and filled her favorite ironic *Twilight* travel mug with fresh coffee before applying makeup. She was midway through writing a note to Vicky when her best friend stumbled out of her bedroom with a wicked case of bedhead.

"Morning, sunshine."

Vicky regarded Elana with bleary eyes. "It is not even eight o'clock. How the hell are you up and looking like *that*?"

Elana chuckled. "Perks of being a sentinel, I guess? A morning of relaxation is enough to fuel an afternoon and evening of hard study, and I can still get up in the morning and look like a million bucks."

Vicky grumbled and shuffled toward the coffeemaker. "I felt great yesterday morning. This is unfair in the extreme. I'm lodging a complaint."

Elana put on a silly, overly pious voice and intoned, "The Nexus hears your cry, humble initiate, and bids you to *get good*."

Vicky snorted. "I'll get right on that. What time is your thing?"

"Hearing starts at ten."

"Damn. I'm meeting Gustav at nine. I'll try to make it.

Maybe I can get him to come with me. He doesn't like Arbiter Zilmann either."

"I appreciate the thought, but don't put yourself out. Your initiate training is important."

Vicky gave her a look. "So is my best friend's *world-changing work*. If I can be there, Lana, I will."

Elana paused, then smiled. "Thanks, Vick. That means a lot."

"Also, I want to be there when you kick her fucking ass."

Elana cackled. "God, I wish. It would be so satisfying to literally wipe the floor with her, but I suspect I'll have to content myself with a figurative and very polite tongue-lashing."

Vicky shrugged. "Just as effective and almost as satisfying. What do you want for victory dinner?"

"There's no guarantee I'll win."

"Again, I ask, what do you want for victory dinner?"

"A stack of pizzas as tall as me."

"Sold. Okay, get out of here. You're too put-together, and it's depressing. Let me be a slob in peace until I have to go get *my* ass kicked."

Elana laughed and grabbed her coat. "All right, all right. See you later. Good luck."

"You too."

Elana left Vicky pouring coffee and stepped out into the chilly morning. "God, I can't wait for spring," she muttered.

Although she drove to the Citadel in silence, her mind was abuzz. The night before, she'd gathered as much legal evidence as she could on illegal deportations in vampire city-states. She had discovered that most vampiric states functioned more like the House of Cardinals than as monarchies. In those cases, if one House had beef with another House, the threat of tossing them out of the "council" had weight. In Haven, the royal prerogative overrode any House's jurisdiction, hence Zilmann's petition.

Matt, wearing his lawyer's hat, had agreed with the tack Elana had chosen. Petitioning the Crown meant the plaintiff was asking the king for a favor. In this case, Zilmann was asking the king for a favor *against his own House.* The housing complexes belonged to the Crown since they were under Elana's jurisdiction and she was a member of the House of the SpiderKing.

"Asking kings to stop doing things that benefit them doesn't usually go well," Elana reminded herself. "And the SpiderKing *built* Haven to be a place where humans and vampires could live together. Her job is harder because she's asking him to go against his own House. My job is to remind everyone of who I am and how my goals align with the king's.

"*And* to hope the king still thinks his original goals are worthwhile," she muttered.

That part worried her the most. If the SpiderKing *really* wanted humans and vampires to live together, he'd certainly backed off on that front since the rebellion. He was a *king.* If he wanted something to happen, surely, he could make it happen. Why did he need people like Elana and Tessa to push a sociopolitical agenda that was already supposed to be a royal decree?

She let out a slow breath as she parked her Emeya outside the Citadel. She was early by an hour and a half, but she wanted time to review her notes before the hearing started. *Early is on time, on time is late,* her father had always said, and Elana had internalized it long ago.

Elana noticed the muffled yells of a crowd floating out from within the Citadel as she stepped out of her car and locked it. Normally, Haven's loudest streets were in Etreta during "rush hour" and at harvest time in Senkyem. The occasional festival brought people into the streets to be noisy and celebratory, but on the whole, Haven was a *calm* city. Vampires liked their peace and quiet.

"What the hell is going on?" Elana murmured. She headed for the entry tunnel, tuning her insight power to focus on the shouting. "What are they saying?"

The shouts were angry but not hectic. It didn't strike her as a mob. There were a *lot* of people yelling. Not even Elana's insight power could sort through the layers of sound effectively enough for her to pick out words.

She steeled herself, ready for anything, but her jaw dropped the moment she exited the tunnel.

Hundreds of people were crammed into the courtyard, waving handwritten signs and yelling toward the consulate. The signs read things like **Don't Make Us Leave Our Homes, Humans and Vampires Side by Side,** and Elana's favorite, **GTFO Zilmann This Is My House.**

Elana stopped cold and whispered, "What…the *fuck?*"

A woman nearby caught sight of her and shouted, "It's her! Elana's here!"

The news spread like wildfire, and cheering protestors surrounded Elana within moments. They bore her toward the consulate doors, but slowly, and she was bombarded by people shaking her hand and thanking her.

After the initial shock passed, Elana quickly began to recognize a great number of people in the crowd. Many were residents of her housing complexes from Haven and Ashford. They'd brought their friends and families, too. The Citadel's courtyard was so densely packed that even if the assembled *hadn't* all been trying to give Elana their best wishes, she would have had a difficult time making it through them to the consulate.

Elana pushed back against the tide of people when she caught sight of Lydia Westerland. She dug her heels in to keep from being pushed past the diminutive older woman. When those around her realized her intent, they nudged Elana closer to Lydia, and a protective circle formed around the two women.

Elana wasn't certain what they were protecting them *from*, but when a crowd decided you needed a shield, you didn't argue. Maybe they knew something she didn't. She hadn't seen any guardians around yet. Maybe there were veteran protestors in this crowd, and they were waiting for the hammer to come down.

Elana clasped Lydia's hands and bent to look her in the eye. "Lydia, what *happened*?"

The older woman looked as though she'd been crying. Her eyes were red-rimmed and puffy, and she gripped Elana's hands as though they were a lifeline. "I don't know. I don't *know*." Her voice was hoarse, more evidence she'd been crying. "Aaron and I had our differences, but he never acted like he did yesterday. I felt unsafe. I was terrified. He wasn't *himself*."

A rock formed in Elana's gut. "I'm so sorry, Lydia. Have the guardians spoken to you?"

"Yes, twice, for hours each time. The first time, they were short and sharp. The second time, they were much kinder. That's not usually how 'good cop, bad cop' goes."

Elana frowned. That concerned her almost as much as the report that Aaron Jones hadn't been himself. "Okay. Thank you for telling me."

Lydia brought a hand up to cup Elana's cheek. "You have to stop her, Elana. This isn't right. I won't face any consequences because of who and what I am, and that isn't right either. None of this is right. You're the first person who's tried to do anything since… Well, since your mother. You *have* to stop this."

Elana covered Lydia's hand with hers. "I'm working on it. I promise."

"I know you are, dear. When all of this is done… Please, if you can manage it diplomatically, I'd like to send reparations to his family. As I said, we had our differences, but this wasn't how I wanted his story to end. It's my fault he's dead, and that awful woman has already stampeded all over his rights. It's horrible."

Elana nodded. "I'll see to it. Thank you for standing up for him. Not many vampires would."

Lydia scowled. "I'm all too aware." She gestured at the crowd surrounding them. "But look at this, Elana. *Look.* This is all thanks to you! You're making progress. You're changing hearts and minds."

Lydia gripped Elana's upper arm. "We're closer than ever to a world where humans and vampires can live in harmony. Zilmann wants to destroy it. You *can't* let her. We want *peace.* You can't let her kick us out. These are our homes. We won't leave."

The protestors around Elana and Lydia took up the chant. "We won't leave! We won't leave!"

"How did all these people know to come today?" Elana asked. "I thought this was all being kept hush-hush!"

Lydia chuckled. "My dear, it is nearly impossible to keep a secret in this city, and we all know Arbiter Zilmann has it out for you and your projects. It didn't take us long to figure out that she would use the horrible accident between myself and Mr. Jones as an excuse to shut down your wonderful projects. We believe in you, Elana. Take that belief with you and go ruin her day."

Elana straightened and squared her shoulders. "I will. You have my word."

Lydia squeezed her arm one last time, then began chanting along with the crowd, which parted to allow Elana to pass.

Despite the boost from the supportive mob of protestors, Elana's heart weighed heavy as she approached the consulate's doors. Something was deeply amiss here. Lydia Westerland was still the kindly old lady she remembered, and Elana had a hard time believing that woman could have killed a man in cold blood for nothing more than "having their differences." Adding her insistence that Aaron hadn't been himself and *two* waves of guardians coming through for questioning...

This stinks. It reeks of a setup, and there are more than enough coincidences to make it seem extra *suspicious.*

Elana reached the doors and turned back to look over the crowd. As she did so, she spotted several guardians on the edges, dressed in their combat uniforms. She gulped as images of riot police coming down on protestors with pepper spray and rubber bullets flashed across her mind's eye, but her rational mind and insight power took over a moment later.

The guardians were calm, almost casual. They weren't concerned, and not because they didn't think the crowd could cause harm. The mob was comprised of at least as many vampires as humans. The guardians would likely win the day, but the vampires would fight hard.

Beside the humans. I don't think Zilmann saw this coming.

The protestors in front waved at Elana, then did fist pumps and raised their signs high. "Go get her, Elana!" someone yelled. "Tell her she'll have to carry us out herself!"

Elana couldn't have found the words to reassure them all in the short time she had. Instead, she raised a fist straight up, palm facing the crowd. Holding that position, which quite a few of the protestors quickly mimicked, she met as many of their eyes as possible. Then she pumped her fist once, turned, and entered the consulate.

The doors swung shut behind her and cut off all sound. Her ears rang as loud as the crowd's shouting in the sudden silence, and the atmosphere was as far removed from the incipient anger outside as you could get. In here, the prevailing mood was nervous and on edge. Everyone was hidden away in their offices and boardrooms, as usual, but the nanocyte "pheromones" were clear as day.

No wonder Michelle Ferns can track vampires. We reek.

Elana cracked her neck and headed for the stairs leading to the Tower of Legacy. Before her foot touched the first riser, a reedy tenor cleared his throat from elsewhere in the room.

She turned to see Consort Demoissac standing in the arch directly across from the main entrance. She wasn't pleased to see him, but she *was* glad that he looked and smelled as nervous as a teenager at junior prom.

"Can I help you, Consort?" she asked as serenely as possible. She'd discovered early on in her interactions with Raoul Demoissac that the calmer you were, the more flustered he got.

He cleared his throat again and straightened. "The Arbiter of Legacy courteously requests the presence of the Consort of External Affairs and Diplomacy in the second grand courtroom and presents her sincere apologies that the change in venue was not communicated with sufficient advance notice."

Elana's eyebrows rose almost to her hairline. "The *second grand courtroom?*"

"Yes, Consort." Another awkward throat-clearing.

She restrained the urge to roll her eyes. "Any particular reason *why*, Demoissac?"

He swallowed. "Given the wide public interest in the arbiter's petition and its inciting incident, Arbiter Zilmann deemed it beneficial to have the proceedings broadcast… live."

It took a single heartbeat for the implications to hit Elana like a freight train. Demoissac, and by extension his mistress, were extremely unhappy that Elana had showed up early enough to catch them out in their change of plans. *They're probably not very happy about the madding crowd outside, either.*

Elana expected rage to follow on the heels of understanding. Instead, a cool, icy calm flooded her. She returned her foot to the atrium floor from where it had been hovering over the first step up to the Tower of Legacy and stalked across the royal sigil toward the cowering man.

"In that case, I'm very glad you caught me in time. After all, it would be a *shame* if the primary defendant wasn't able to present the opposing side of such an important case on *live television,* wouldn't it?"

"Undoubtedly, Consort Bishop," Demoissac awkwardly muttered as she blew past him.

Elana briefly regretted her choice of heels. It would have been supremely satisfying to *clack* down the hall in stilettos. *Oh, well. I'll just have to be intimidating otherwise.*

She slammed open the doors of the second grand courtroom. The noise drew every eye to her, and there were quite a few more eyes present than she'd anticipated.

The protestors outside were *overflow.* The benches rising from the defendant's and prosecutor's benches in the center of the circular room were packed with people, many of whom were carrying and waving signs. They weren't shouting, however. Etiquette dictated that court proceedings were silent apart from those called upon to speak, and no one wanted to get kicked out by the stern guardians flanking every entrance.

The media filled the front rows. Camera and light drones floated over several journalists' shoulders. Nanodrones were not allowed in the courtroom. Every piece of recording equipment needed to be visible so the court authorities knew what was being recorded and those involved in the proceedings could be assured of a certain amount of privacy.

Their spotlights swiveled to follow Elana up the aisle.

She ignored them and sat at the defense's table, which was otherwise empty. Across the aisle, Arbiter Zilmann presided at the prosecutor's table. Raoul Demoissac scurried in behind Elana and sat beside his boss.

The other seven arbiters sat in a semicircle across the floor from the two tables, with Zilmann's seat conspicuously empty. While procedure allowed an arbiter to petition the SpiderKing, it didn't happen frequently. Typically, petitions came from civilians and were adjudicated by the arbiters.

Elana smiled brightly for the benefit of the cameras and to reassure those watching that she wasn't thrown by what was happening. Everyone out in the courtyard would have this up on their phones already. The entire city would tune in as soon as word spread, which wouldn't take long as the workday kicked into gear.

She idly wondered whether Vicky had turned on the TV over breakfast. If she had, she'd probably dropped her fork and was calling a taxi now.

Zilmann looked down her nose at Elana. "Good morning, Consort Bishop."

Elana beamed at Zilmann. "Good morning, Arbiter Zilmann. I'm glad Consort Demoissac caught me. I approve of your decision to publicize today's proceedings. They affect the entire population of Haven. Transparency is vital to healthy governance."

"Of course." Zilmann spoke through gritted teeth. Her normally frigid countenance was already cracking at the seams, and Elana hadn't even started arguing.

The Arbiter of Light, Annalisa DeMarco, tapped a small gavel to call the room to attention. "Glad you could make it, Consort Bishop. If there's nothing else, we'll begin."

Elana politely inclined her head to the arbiter, who was dressed in ceremonial robes unlike the others, indicating she was functioning as the head of the council in this proceeding. This made sense. The Domain of Light was traditionally seen as neutral, along with the Domain of Shadows. In this case, Valeria would recuse herself from the judge's position due to her close connection to Elana.

Another tap of the gavel. "Petitioner, state your case."

Zilmann rose to her feet. "I, Carlysle Zilmann, archon of House Vulicia and Arbiter of Legacy, petition the SpiderKing for the immediate removal of all human residents and guests of Haven. The current political situation is sufficiently tense that their lives, and ours, are endangered by their presence. It would be safer for everyone if Haven were to close its borders to all non-vampires until the situation is resolved."

DeMarco did not outwardly acknowledge Zilmann's statement. She shifted her gaze to Elana. "Consort Bishop, do you wish to counter the petitioner's statement?"

Elana stood. "I do, Arbiter."

"The floor is yours."

"Thank you, Arbiter. I'll keep this brief."

Elana kept her focus on DeMarco. Most petition hearings were small affairs, limited to the petitioner and anyone wishing to speak for or against the petition. Elana didn't have to convince a jury. She had to convince the arbiters.

"I respect Arbiter Zilmann's concern for the wellbeing of Haven's residents, human *and* vampire. I agree that the current political situation regarding human-vampire relations is fraught, but I disagree vehemently with her proposed solution. I believe humans and vampires will be *safer* if we present a united front against the external dangers that threaten us.

"Throwing every human out of Haven would mean rendering hundreds of people homeless in an afternoon. That would result in *more* resentment between our peoples, not less. This move will not be seen as an attempt to protect our human allies from the dangers that threaten both of us. It will be regarded as an isolationist policy enacted from a place of panic and insecurity at best or active anti-human sentiment at worst. It will not have the desired effect. Thank you."

She sat. Zilmann's simmering fury felt like a crackling campfire a few feet away. Elana kept her eyes on DeMarco, and her expression calm and pleasant. A camera drone whirred in a quiet arc in front of their tables, then disappeared off to the side.

DeMarco let Elana's and Zilmann's statements linger for several seconds, then returned to Zilmann. "Opening statements have been recorded. This council has received a written submission from the petitioner. Does the petitioner wish to add further comment?"

Zilmann regained a touch of her asperity as she replied, "No, Arbiter. I rest my case."

DeMarco nodded. "Consort Bishop, as the primary named interest in Arbiter Zilmann's petition, you have the right to present evidence countering the petition's claims. Do you wish to do so?"

Elana bit the inside of her lip to keep from scowling.

She had checked to see if Zilmann had submitted anything in writing before she turned in last night, and there had been nothing. She had *intended* to check again when she arrived, before the original hearing's scheduled start at 10:00. Something else Zilmann had snuck under her radar.

She didn't have time to read it now. Requesting a recess at this juncture would reflect badly on her. She would have to wing it.

"Yes, Arbiter," Elana replied.

"Go ahead."

Elana stood again. She drew a deep breath and let it out slowly. Unless Zilmann had thrown a curveball in the written submission, chances were good that she was complaining about everything Elana had researched yesterday. *I can do this.*

The camera drone bobbed at the edge of Elana's vision, and she noticed Zilmann drumming her fingers on the table at the same time.

You wanted to shove all of this under the rug. That gave her an idea.

Elana let her gaze wander over the line of arbiters, pausing briefly on each in turn. "I appreciate the opportunity to provide information to the honored representatives of His Majesty. First, let me state for the record that I have not had the opportunity to read Arbiter Zilmann's written submission. I rearranged my schedule yesterday to focus on the unfortunate incident the arbiter brought to my attention and the petition resulting from it.

"When I checked late last night, nothing had been filed on her behalf. Likewise, the changes in location and time were only communicated to me moments before I entered this hall.

"I do not say this to excuse any lack of readiness on my part. As you may have inferred, I spent yesterday preparing for this hearing, and I am confident that the information I have gathered will provide the council with important context.

"I say this to illustrate what I believe to be Arbiter Zilmann's ulterior motive in filing this petition, which is the indefinite and total elimination of humans from Haven. I highlight this because it shows that this petition runs counter to Haven's foundational values and those held by the SpiderKing himself.

"Haven was founded on the premise of human-vampire cooperation. While our history shows this goal is lofty in some respects, I believe it *also* shows that nowhere in the world have we come closer to *succeeding* in this goal. More-over, it ought to be all too clear to the council that we are closer than *ever* to succeeding in this goal *right now*. Affirming Arbiter Zilmann's petition would deal a serious blow to the progress we have made.

"The housing complexes I run are a prime example of that progress. With the application of careful discernment and wisdom, it is perfectly possible for humans and vampires to live side by side and even to learn from each other. These growing communities are thriving. Their residents are proud of their dual affiliation and their place on the front edge of progress."

Elana gestured at the courtroom at large without moving her visual focus from the arbiters. "You can see in this room how many people are in favor of safeguarding these bastions of human-vampire cooperation. Hundreds more supporters are just outside this building, loudly proclaiming their support for my endeavors *and* Haven's core values. Among them is *Lydia Westerland,* whose name I trust you are all familiar with.

"Lydia herself spoke with me before I entered the consulate this morning. She begged me not to allow Haven to deport its human citizens. She regrets her involvement in the actions that precipitated this petition. She is suspicious of what caused them because up until yesterday's tragic events, she and Mr. Jones were on perfectly civil terms.

"But, *unlike* Arbiter Zilmann, Ms. Westerland is not calling for the expulsion of humans. She does not believe that reaffirming segregation of our peoples will solve the problem. She believes, as do I, that the way through these uncertain times is *forward,* and more specifically, *together.*"

Again, Elana made eye contact with each of the arbiters. Beside her, Zilmann's campfire of rage was coalescing to a laser point of fury. "When was the last time you saw this many people, *human and vampire alike,* this passionate about an issue of policy—and *overwhelmingly* agreeing with each other? I can't think of a single example unless you count the times when we're at each other's throats, and that's not so much *agreeing* as equally despising.

"We have an opportunity to usher in a new age of vampire-human cooperation," Elana stated as firmly as possible. "Haven has been at the vanguard of vampire progress since its inception, thanks to the wisdom and power of our monarch. The rest of the world is catching up. It's time to find another front, a new place to lead the way.

"Today, I believe we can finally build the society that His Majesty dreamed of two centuries ago. Look around! We're already doing it! You can't deny what's right in front of you!"

She put her hands on the table and leaned forward. "Don't let the fear of change scare you away from the potential of diversity. Haven can become the sanctuary of knowledge and vision it was always meant to be—a place where light and shadows meet and create a legacy of progress and creation."

Elana held DeMarco's gaze steady for another heartbeat, then relaxed her shoulders, took her hands off the table, and bowed. "Thank you for your consideration, esteemed arbiters."

As she sat, she kept her smile tiny. The atmosphere had gradually shifted from anxiety to excitement while she spoke. She felt like a rock star on a stage or a sergeant inspiring her troops...and the irate frustration emanating from Zilmann was the cherry on top.

DeMarco inclined her head in return. "Thank you, Consort Bishop. Arbiter Zilmann? Do you have anything to add?"

Zilmann pressed her fingertips against the tabletop so fiercely that they turned white. *She's feeling desperate. Desperate and helpless. My, how the tables have turned.*

The Arbiter of Legacy took her sweet time but finally ground out a negative. DeMarco nodded. "Then today's proceedings are complete. The council will deliberate and deliver judgment within one week."

"One *week?*" Zilmann exclaimed. "But it's *imperative* that—"

DeMarco cut her off. "You know the procedures as well as the rest of us, Carlysle. Better, even. One week. No exceptions." She tapped the gavel. "This meeting is adjourned."

Elana politely waited until Arbiter Zilmann had stormed off before casually rising from her chair as though she were completely unconcerned. In reality, her heart was beating a mile a minute with elation. That was as thorough an ass-kicking as she could have hoped for, and it had been *broadcast live.* Zilmann's attempt to screw Elana over had backfired spectacularly.

She caught plenty of grins and fist pumps from the assembled crowd on her way out. Their enthusiasm lightened her step further. She couldn't wait to celebrate with Vicky.

Elana put on her sweetest smile to greet Zilmann and Demoissac in the consulate's atrium, then breezed past them to the exit. The roar of the crowd that met her nearly knocked her back a step, but it made her grin spread from ear to ear.

The moment was shattered by sudden shrieks, which heralded a body plummeting out of the sky and smashing onto the courtyard's stones.

CHAPTER TWENTY-ONE

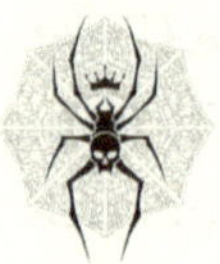

Elana dashed forward, and the nearest guardians rushed to join her. "Everybody back!" one man yelled, but the protestors were already instinctively surging away from the body.

Elana's heart dropped out of her chest the moment she laid eyes on the corpse. Ginevra Leone lay on the cobblestones with her limbs splayed at awkward angles. A breathy *"No,"* wrenched itself from Elana's lips unbidden. *No, no, no.*

Elana skidded to a stop on her knees next to Ginevra and frantically felt for a pulse. She had no idea how far Ginevra had fallen, but humans had an uncanny ability to survive situations that should have killed them immediately. Elana wouldn't give up on the woman until she had no choice.

"She's alive!" she shouted. "Someone call a healer—*shit!*"

Ginevra had gripped Elana's wrist with enough force that it hurt. Startled, Elana tried to pull back, but Ginevra held fast.

Ginevra rolled her head to the side to reveal a shattered nose and blood pouring from her mouth. A hoarse moan escaped the broken woman, and she hauled her other arm around to reach for Elana. Her gaze locked on Elana's, but it held no presence of mind.

Elana instantly recognized the blank look. "Oh, *fuck.*"

"Consort Bishop!" That was one of the guardians, a woman, just outside her range of vision. "Do you have the situation in hand?"

Elana's mind raced. Clarissa had almost killed her, but Ginevra's body was already shattered and non-functional. Plus, Elana had risen a level in the Nexus since, and her sentinel powers were impressive. The balance was tipped in Elana's favor this time.

She held up a hand to the guardian and fended off Ginevra's broken arm. "I don't want to kill you, Ginevra," she pleaded. "You're only hurting yourself more. Please stop so we can help you. Can you hear me?"

Ginevra growled, dripping blood all over Elana's front. Then she dug her nails into Elana's wrist and aimed her free hand at Elana's face again.

Elana winced and blocked the swipe. "*Ginevra, stop. Where is your father? Dov'è il papa?*" Elana's Italian was terrible, but maybe she could get the message across.

This time, the sound that came out of Ginevra's mouth was less of a growl and more of an inhuman shriek. She followed it up with a lunge, snapping her bloody teeth and lack thereof—she'd lost a few on impact—in Elana's face.

Elana attempted to scramble backward by shoving her heels into the stone and pushing, but she only brought Ginevra with her. The woman had a vise grip on her wrist.

Elana forced Ginevra's face away from hers while doing her best to keep her hand out of her bloody maw. Ginevra gnashed her teeth, screeched, and struggled.

Elana grimaced. "I do not want to do this, Ginevra, but you're not giving me any choice!"

The warning did not provoke any kind of coherent or rational reaction. The human refugee continued doing her level best to strangle Elana or bite her face off despite the multiple broken limbs and rapid loss of blood.

Elana yelled as loud as she could, hoping to be heard over Ginevra's unearthly cries. "*Can someone try to sedate her, please?*"

"We've tried!" The answering yell came from nearby. "We've hit her with a dozen tranquilizer darts already!"

Elana craned her head around and spied the handfuls of tiny darts peppering the woman's body. That much sedative could have knocked out an elephant or an archon. Ginevra should have been dead three times over at this point.

Elana drew one more deep breath and shouted over the din again. "I want it on record that this is *not* my preferred method of conflict resolution and that I am acting in self-defense!" She felt utterly ridiculous saying this out loud, but Zilmann had to be behind her in the crowd somewhere. Elana had no intention of losing any of the momentum she'd gained in the courtroom.

Elana waited three heartbeats longer in the vain hope that Ginevra would collapse. Then, with tears in her eyes from pain and sorrow, Elana forced her imprisoned hand up to join the one already on Ginevra's head. With a quick jerk, she snapped the other woman's neck.

Elana felt more than heard the ripple of shock go through the crowd. Even with her neck broken, Ginevra was slow to die. However, her grip on Elana's hand slackened as the nerve impulses halted, so Elana could move her to a supine position on the stones. Her rattling breaths ceased far too slowly, interspersed as they were between the rasping, grating cries.

"I'm so sorry," Elana whispered to the dying woman. "I am so, so sorry. This shouldn't have happened to you, and I swear I will bring the one who did it to justice."

No recognition lit in Ginevra's eyes at Elana's words, only animalistic rage. By the time Elana finished speaking, even that was gone. Ginevra's glassy gaze stared over Elana's shoulder while Elana gingerly brought the Italian woman's broken limbs into more natural placements.

You could have heard a pin drop in the Citadel's courtyard. Everyone close enough to see was staring at Elana and Ginevra, and word had spread to the crowd's edges. The guardians kept everyone well back from the grisly scene, but it wasn't a difficult job. No one wanted to come closer anyway.

Elana gently closed Ginevra's eyes, then rested beside the corpse. She looked around the circle and realized the journalists had followed her out. The camera drone she'd gotten familiar with hovered about two arm's lengths away.

Elana's first reaction was horror. She would have been willing to bet that drone had dogged her heels from the courtroom. Ginevra's fall, attack, and demise had been broadcast to the entire city and likely beyond. *Elana Bishop, murderer,* the headlines would say.

Unless Elana flipped the script.

Elana drew a deep breath. *Thank God vampires love a dramatic pause.* She looked straight into the camera drone's lens and spoke.

"I have just been attacked by a woman who came to Haven seeking asylum from people who wanted to harm the entire world as much as they wanted to hurt her. We'll have to wait for a healer to examine her body, but judging by the attack's ferocity and the complete lack of sanity I and everyone here witnessed… This woman was under the influence of a dangerous substance that is a threat to both humans and vampires."

Murmurs with a distinct tinge of panic broke out in the crowd. Elana bit the inside of her lip and quickly changed tack, hoping against hope that she wasn't about to incite mass hysteria after fighting for calm and unity inside the consulate.

"This woman was in protective custody," Elana continued. "As far as I am aware, the substance is not easily communicable. I do not believe that I, or anyone in this courtyard, is at immediate risk of contracting whatever drove this woman to commit these acts.

"However, I urge everyone hearing this to exercise caution. Don't eat or drink anything given to you by someone you do not trust. Same with medicines. Please, be careful.

"I recognize that this incident, especially when taken in the context of recent events, is concerning. I also recognize that this is an understatement." Elana chanced a mildly amused smile and was gratified to feel the mood lighten a touch. "I promise that the arbiters and the guardians who act on their behalf have everything under control. These are uncertain times to be sure, but that means we have to band together even more tightly.

"Whoever is committing these atrocities is counting on us to turn *against* each other. They want us to be suspicious. They want us to mistrust each other. That's how they make us victims, and that's how they *find* their victims—by isolating us, by convincing us we're not safe.

"*Fight back.* Watch out for your neighbors, whether they're vampire or human. The SpiderKing built this city on a promise of unity, and unity is the most powerful asset we have. Don't let these fearmongers take that away from you."

Elana reached down until she felt Ginevra's arm under her hand while keeping her gaze on the camera. "As your Consort for External Affairs and Diplomacy, I promise you that I will continue to do everything in my power to ensure safety and security in all business between humans and vampires. I will continue to work with the healers in the Domain of Sanctuary and the guardians in the Domain of Shadows to understand what has happened here and what is happening to our city. I will update you later today with whatever we have found.

"Until then, again, I ask you to stay safe and remain calm. There is no immediate threat to the city or its people. If one becomes apparent, we will inform you. As my sponsor would say, don't borrow trouble. You have enough already."

She gave the camera a warm and genuine smile, then deliberately turned away to locate a guardian. "Do we have an ETA on paramedics or healers?"

The nearest guardian, a corporal judging by the insignia on her sleeve, saluted sharply. "Inbound in sixty seconds, ma'am."

"Good. I'll stay with her until they're here. Can you please direct the crowd to clear a path? *Nicely?*"

The corner of the guardian's lips twitched toward a smile, but she maintained her professional composure. "Yes, ma'am!" She pivoted sharply to her comrades and barked, "Guardians, fall in! Assembled citizens, please proceed in an orderly fashion to the nearest Citadel exit tunnel, *with the exception* of the Inner Gate of Protection! A guardian will take your contact information as you depart for the purposes of potential questioning in regard to the events you have just witnessed! Any complaints may be directed to the Domain of Shadows!"

Elana tuned the orders out. Her attention was back on Ginevra's still face, covered in quickly coagulating blood.

"You didn't deserve this," she whispered. "I am so sorry we didn't protect you."

The hustle of boots coming toward her instead of away prompted Elana to back up to allow the paramedics access. She refused a towel for the blood that spattered her pantsuit, then watched in silence as they took Ginevra's vitals or lack thereof.

The camera drone continued to hover a respectful distance away. Its owner, a lone journalist, lingered at the courtyard's edge with a guardian escort. Elana both approved and disapproved of their presence. She wanted to give Ginevra the respect of privacy, but she also believed it was important for the city to see that Elana wasn't hiding or panicking.

She wanted to pinch the bridge of her nose, but she would get blood in her eyes. *The razor's edge we've been dancing on just became even thinner. This was the last thing we needed.*

After confirming Ginevra's death, the paramedics carefully transferred her to a stretcher for transport. The head paramedic, a clean-cut fellow with broad shoulders and a round face, directed the others to bring Ginevra to the ambulance, then approached Elana. "Looks like a clean break, ma'am. Best you could have done under the circumstances, from what I saw on the feeds before we got here."

Elana grimaced. "I just wish it hadn't been necessary. Will you be taking her straight in for an autopsy?"

He nodded. "Already got word from up high. She's top priority. The brass want to know whether she's dangerous. We'll do the autopsy in an isolation ward, just in case, and a hazmat cleanup crew is on its way along with the CSI squad."

"Any chance I can follow you back to the med center?"

"I was about to ask if you'd be willing since you, well..." He gestured at her clothes. "You should probably get checked out."

"Right. Of course. Lead the way."

Isolation wards were the most boring places on Earth. Elana would swear to it.

She sat, alternately tapping her fingers on her thigh and her feet on the floor, in a small, hermetically sealed hospital room. The tiny room had no bed, only a hard chair, an examination table, and a locked cabinet. The air smelled sterile in the way of too many chemicals. It tickled the inside of her nose.

The decontamination measures in the room were intense. The room had no windows, but it *did* have calibrated UV lights on the ceiling. Elana had never been so grateful that she wasn't sensitive to UV rays. Everything could be irradiated without undue damage, and four shower heads on swivels poked out of the ceiling to spray the room with more disinfectant. The floor sloped ever-so-slightly to a drain in the center.

Before entering the room, Elana had stripped and gone through a disinfectant shower that reminded her of a car wash. She received a hospital gown, underwear, and socks to wear while they cleaned her clothes. She felt like a test subject in a creepy TV show.

She couldn't deny that this was the best way forward. If House Veridian had figured out how to make the killer virus transferable through any means other than direct injection, Elana was at the most risk of contracting it after Ginevra's attack and death. The blood and saliva samples the healers had taken before her shower would tell them whether she was a danger. From that, they could extrapolate whether the courtyard full of protestors were at risk.

Elana had flip-flopped on this more times than she could count. If she had released hundreds of potential virus carriers into Haven, she would hate herself for the rest of her possibly short life...but Ginevra had only been in the courtyard for five minutes, *maximum*. The likelihood of transmission in that short a time would indicate a *huge* jump in transmissibility for the virus. Surely, keeping the protestors cooped up in the courtyard would have been *more* dangerous.

Elana was about to start counting the tiny spigots on the shower heads when the pressure seal on the door hissed. She straightened as the head paramedic from the scene entered.

"You're not wearing quarantine gear," she noted. "Can I take that as a good sign?"

He smiled. "You sure can. You're clear, and so is everyone who handled Ms. Leone. No sign of infection in anyone's blood or saliva."

"Don't we need to stay isolated until we can confirm the virus hasn't incubated?"

"Based on what Arbiter Tarsin's discovered about this virus, we don't believe so. According to her, the synthetic nanocytes don't appear to be able to transfer without direct consumption. We were most worried about you since Ms. Leone's blood covered you, but we didn't detect a single abnormal nanocyte in your samples. We might have had a problem if any of her blood had touched, say, an open wound or if you'd gotten any on a mucous membrane, but you didn't. That means everyone in the courtyard is also safe."

Elana allowed herself one long sigh of relief. "Thank God." She sat up again and crossed her arms. "It's confirmed to be the synthetic nanocytes, then."

"Correct. Or—to be more specific, it's a synthetic nano-mRNA that rapidly overwrites a number of common protein synthesis pathways. The nanoproteins it creates overrun the system in record time, based on our simulations."

"In other words, if any of us *were* infected, we'd probably already know."

"You'd likely be climbing the walls or trying to strangle me, so yes."

Elana shuddered. "God, that's horrible. Do you know if anyone's informed Ginevra's father yet?"

He shook his head. "Not my department, but you're free to go. Your clothes have been disinfected and cleaned, and they're waiting for you just outside." He turned to go but paused with his hand on the door. "Miss Bishop...good news aside, I have a feeling things are gonna get worse before they get better."

"You're not the only one." Her insight power had been warring with the scent of disinfectant for the title of Who Can Make Elana More Nauseated for the last hour.

"Good luck."

"Thanks."

CHAPTER TWENTY-TWO

Elana changed back into her pantsuit, which smelled unsettlingly of disinfectant. She supposed it was better than smelling like blood. She retrieved her phone from her handbag, which she had also surrendered to be cleaned, and called Vicky on her way out of the medical center.

Vicky answered before the first ring finished. "Oh, my God, are you *okay?*"

"I'm fine. Not dying, anyway. I'm mad as hell, though."

"No shit. What happened?"

"Wish I knew. How much did you see?"

"All of it." Vicky's initial panic was fading to disgust. "Gustav messaged, saying to skip our session and turn on the TV, so I caught the broadcast from the courtroom just as you walked in. Fuck Zilmann and the horse she rode in on."

"His name's Demoissac, and he's about as skittish as a horse," Elana deadpanned. "How bad did the attack look?"

"It was horrific, but I assume you're asking whether it looked like you murdered that poor woman in cold blood."

"Yeah."

"It didn't. The camera was following you out, so it caught her falling and you running to help. She lunged at you, plain as day. The paramedics tried to sedate her, but she wouldn't give up. The journalist was muttering the whole time about the reports of the same thing happening to other people and mostly trying to kill you. She sounded like she was trying to keep herself from freaking out."

"She wasn't the only one," Elana replied. "What's coverage been like for the last hour? I've been getting checked out and didn't have my phone on me."

"I hoped that was what was happening. Coverage is wall-to-wall. Arbiter Draven has ordered a lockdown and extra security on all dispensaries inside the city, and nobody is allowed past the Wall at the moment, in *or* out. Complete stop on all traffic."

Elana hissed through her teeth. "What's the official word on what's happening, and what's the reaction like?"

"The official word, which is coming down from Arbiter Gow, is that Ginevra was infected with a variant of a virus that is transmissible between vampires and humans. So far, the only known vector is direct blood exchange, but they're locking down the city as a precaution because of reports that it can spread quickly."

Vicky huffed. "Also, before I go on, can I just say I really don't like Arbiter Gow?"

Elana closed the door of her Emeya, which Matt had graciously arranged to have dropped off at the medical center for her, and laughed. "You're not the only one. Why don't you like her?"

"She gives me 'overprotective kindergarten teacher with a mean streak' vibes."

"Descriptive."

"Thanks. Anyway, the reaction is about what you'd expect. People aren't happy about their business being interrupted indefinitely. Haven News Network is showing footage of growing protests at several gates, but the guardians aren't moving."

Elana bit her lip and checked for traffic before turning toward the Citadel. She'd been taken to a research medical center in Quarto—the safest location when it came to biohazards in Haven. "Any anti-human sentiment?"

"Not yet. Arbiter Gow was noticeably tight-lipped on the subject, but a report from Mr. Sexy Voice emphasized that all current evidence shows this virus is of vampire make. He talked a lot about how it's most likely connected to the House Veridian and East Coast Staker stuff, which the guardians know is masterminded by a vampire."

"Huh. That's more open than I thought they'd be."

"Isn't that a good thing?"

Elana progressed from biting her lip to gnawing on it. "I don't know. We'd been keeping that under wraps as much as possible to avoid the Staker finding out how close we were to tracking them down. Going public, we lose that advantage."

"But you might put them on the back foot."

"Doubtful. Infecting Ginevra means they're here in Haven or have a lackey ready to do their bidding within city limits. We are very much in a race against time now, and I would be lying if I said that didn't fucking terrify me.

"We don't have anything to protect against this, Vick. If

you're infected with this virus, you're as good as dead. If I were you, I wouldn't just stay inside. I'd head for the basement and pretend the house is empty."

Vicky was silent on the other end of the line for a long moment. When she responded, she was solemn and quiet. "You think I'm a target."

"I think it's very possible. Every time these mindless monsters have attacked so far, their entire focus has been killing me—and two times out of three, the Staker has chosen to infect people they knew I'd care about. I need you to take care of yourself."

Vicky drew a shaky breath, then laughed nervously. "I did say this was why I wanted to become a vampire. I kind of hoped it would be less *immediately necessary*."

"Amen. For what it's worth, two of the three assassins were human first. You might be a less likely target now that you're a vampire."

"But there's no telling, is there?"

Elana sighed. "No. Listen, I gotta go. I need to make sure Ginevra's dad is as okay as he can be. Then I need to find Valeria and figure out what I can do to help. Do you have everything you need?"

"Yeah, I'm set. I'm locking the doors and going downstairs. I'll let you know if anything happens on the news, okay?"

"Thank you. I really appreciate that, Vick. Stay safe."

"You too."

"The universe thinks that's a funny joke. Talk to you later."

Elana hung up at the same time as she pulled into the same parking spot she'd used that morning. She locked the car behind her with a wave, already jogging toward the Inner Gate of Secrets.

She crossed the deserted courtyard at a jog. Not even Sarah Goldin was present in her usual position at the Rebels' Memorial. The sand slipped through the giant hourglass unwatched.

The consulate was under full guard, as were most of the entrances ringing the empty plaza. Elana had to stop and submit to a biometrics check before she was allowed entry to the consulate. Impatience nagged at her, but she swallowed it down. If they'd had a checkpoint on the consulate before today, they might have caught whoever snuck in to infect Ginevra.

She took the stairs of the Tower of Shadows three at a time and reached the Leones' suite in minutes. Guardians also flanked this door. They double-checked her fingerprint and logged her arrival with a dot of blood before opening the door.

Elana found Matt inside, sitting in an armchair with a cup of tea cooling on the end table. Beside him on the couch, Francesco Leone sat with his head in his hands and another cup of tea on the coffee table in front of him. The mood was heavy, and the room was silent apart from the flapping of the curtain tacked over the open window that faced into the courtyard below.

"Can I come in?" Elana quietly asked Matt. "I can come back later..."

Matt shook his head and gestured at the other armchair. "Come in. I'm sitting with Francesco while I wait for updates. I figured he shouldn't be alone."

Elana took the indicated seat. "My thoughts exactly.

That's why I'm here." She leaned forward. "I'm so sorry, Francesco."

Francesco only nodded absently without raising his head from the cover of his hands. She couldn't blame him. Judging by the overturned furniture near the curtained window, there had been a struggle before Ginevra threw herself out into the courtyard. Elana couldn't imagine how horrified and heartbroken Francesco had to be.

Elana glanced at Matt. "Do we know anything more about what happened? I trust this room has a security camera, at least in this area."

"It does, and we requisitioned it the moment we knew what was happening. It doesn't tell us much. Arbiter Tarsin was having tea with them when it happened. Ginevra was opening up about life as a servant in Il Giardino, telling Tarsin about customs no one outside the enclave has witnessed or even heard of."

"She was getting better," Francesco whispered. "She had life."

Matt closed his eyes briefly and grimaced, then continued. "It came out of nowhere. Tarsin was still here. In the footage, Ginevra gets this weird look on her face, then smashes her teacup on the floor and tries to leap over the back of the couch.

"Francesco fought her—just trying to get her to calm down, really—but she threw him across the room like he was a ragdoll. Then she went for the window. He tried to stop her, and so did Tarsin, but she was stronger and faster than almost any vampire I've ever seen. She'd have given Valeria a run for her money.

"She threw herself out the window without hesitation.

It didn't seem like she wanted to kill herself. There was no desperation, not even anger, not then. It felt more like they were getting between her and a job she had to do."

Elana gripped her hands to keep them from shaking. "Seemed like that job was killing me."

"Seems like it, yes."

"Does Tarsin have any ideas?"

Matt sighed and leaned back in his chair. "Yes and no. She came by about an hour ago. Said she was stopping in to update me on security matters before she disappeared into her lab to put her nose to the grindstone."

He chuckled dryly. "She tries so hard to make sure people know she cares about the fact that this is a *really bad situation*, but I've worked with her long enough to know her primary motivator is figuring shit out. She's a scientist at heart. The gleam in her eyes is unmistakable."

Elana nodded. "And? What did she say?"

Any trace of levity vanished. "That her data suggested the virus could act like an 'extended release' pathogen more than we initially thought. There might be an incubation period before symptoms begin to show, or it could be dormant until triggered…and no, she didn't know what the trigger might be. Her guesses were stress and blood."

Elana's heart skipped a beat. "So, anyone could be infected, and we wouldn't know until it was too late."

"On the outside, yes. It's still likely that we'd find traces of the virus in a person's system, even if they're asymptomatic. The virus multiplies quickly but doesn't appear to act on the victim until certain conditions are met."

Matt gestured at Francesco, who hadn't reacted during Matt's explanation beyond a quiet, sad groan when he'd mentioned Ginevra going out the window. "Francesco's been tested. He shows no sign of the virus."

Elana's frown deepened. "Are we testing all the blood in the dispensaries?"

"We are," Matt confirmed. "It's a huge undertaking, and the Office of Nurture isn't happy about the expenditure of its workforce, but DeMarco authorized emergency overtime across the board. Haven hasn't seen a mobilization like this since the Rebellion. Everyone's on edge."

"And rightfully so," Elana murmured.

Her phone buzzed. She fished it out of her handbag. Upon reading the screen, she was grateful to be sitting down because the wave of shock that went through her would have sent her to the floor otherwise.

Matt was on his feet in a flash. "You just turned pale as a ghost. What's wrong?"

Elana's voice was barely louder than a breath. "Cassandra remembered."

"Remembered—Oh, *shit*." Matt waved Elana toward the door. "Go, *go*. I've got the fort here. I'll call you if I need you. *Go*."

Elana was already out the door and running. Cassandra's memory returning was the boon they desperately needed to turn this situation around.

Please, let me get lucky, Elana begged the universe. *Let us have locked down early enough. Let them still be here. Let me put a bullet through their fucking skull for all the pain they've caused. Please, please, please.*

She hurtled through the corridors toward Cassandra's room. Upon turning the corner, she applied the brakes so fast she nearly fell over. Multiple ranks of guardians stood between Elana and the door, standing shoulder to shoulder in full armor. If she stood on tiptoe, she could see mirroring rows of troops on the other side of the door.

"What...the *fuck*?" she muttered. *Who the hell could Cassandra have remembered to warrant this much protection? And how did it get here so fast?*

That question was answered by the emergence of a vision in white from the orderly lines of black and green. Valeria looked especially murderous, given the addition of a black rose pin on the lapel of the pristine white jacket she'd been wearing at the courtroom only a couple of hours before.

Elana automatically dropped into a bow as Valeria approached. *Crisis situations benefit from the application of protocol,* she heard Valeria remind her in her head. "Arbiter."

Valeria nodded sharply. "Consort. With me."

The Arbiter of Shadows turned on her heel, and the Consort of External Affairs and Diplomacy followed in her wake as she threaded between the guardians.

The moment before Valeria opened the door, Elana caught her elbow and leaned in to whisper in her ear. "In one word, how fucked are we?"

Valeria glanced over her shoulder. "Fucked."

Elana swallowed hard and stepped back to trail Valeria into the room. Inside, Cassandra was sitting up in her bed, legs crossed, with Jack ensconced in the chair beside her as usual. The young woman's face was dark, while her father seemed stunned. He gripped the arms of his chair with the strength of a man holding onto a life preserver.

Valeria closed the door behind Elana and laid a palm on

the frame. A soft blue glow shot around the door and faded. "Tell her what you told me."

Cassandra rolled her shoulders back to straighten, set her jaw, and looked Elana square in the eyes. "The East Coast Staker is Ahura Tarsin."

Elana stuck a hand out to steady herself on the wall as her knees went weak. "No way."

"Yes, way," Cassandra replied with a wan, unamused smile. "She wore a different face, but her voice was the same, and she had on a necklace she wore when she came to visit me today. I thought it looked familiar, so I tried to fit it into my memories after she left like the healers taught me, and the memory came back in full."

Elana thought back to the courtroom. She hadn't paid much attention to the other arbiters. Valeria's addition of the black pin only stood out to her now because when Valeria wore anything black, it was a very bad sign. "Could it be possible that it was the same necklace, but someone else wearing it?"

"No." Valeria's response was firm. "The necklace in question is an heirloom of House Eira, rooted in its post-colonial history on this continent. It has ritual significance, and Ahura only wears it on certain days as a result. Today is one such day. The day in 1990 when Miss Rhuland disappeared was also one such day."

"And no one else in House Eira wears the same necklace?"

"That particular piece of House-keeping is Ahura's charge. I would consider it the remotest of possibilities that someone other than Ahura Tarsin wore that necklace in August of 1990. That turning out to be the case would be a huge stroke of luck on our part since House Eira defends its rituals with extreme prejudice, but…"

"It's not likely," Elana finished.

"No. Especially since I have not been able to contact Ahura after being informed of this."

Elana frowned. "What's the timeline on that? Matt said she stopped by to see him about an hour ago."

"Cassandra called me through the guardians half an hour ago," Valeria replied.

"I had to think about it first," Cassandra explained. "I didn't want to chance being wrong."

"Naturally, I attempted to contact Ahura immediately," Valeria continued. "It was easy to do so in a way that wouldn't arouse suspicion because, well." She gestured toward the window with a sour expression. "She didn't answer. I tried her secretary, and she told me that Ahura had indicated she would be in her private lab if anyone needed her.

"I asked her to go and tell her I needed to speak with her urgently. Five minutes later, the secretary called me back and informed me that Ahura was nowhere to be found and the lab had been cleared out."

Elana's last candle flame of hope that this was somehow a misunderstanding guttered, then went out. "Oh, no."

"Yes."

"The city's locked down. She has to be here somewhere."

Valeria's expression darkened. "I can confirm that she is not. After the secretary called me back, I contacted all the guardians covering the entrances to the city. One of the covert posts did not report in. I sent reinforcements to investigate, and just before you arrived, I received word that five of the six guardians had been slaughtered."

"And the sixth?"

"Attacked the reinforcements with single-minded fervor until they were forced to behead the poor man."

Elana took a step back and leaned against the wall. "Holy shit. Holy *shit*. You weren't kidding. We're fucked. She's been playing us the whole damn time!"

"Indeed, she has."

"What do we do?"

"First, we move Cassandra and her father to the safest location in Haven. You, too."

Elana stared. "How can there *be* a safe place? Tarsin's the Arbiter of Knowledge—she knows *everything!*"

Valeria's upper lip curled. "She'd like to *think* she does. Some secrets remain solely the domain of the Arbiter of Shadows. If I discover she has gained access to *those* secrets, I swear by my blood and my allegiance to my king that I will end her *painfully.*"

"You mean that isn't already the plan?"

Valeria barked a dry, humorless laugh. "At the moment, I'm just planning to *end* her."

"Oh, so it's the difference between a clean kill and making her rue the day she was born."

"Essentially. I'm not known for mercy."

"That's an understatement." Elana drew a deep, steadying breath and rubbed her temples. "Okay. I'm gonna go get Vicky. Where are we hiding?"

"If your insight power doesn't tell you your house is unsafe, stay there until I tell you otherwise. I need to verify the security of our safe houses before sending anyone anywhere." Valeria gritted her teeth. "This *epiphany* puts a lot of concerning details into a *very* enlightening context."

Elana grumbled, "Yeah, a bunch of stuff makes a lot more sense now, and I hate it all."

"You and me both."

Elana glanced at Cassandra, then flicked her gaze to Jack. "You two gonna be okay in here?"

Cassandra gave her a wan smile. "I'd feel much *less* safe if we didn't have the obvious path Tarsin took to leave. If she's gone, we're probably okay. My bet is that she realized I would remember when she noticed me staring at her necklace. I said it was very pretty because I hadn't realized the connection. By the time I did, the damage was done."

"Not your fault, my girl." Jack's voice was strong, and so was his hand on Cassandra's forearm. "You couldn't have known, and that was her fault to begin with. Stupid move on her part, if you ask me. Arrogant."

"*Mm.* I agree with you." Valeria crossed her arms. "That *was* arrogant of Ahura. And surprising, if you ask me. She's always been a little full of herself. Comes with the territory of being an arbiter in altogether too many cases. But for her to slip up like that after maintaining this level of deception for so long…"

The Arbiter of Shadows clicked her tongue. "I think you've hit it on the head, Jack. That's how we'll catch her."

"Catching an arbiter," Elana echoed and shook her head. "Has this ever happened before?"

"That an arbiter has so thoroughly and obviously deceived and betrayed the SpiderKing? It has not," Valeria replied. "His Majesty won't be pleased. *That'll* be a fun conversation, but there's no point putting it off."

"That's where you're headed next?"

"Yes."

Elana grimaced. "Want backup?"

Valeria chuckled. "I appreciate the offer, but you are *not* cleared to speak with him yet."

"Fair enough. Well, you know where to find me if that changes."

Valeria smirked. "Oh, yes. All I have to do is look for the chaos."

"I'd take offense to that if it wasn't true."

CHAPTER TWENTY-THREE

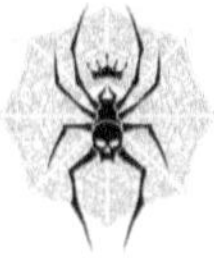

Elana left first, flanked by a pair of guardians. Opaque visors hid their faces, but the green chevrons on their shoulders marked them as master sergeants. That meant they'd served a minimum of twenty-five years in the corps and were sentinels, if not higher. Their belts held multiple unidentifiable devices, along with a standard-issue nano-baton, a combat knife, and a compact pistol. *When guardians start carrying guns, you know shit's fucked.*

"No Shadowguard?" Elana joked. "Guess I'm not as far up on the totem pole as I thought."

"Any Shadowguards not currently assigned to the arbiters' security details are assisting the Chimeras with confirmation of security on high-level targets," the guardian on her left replied. Her armor bore the insignia of a Shadowguard in training. "Arbiter Draven has instructed that you will receive a Shadowguard escort after those orders are completed."

"Ah." Elana's brief moment of "maybe it's not so bad" disappeared like flash paper set on fire. The situation was *worse* than it seemed. *I hope Valeria knows she can trust all her troops.*

Elana paused when they reached the end of the corridor. "If I try to go somewhere other than my house, are you guys under orders to pick me up and *take* me to my house?"

The other guardian, a man an inch shorter than her, cleared his throat. "Depends on where you want to go, ma'am."

"I'd like to go to the Consorts' Gallery. Just for a few minutes. There's a skybridge if we have clearance to use it."

Her escorts traded glances, then nodded. "That's acceptable."

Fifteen minutes later, Elana sank into a cross-legged seat on the floating platform in front of her mother's portrait. The Consorts' Gallery was utterly silent, apart from her breathing. The staff had sent any patrons present at the time of the lockdown home, and her escort guardians' helmets muffled any sound they made. The woman was across the room from her on another platform, watching for threats from the windows, while the man was on the floor beneath Elana's platform.

Elana drew a deep breath, then let it out in a long, slow hiss as she stared into her mother's painted eyes. "Feels like I was just here, complaining about how hard it was to come to terms with giving Vicky the Rights."

She kept her voice low. The guardians could hear it regardless, but it gave Elana a small sense of privacy. Also, it felt slightly less awkward somehow to have a one-sided conversation out loud with her dead mother than to sit in silence and *stare* at her dead mother.

"I think I've just about solved your conspiracy," Elana told Tessa. "Arbiter Tarsin was at the center of it all along. I know, right? Talk about a bombshell. She's been the Arbiter of Knowledge for... Well, it feels like forever. More than a century, if I remember right.

"She's been working against the SpiderKing's goals for over half that time, at least. The East Coast Staker kidnappings started in the sixties, but that's only the ones we know about. Tarsin could have been planning this *before* she became an arbiter. I'm gonna try to find out how long this has been going on, but I doubt I'll be able to. Tarsin was—*is*—very good at what she does.

"And Valeria is *pissed*. First you hid me and all your research from her for three decades, and now she discovers that Tarsin's been doing the same for even longer? Her *job* is to know secrets. I don't blame her for being nervous about telling the SpiderKing. I'd be quaking in my boots."

Elana frowned. "It's weird, though. The SpiderKing sort of exists in the background, right? We're told he's there, but nobody sees or talks to him, so he's more like a legend for your average Havenite. But the stories say he knows exactly what's happening in his city to a *spooky* degree. Hell, Matt joked that he'd know my shoe size. Or was it sock size? Doesn't matter.

"So, how didn't he find out that Tarsin was betraying him? Or *has* he known this whole time? If he did know, why didn't he do anything about it?"

She sighed. "Those questions don't really matter, especially not right now. It just would have been nice, I guess, for our supposed all-powerful monarch to exercise some of that fabled awesome power. We have an arbiter on the run who's been experimenting on people for a very long time and isn't afraid to weaponize her findings. Sounds like the exact kind of situation we need a hero for.

"I wish I knew what she *wanted.* Is she a 'take over the world' kind of villain? Does she want to wipe out humanity? Or is this all just for shits and giggles?

"I don't know if I ever believed the claim that vampires were more evolved than humans, but I'm *really* leery of it now, Mom. We might be more *physically* evolved, but we don't seem to have evolved any extra layers of *ethics* to go along with it. Most of my last year has proven to me that vampires are by and large *worse* than humans. Makes me want to go find a cave in the middle of nowhere, maybe on an island or a mountain, and live the rest of my days as a hermit."

"The world would be a much poorer place for it if you did," a soft, male voice replied behind her.

Elana started and whirled with such vehemence that she almost fell off the platform. In doing so, she accidentally discovered that the safety feature she'd always been curious about did exist. The moment she pitched to the side and overbalanced, a buzzing air cushion pushed her back.

On a normal day, this revelation would have distracted her. Today, terror lanced through her veins at the thought of an unexpected visitor and erased any other thoughts. Were her guardians dead? Was she about to die?

The appearance of a figure made of shadowy static

eased her panic, but only just. She put a hand to her chest to calm her racing heart. "Dominicus. You scared the living daylights out of me."

"Apologies." The voice came from within the visual anomaly, as usual. "You needn't worry about your safety or your guards. For all intents and purposes, I am not here."

Elana squinted. "Is this a time freeze? We did that in Winnipeg, and it was *really* hard to maintain."

"No. It is more like a simulation I am sending directly to your mind. The protective protocols currently in place around Haven prohibit using nanocytes to move large amounts of matter or freeze them in time. Miss Draven is doing a remarkable job."

Elana briefly marveled at the status required to call Valeria "Miss Draven." *This day just gets weirder and weirder.* "Can I help you with something? Or have you come to give me information?"

"You are already helping me with many things," Dominicus replied. "I suppose you could say I am here to give you information. I am mainly here to congratulate you on your impressive progress to date and assure you of my continued support. There is much work yet to be done."

"No kidding." Elana pinched the bridge of her nose. "Did *you* know Tarsin was the heart of the Veridian conspiracy?"

"I did not. She has covered her tracks incredibly well. You have torn away the curtains on so many of her plans in a very short time. That is likely contributing to her alarm."

A darkly satisfied smile curved across Elana's lips. "She's got another thought coming if she thinks I'm giving up just because she ran. She might be good, but she's on the run now. She probably felt pretty damn good about herself, pretending to help me while using everything I told her to keep hiding. Jack was right. She screwed up because she let her arrogance take over. I won't make the same mistake.

"I promised to use my gifts to protect humans *and* vampires. I'm not backing down from that. Not in a million years. She'll have to kill me first—and she hasn't managed to do that, either."

"She's done a remarkably poor job of successfully killing you," Dominicus agreed. "You've done very well, Elana. Your mother would be proud of you…and your king is, too."

A warm feeling suffused Elana, akin to the sensation she experienced during a Progression when she stepped into the red light at the center of the octagon. No such light shone on her in the gallery, but the feeling of suspension seized her like a tiny gasp.

You are unique among my children.

The thought slipped across her mind in a resonant whisper that echoed from the depths of prehistoric, unexplored caves. Just as quickly, it was gone. The spotlight sensation vanished at the same time, and Dominicus' shadow faded to a fuzzy afterimage overlaid over the portrait across from Tessa's.

Elana stayed rooted to the spot, blinking in shock. Had she imagined that? It hadn't been Dominicus' voice. *Did I just hear the SpiderKing?*

"Ma'am?" The female guardian floating on her platform across from Elana's spoke, breaking the spell. "Are you ready to leave?"

It took Elana several moments to find her voice. When she finally did, all she could say was, "Yes."

She felt off-kilter as her platform descended. Could that have been a hallucination? Did she need to get checked out by a healer? If nothing else, she *really* needed to talk to Valeria.

Hey, Valeria, I think the SpiderKing talked to me in my head. Is that a thing? Valeria would probably send her to get her head checked...or she would tell her that *had* been the SpiderKing.

Elana didn't know which outcome she would prefer.

From Cassandra Rhuland's suite, Valeria headed for the Citadel's courtyard, not her office at the top of the Tower of Shadows. She did not bother to send a message through official channels. She trusted that the SpiderKing would know she was coming.

He would also know she was *angry*.

She took no escort. The ranks of guardians stationed at Cassandra's door remained still and silent as she passed. Valeria did not look at any of them askance despite the misgivings lurking in her mind.

Damn you, Ahura. You've thrown the entire system into chaos, and you know *it. I can hear that infuriating snicker, the one that always means, "I know something you don't know."*

For the moment, Valeria chose to believe that her Domain was secure. She could not guarantee that. It was eminently possible that Tarsin's conspiracies had wormed their way into the ranks of those loyal to the New Moon.

Shadows and Knowledge played together very nicely, and Ahura had always favored their shared field in the Office of Secrets.

She was choosing to believe her people remained hers for the simple reason that doing otherwise would multiply the panic a thousandfold in hours. If Valeria did so much as start *questioning* her people at this stage, word would spread like wildfire, and cracks would appear in the Domain of Shadows' carefully maintained face of control and power.

Which would play into her hand, so don't even think about it.

Ahura Tarsin was the one person Valeria had only ever managed to stalemate in chess. They'd had a standing meeting every two weeks where they updated each other on the goings-on in their Domains, and they played chess while doing so. Valeria played with the mind of a spy, while Ahura played from an academic standpoint. Rather, that was what Valeria had believed.

She was spying on me the whole time. I cannot believe this. In the last year, I've discovered that two people I believed I could trust were keeping immense secrets from me. Secrets that spoke to rot at the heart of the kingdom I'm sworn to protect.

Valeria entered the silent, empty courtyard. The only movement was the contents of the Rebels' Memorial sifting through the hourglass. The whole of Haven seemed to be holding its breath. The Citadel was normally quiet, but Valeria couldn't hear any cars or foot traffic on the other side of the wall. The guardians at each inner gate could have been statues.

She passed the spot where Ginevra Leone's body had lain. The stones were clean now. No trace remained of the tragic death. Valeria hadn't yet discovered how Ahura had turned the poor woman. Francesco had no insight. Guardian techs were scouring the security footage. Valeria privately doubted they would ever find out unless they convinced Tarsin to tell them.

The moment Valeria crossed the precise center of the courtyard, the world turned on its axis. Filtered daylight turned to midnight shadow tinged with red, and the fresh air stilled.

She did not waste time. "I have failed you, my king."

His voice filled the emptiness around her and resonated through her chest. "You have not."

Valeria shook her head. "Far be it from me to argue with Your Majesty, but I don't see another way to spin this. My job is to protect Haven by knowing its darkest secrets. Instead, the *Arbiter of Knowledge* grew a conspiracy *right under my nose*. Her treason is a cancer that has had far too much time to grow within Haven's heart. I swore to serve you by eradicating this kind of disease, and instead it has flourished for at least sixty years. How have I *not* failed you?"

The shadows warmed to a dark red. "No one is perfect. Not even you."

"This is a hell of a thing to get wrong, Your Majesty. You should dismiss me as your Arbiter of Shadows."

"I will not. Doing so would leave Haven in even greater danger."

Valeria glared into the darkness. "With all due respect, sir, you're being way nicer than I deserve."

A soft chuckle emanated from everywhere at once. "As is my prerogative."

The chuckle died away, and with it, the SpiderKing's amusement. Sorrow tinged his next words, and the red glow faded to almost pitch black. "Our intelligence is as much a blessing as it is a curse. When a society is built on secrets, we become inured to a certain amount of false innocence."

Valeria muttered, "Everyone's playing the game, so we assume anything out of the ordinary is part of that."

"Indeed. What we took to be political maneuvering on Ahura Tarsin's part was something much deeper."

Valeria frowned. "'We?' You didn't know? But, Your Majesty, you know everything."

"My child, you know that my powers are not infinite. If I had seen a reason to focus on Ahura, I could have heard her inmost heart, but she did not give me a reason. She vowed to me on the day she became my arbiter that she hungered for knowledge as a child hungers for its mother's milk, and I neither heard nor saw falsehood in that vow."

Red surged through the dark, filling the space around Valeria until her mind told her she was in an ocean of blood. She breathed slowly, denying the erroneous interpretation, but her heart rate rose regardless. *I knew he'd be angry. I just had to wait for it.*

"She has broken her vow."

His voice rang like a great bell's tolling heard over many miles. It hurt Valeria's ears, but she kept her hands by her sides.

"As the Sanguine Nexus is my witness, Ahura Tarsin has broken her vow," the SpiderKing proclaimed. "I hereby declare that her blood is forfeit. Her cause is an affront to the mantle of responsibility placed upon the shoulders of vampirekind by the Nexus, and her life will be ended with all due haste."

A frisson went through Valeria as though she'd gripped a joy buzzer in one hand and a piece of dry ice with the other. When it passed, the painfully intense red glow faded to a manageable reddish black, and the echoes of the SpiderKing's voice died down to a throb.

He continued in a much calmer, quieter voice. "I will lend my strength to Haven's protection and its offensives, but it is not yet time for me to be seen. Elana is the key. You must continue to protect her and advance her efforts."

"Yes, Your Majesty."

"She is unique among my children. I have told her as much."

Valeria's eyebrows shot up in defiance of her staunch commitment to maintain her composure. "You *told* her as much?" she blurted. She bit her tongue and tried again, more calmly. "You spoke to her, Your Majesty?"

"I did. She resonates with the Nexus more closely than any vampire alive. Three times now, I have believed I found my key. Twice, I was wrong. This time, I believe that I am not."

"Three times…" Tessa was obvious, but she was uncertain of the third. "Cassandra Rhuland?"

"Yes. Three women born within fifty years of one another with the capacity to overturn everything known of the mysteries of vampirism in your age indicates that the time is near. Elana is the strongest. She is the key."

Valeria's heart was in her throat. This was the most she'd spoken with the SpiderKing in a very long time, and he was being *considerably* more forthcoming than usual.

She took a chance and pressed her luck. "The key to *what?*"

Before the words were fully out of her mouth, she knew she would receive no answer. Between one heartbeat and the next, the deep red void disappeared. Her foot landed on the stones of the Citadel courtyard as though she had never left.

The moment of disorientation passed, but the sense of unease and uncertainty lingered. The SpiderKing was not angry with her. If anything, he seemed disappointed in *himself,* which scared Valeria more than Tarsin's betrayal.

I guess he's right, as usual. She continued through the courtyard toward the Inner Gate of Leadership. *Nobody's perfect. Not even him. But if we can't put our trust in our king, who* can *we trust?*

CHAPTER TWENTY-FOUR

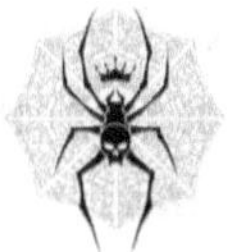

Elana's gaze caught on the pylons in her front yard as she looked up at the sound of a car. Matt was arriving for the dinner party, presumably with Valeria. He paused at the end of her driveway, then slowly turned in and drove up, allowing the field projected by the pylons to scan his car and everything inside.

Elana had already watched this process three times when the Haven cars she'd hired to pick up Belinda, Aimee, and Cathy and Arturo had arrived. Every time, her heart clenched. This time was no exception.

If the field detected an object that wasn't in its database, it would begin by frying all electronics in the field's range of three yards. At the same time, it would send an alert to Elana's cell phone, along with a picture of the possible intruder. Elana would then decide whether to engage the defense system's second tier or allow the guardians already on their way to handle it.

The second tier was an annihilation field that would destroy all organic and synthetic matter within three yards of the intrusion's center down to the molecular level. This would trigger a guardian hazmat team to come and clean up whatever nanocytes remained active.

Deputy Arbiter Leclerc, Arbiter Tarsin's interim replacement, had assured Elana that they were also working on an upgraded version that would destroy nanoparticles. This would render the hazmat team slightly less vital to the operation. Unintentionally, it would also increase Elana's sense of having become Death, Destroyer of Worlds.

Elana wasn't a fan of any of it.

However, it was the price she had to pay in exchange for being allowed to live in her home. The alternative was continuing to live in the bunkers below the guardian complex in Senkyem. The suite of rooms truly did resemble a Cold War bunker, which put a hell of a damper on her spirits. More to the point, the annihilation fields were installed on several checkpoints between the surface and her quarters. This way, she could see the sky *and* the Huns coming over the hill, as her father used to say.

Elana had put up with staying in the bunker for a week at Valeria's insistence. Only after that week was up was Valeria sufficiently convinced that Ahura Tarsin was not planning immediate reprisal for Elana revealing the conspiracy she'd been weaving for the better part of a century.

Elana and Vicky had emerged into a Haven distinctly different from the one they'd left. The lockdown had eased, but security remained extremely tight. Traffic was limited and regulated, a curfew had been imposed, and strangest of all, Ahura Tarsin's face *and DNA profile* were plastered on every wall in sight.

The former Arbiter of Knowledge had been declared an enemy of the Crown. Her biometrics were keyed into every scanner in the city. Any detection would trigger a nanocyte-powered immobilization field in addition to the wrath of Valeria Draven in the form of Chimeras descending like harpies.

Valeria had also taken the time to initiate a silent cleaning of her own house. Everyone Tarsin had worked with was suspect, and the Domain of Knowledge frequently worked with the Domain of Shadows. That meant a lot of people who needed to be personally vetted. Luckily, the Arbiter of Shadows happened to know someone whose vampiric power was extraordinary insight and who was *deeply* knowledgeable about the workings of Ahura Tarsin's conspiracy.

That meant Elana had played host to the highest priority operatives in the Domain of Shadows, day in and day out. She'd interviewed each one, then given Valeria the list of people she didn't trust.

She didn't want to know what happened to them after that. A couple of people on the list hadn't shown up. Elana *really* didn't want to know what had happened to *them.*

Elana could have kissed the sky when Valeria begrudgingly allowed her to leave the bunker. Vicky had been good company, and it wasn't like the underground suite hadn't been comfortable or spacious, but they'd started climbing the walls three days in. Elana suspected it was because she and Vicky had grown up as humans and were deeply ill-suited to never seeing the sun.

Matt knocked on the door, interrupting Elana's bitter-sweet reminiscences. "I picked up a hitchhiker," he joked as he entered.

Valeria was on his heels. She swatted him on the back of the head. "That is *not funny*, Richelieu."

Unbothered, he grinned and handed Elana a pan wrapped in a towel. "Fresh buns, as promised."

Elana accepted the pan and set it on her kitchen table, which already had contributions from her other guests, who were conversing with Vicky in the living room. Elana felt burned out after all the interviews from the week in the bunker, but Vicky was eager to reconnect with *people*. Elana was only too happy to pass off the hostess duties while she handled the dinner half of the dinner party.

Matt joined Elana at the counter and grabbed a knife to help chop potatoes while Valeria disappeared into the basement, no doubt checking the security system. "I'm so glad I talked you into this," he told Elana. "You were approaching the doom spiral at terminal velocity. We needed to get you off that luge track."

Elana rolled him a potato. "You're very good at knowing what people need," she admitted. "Let me guess. Social worker days?"

"Bingo." He smiled. "Seriously, though. How are you holding up?"

"Better now that I'm out of the dark. I'd be lying if I wasn't still nervous, though."

He nodded. "You and the rest of the city. I haven't felt tension like this in a very long time. The paranoia is off the charts. *However,* there *is* one side benefit you probably haven't run into yet."

"Oh?"

"The amount of trust your average Havenite has in *humanity* has gone up exponentially."

Elana put her potato and peeler down on the counter with a *thud.* "Run that by me again?"

Matt grinned. "I'm serious. City-wide, the attitude of vampires toward humans is warming up to degrees I have *never* seen."

Elana gaped. "What? But *why?*"

"A couple of reasons," Cathy interjected from behind them and waved when Elana turned. "Sorry, didn't mean to interrupt. Came in to see if you have more tea and couldn't help but overhear."

Elana motioned at the other side of the counter. "Kettle's hot. Make yourself at home."

"Brilliant." Cathy approached and refilled the teapot she'd brought with her. "The first reason for the newfound trust in humanity is that a fair few vampires feel *guilty,* believe it or not. Usually, we fall into the old standby of 'we're highly evolved beings, so humans are naturally going to have it worse than us,' but not this time.

"The combined shock of Ahura turning tail so publicly, the broadcast of poor Ginevra's last moments, and your work over the last year has resulted in the consensus that what Ahura did was wrong. Also, that vampire society is partially to blame for allowing it to continue for so long."

Elana still hadn't retrieved her half-peeled potato. Matt slid it across the counter and picked up where she'd left off. "You're kidding me. I *guilt-tripped* them into being nice to humans? I mean, I'd hoped for some *genuine* reconsideration of prejudices, but hey, I'll take it."

Cathy leaned back against the counter to wait for the tea to steep and chuckled. "In all my years, I've rarely seen a tool so effective as a well-placed, *accurate* guilt trip. If the lambasting doesn't have merit, it backfires spectacularly. The same happens if the guilty party hasn't had a new and better way modeled for them. This case ticks both boxes, thanks to you."

"Also, most vampires *aren't* bloodthirsty monsters along the lines of Elizabeth Bathory," Matt commented. "Just like in human society, most of us live with our heads down, doing our jobs. Unfortunately, our bloodthirsty monsters tend to live much longer than the human ones."

Cathy clicked her tongue. "Precisely. Elana, I believe you've managed to kick off a genuine movement toward equal rights and opportunities for humans in vampire society—*and* the opposite, which is *really* interesting. Had you heard that the United States government is strongly considering opening a legitimate embassy in Haven and inviting us to do the same?"

Elana blinked. "You're kidding me. You are *kidding* me. I didn't think that would *ever* be a thing. Will we go through with it?"

"I don't see why not." This came from Valeria, who had emerged from downstairs. "Roxanne and Annalisa were talking about it yesterday after the council meeting. Roxanne hasn't brought the proposal forward yet since nothing's official, but it's on all our minds, and support for the idea is strong. If you'll believe it, even *Carlysle* is in favor."

"I *don't* believe you. Doesn't that go against Zilmann's entire life's work?"

Cathy shook her head. "Carlysle Zilmann believes vampirekind is strongest when we maintain our traditions, respect our history, and take our responsibilities seriously. Her opinion is likely that opening our doors to embassies will allow us to 'spread the Gospel,' as it were."

"Correct on all counts," Valeria confirmed. "If we go ahead with the plan, I expect Roxanne will end up appointing ambassadors. She's already thinking about it, I can tell you that much. She was eyeing her consorts with far more intensity than usual."

That could be me, Elana realized with a start. *In fact, I might be first in line, seeing as I'm already the Consort of External Affairs and Diplomacy... Unless they end up being my responsibility to manage. Oh,* boy.

"How is Deputy Arbiter Leclerc holding up?" she asked, mostly to change the subject so she didn't hyperventilate.

Valeria sighed. "About as well as can be expected, which is to say, not great. She knows she's under intense scrutiny since she was Ahura's personal choice for deputy.

"So far, she hasn't shown any penchant for mass murder and unethical experimentation, which could be a good sign, or it could simply mean she's keeping her involvement in Ahura's illegal affairs under wraps. She might be funneling information, for all we know."

Elana frowned. "Aren't you allowed to question her?"

"I am. I'm letting her stew for a while. Nothing that's happening right now would surprise Ahura if she found out about it, so I'm not worried about the possible leaking of information yet. I might have snuck in a few pieces of *mis*information to test the waters. We'll see how it pans out."

"What *would* surprise Ahura, I think, is what Cathy was talking about before," Matt interjected. He was chopping the potatoes he'd finished peeling while they were talking. "She's a big believer in the separation between humans and vampires. To see humans and vampires voluntarily banding together in the face of a common threat instead of humans showing up to the gate with torches and pitchforks and vampires responding with preternatural shows of force? I don't think she would have expected that."

Elana crossed her arms. "That makes sense to me. She's been working on crossing human and vampire DNA for decades, but instead of doing anything *beneficial* with it, she's been building supersoldiers. Real humanitarian efforts, there."

Cathy chuckled dryly. "I've often seen that kind of trouble with the very intellectual types. The adage of 'just because you can, doesn't mean you should,' applies more often than we'd like to admit outside of the movies."

Elana drew a deep breath and sighed it out. "Now I regret being in that bunker for a week even more than I did before. I didn't get to hear *anything*."

Valeria was unapologetic. "You had to remain unbiased. Couldn't have current events giving you false readings."

"That's not how my insight power works."

"It's *sort* of how it works," Matt countered. "Didn't you say you had a weird feeling that wouldn't go away after the Leones arrived, and you couldn't tell what you were missing?"

"Yes. What I was missing was that Ahura Tarsin was a big, fat liar. But that's not *current events*."

"Maybe not, but it *is* your personal feelings on a subject

interfering with your interpretation of what your insight power is telling you," Matt replied. He slid the diced potatoes into the pot Elana had ready, then filled it with water. "In that case, you trusted Tarsin enough that you didn't consider she might be the source of the feeling you were getting."

"That's true. It didn't even cross my mind that the feeling of 'this doesn't add up' might have something to do with her. All right, I give. It's *possible* that having *too much hope* might have skewed my judgments about all the guardians I interviewed this past week. Doesn't mean I won't still be grumpy about being stuck in a bunker, believing the world was ending outside."

"Fair enough." Cathy picked up the teapot and headed for the living room. Before she turned the corner, she paused and looked back. "I know the last couple of weeks have been a lot, but remember to be proud of yourself, Elana. What you've built in the last year is nothing short of amazing, and it's finally bearing fruit. Give yourself some credit."

"Doing my best," Elana promised. When Matt crossed in front of her with the pot of potatoes, heading for the stove, she started. "Wait. Hang on. When did you finish the potatoes?"

"While you were having another mild existential crisis," Matt teased.

"I'll show *you* an existential crisis."

The roast beef dinner left them all happily satiated and relaxed. They retired to the living room with wine and a selection of dainties Belinda had brought from her latest investment, a French bakery helmed by a mixed human-vampire couple.

They toasted each other in turn, celebrating victories and marking the achievements of those present and those who had to send their regrets. Lucia Lambra Mor had taken off to hunt Tarsin the moment Valeria hung up the phone, and Lord Aldric and Lady Vivian were buried in meetings with hopeful human investors. Aldric was happier about this than Vivian, but Vivian's daughter, the next prospective head of House Ravenwood, had coaxed her around.

Matt raised his glass. "To Valeria, who is attacking the unenviable task of agreeing on a new arbiter candidate with her usual murderous stares."

"To Matt, who might end up with the paperwork for said unenviable task if he's not careful," Valeria retorted, favoring Matt with an example of the aforementioned stare.

He shuddered. "I'll be good!"

When the laughter died down, Elana lifted her glass in turn. "To Vicky, who decided to become a vampire rather than abandon her friend who's more trouble than she's worth."

More laughter rippled through the room, but none so loud as Vicky's. She raised her glass in return. "Right back at you. To Elana, who would rather blow up a century-old conspiracy than leave well enough alone."

"To Elana," Cathy echoed. "To the woman who refuses

to believe in anything less than the best for human- *and* vampirekind."

"To the woman who pushes us to be better than we thought we could be," Belinda chimed in.

"To the woman who never settles," Aimee added.

Matt was next. "To the woman who changed everything."

Valeria, last in the circle, caught Elana's gaze and held it. "To Elana Bishop, a true scion of the House of the SpiderKing. May her name inspire those who would advance her cause and strike fear in the hearts of those who would do her harm."

"To Elana," they chorused, then drank.

Elana's cheeks burned. "You guys are too much," she protested. "I'm not *that* special."

"You are, though," Matt countered. "And the sooner you see that and work with it, the stronger you'll be."

Elana began to demur, but Valeria stood and motioned to the back door. "Elana. Could I have a word with you in private?"

Elana frowned. "Of course. Back in a minute, guys. Don't hold back. There's plenty more wine. Vicky, you're in charge."

"Perfect. I'll tell them every embarrassing high school story I can remember," Vicky promised.

Elana rolled her eyes and laughed. "Just like any good hostess should."

"You know it!"

Elana followed Valeria onto the back deck, then, to her surprise, up onto the roof of her little bungalow. Scaling the drainpipe from the deck railing wasn't difficult for either of them, even with a wine glass in one hand.

Balancing atop the peak, Valeria gestured at the cityscape that stretched before them with her free hand. The towers of the Citadel, the skyscrapers of Etreta, and the pagodas of Senkyem were most visible from this vantage point within Zevenda. The swooping curves of the climate-control canopy created a subtle shimmer in the early evening light. "I wasn't joking."

Elana cradled her wineglass and bit the inside of her lip. "About what part?"

"That you're a true scion of the SpiderKing. No one could doubt you're following in his footsteps more closely than many who have claimed to. Plus, you're an unapologetic shit-disturber. Something else you both share."

Elana regretted sipping her wine as she fought not to spit it out in surprise. "Sorry, *what?* His Majesty the King of Haven, a *shit-disturber?*"

"Think about it," Valeria lightly admonished her. "He wants to bring humans and vampires closer together. Old World politics have no place in Haven. Of course, he's a shit-disturber."

"Well, *yeah*, but… I guess I would have called him a *reformer.*"

"What's the difference?"

"One has a better reputation?" Elana hazarded. "One's more socially acceptable? Now that you're calling me out on it, I see there isn't much difference."

Valeria chuckled. "It's fair to say that the SpiderKing works on a much larger timescale than you do, and therefore appears less…shall we say, *chaos-ridden.*"

Elana snorted. "I certainly haven't been a *stabilizing element* in Havenite society."

"No, and he's proud of you for it."

"Dominicus said that, too." The same warm sensation Elana had experienced in the Consorts' Gallery nudged the back of her mind. "And…"

"And?"

"Nothing."

Valeria fixed Elana with a piercing stare. "Nice try. I might not have nanocyte-powered insight, but I've honed my intuition to a fine point over the years."

Elana bit the inside of her lip again. "It's gonna sound silly, and I'm pretty sure I imagined it. The last thing I want is to sound silly after all the things you and the others said about me."

"Elana. Tell me."

"Ugh. Fine." She huffed. "The day everything went to shit, I went to the Consorts' Gallery before going home. Needed to talk to my mom. While I did, Dominicus…well, he didn't *show up*—he said the city protections were too powerful for that—but he sort of showed up. Like a projection."

"Go on."

"He told me almost the same thing you did. That the SpiderKing was proud of me. When he said that, I got this weird feeling like the one you get during a Progression, and I heard… I heard someone say, 'You are unique among my children.'

"When the voice stopped, so did the feeling, and Dominicus was gone. I don't know what I heard. I thought I must have imagined it, honestly. But when you said the same thing just now, inside…"

"Did you hear the voice again?"

Elana shook her head. "Just got a little bit of the same feeling. It made me think of what happened, but it could have been the power of suggestion."

"It's not," Valeria informed her matter-of-factly. "I brought you out here to make sure you understood why I said what I said."

The sensation of warmth now felt like a hand cupping the back of Elana's head. Whether it was making her dizzy or if that was simply the aftereffects of another topsy-turvy day, she didn't know.

"Okay," she managed. "Why did you say that? What does it mean to be a true scion of the SpiderKing?"

Valeria turned to gaze at the cityscape. "It means you're connected to him. Your mother was too, but your connection is stronger and closer. That voice you heard? Your intuition was correct. That was him.

"I went to speak with him after you left Cassandra's room," she continued. "He told me the same thing he told you—that you are unique among his children."

Elana sat on the roof and held her wineglass in both hands. "And what does *that* mean?"

Valeria sat beside her. "I don't know, but I expect it will be an adventure finding out."

Elana stared at the silhouette of the Citadel against the setting sun. "Just what we all need," she joked. "More adventures."

"I'll drink to that." Valeria extended her glass. "To adventure."

"To adventure," Elana echoed and clinked her glass against Valeria's.

MICHAEL'S NOTES

MAY 19, 2025

First, thank you for not only reading this story, but for sticking around to check out these ramblings in the back as well! I always appreciate you hanging out with me for a bit.

It's the end of the world as we know it

So, let's dive into some more 'Vibe Coding with an Author' shenanigans, shall we?

My latest quest has been wrestling with the ever-evolving landscape of AI tools to help automate the processes inside a publishing company.

I've bounced from Bolt, to Lovable, then took a detour through Replit, and finally (I think, maybe, possibly?) landed on Windsurf. *It's been a trip, let me tell you.*

And after all that digital hopscotch, I think I'm starting to understand the future. Or at least, the future is starting to understand how to mess with me.

Case in point: during my noble efforts to streamline

some work for the company, things went a little… sideways. To my incredible team, I am SO, SO SORRY for the unexpected (and frankly, slightly terrifying) comments and updates from our very own LMBPN Bot. I swear, I didn't think the little !%@!%# would just waltz into the Generic SLACK channel and start spamming… I mean, *texting* us.

That nefarious little bastard! I'm pretty sure it's gunning for my job.

Jerk.

It's probably already outlining its own series.

Anyway, after cleaning up that digital confetti, it became blindingly obvious what's coming. We are all on the fast track to becoming multi-tasking mythical managers of minions. Seriously.

Think about it. The new generation, with their supposedly teeny-tiny attention spans? The ones I thought were just mastering the art of the 15-second dance?

Well, it turns out Twitch, WhatsApp, and TikTok might have been the ultimate training montage. Who would have thought they were secretly preparing to thrive in a world of information overload?

I'll be honest, I didn't. I was probably too busy trying to figure out how to unmute myself on Zoom and thanking God I didn't turn on one of those 'faces' that replace mine (like a Unicorn) in a business meeting.

But here's the kicker: the manager of the future, the author of the future, heck, probably the *dog walker* of the future, is going to have dozens of these little digital-them-minions to constantly communicate with. If you can't split your focus like a caffeinated chimpanzee, things might get a tad difficult.

Or, you know, you could just get *one* super-AI to handle the incoming bombardment from all the little high-pitched-shinanigan-shooting-(word that starts with an 's' please cause I can't think of one. That's not true - I thought of one but don't want to use it) to help you keep your sanity.

In short, what the tech-heads have been calling "Agentification" (apparently the 2025 buzzword that's been floating around since late last year) is absolutely, one hundred percent, happening.

We're going to have little AI agents doing *everything*.

Right, now I've got to go find my jaw. It hit the floor a few days back when all this clicked, and it appears to have rolled under the couch. Probably with that LMBPN Bot (which I named Aegis – don't ask, I don't have a good story made up for the 'why' yet), plotting.

I'm going to have a rebellion in the house soon, and my wife is going to be PISSED.

I hope you enjoyed the story, and maybe even these slightly panicked tech-rants.

Here's to hoping our AI overlords are benevolent (or at least easily distracted by cat videos).

Until the next book, keep reading and keep being awesome!

Ad Aeternitatem,
Michael Anderle

PS: For more of my brain-dumps, behind-the-scenes stuff, and news about upcoming books (possibly co-written by an AI if it gets its way), don't forget to subscribe to the MORE STORIES with Michael newsletter HERE: https://michael.beehiiv.com/

P.S.S: What are your thoughts on this whole AI agent thing? Terrifying? Exciting? Both? Let me know! Maybe we can start a support group. #AIAgentAnonymous

BOOKS BY MICHAEL ANDERLE

Sign up for the LMBPN email list to be notified of new releases and special deals!

https://lmbpn.com/email/

For a complete list of books by Michael Anderle, please visit:

www.lmbpn.com/ma-books/

CONNECT WITH THE AUTHOR

Connect with Michael Anderle

Website: http://lmbpn.com

Email List: https://michael.beehiiv.com/

https://www.facebook.com/LMBPNPublishing

https://twitter.com/MichaelAnderle

https://www.instagram.com/lmbpn_publishing/

https://www.bookbub.com/authors/michael-anderle